THE DELIVERY

THE DELIVERY

MR. AND MRS. STEPHEN B. CASTLEBERRY

CASTLEBERRY FARMS PRESS

All rights reserved, including the right to reproduce this book or portions thereof, in any form, without written permission from the authors.

This is a work of fiction. All the characters and events portrayed in this book (with the exception of the organization Gideons International) are fictitious, and any resemblance to real people or events is purely coincidental.

All scripture references are from the King James Version of the Bible.

Castleberry Farms Press
P.O. Box 337
Poplar, WI 54864

Printed in the U.S.A.

ISBN 1-891907-09-3

e-mail: cbfarmpr@pressenter.com

Visit us at: www.pressenter.com/~cbfarmpr

© Copyright 1999

A Note From the Authors

On the back of the title page of this book it states that all characters in this book are fictional. That's true. However, one of the names is not fictional — Elaine Jackson. Although she is not represented by the character in this book, we wanted to use her name anyway, in honor of Elaine's love and joy in the Lord Jesus Christ. She has been a blessing to our family and we're thankful that she is our sister in Christ.

We've learned much from godly men over the years. Some of them, like Ryne Dean, read drafts of this book and offered helpful insights. To all of them, we say "thanks!"

The book mentions the work of the Gideons. May God richly bless them as they work to spread the Good News! The Gideons organization has been around since 1899, distributing Bibles at a rate of 45 million a year worldwide. We've been encouraged to see Susie's uncle, Larry Hubbartt, involved in this ministry. If you would like to make a donation or contact them, here's where you can reach them: Gideons International, P.O. Box 140800, Nashville, TN 37214. (615) 883-8533. tgi@gideons.org www.gideons.org

As always, we would love to hear from you.

                              Mr. and Mrs. Stephen B. Castleberry
                                              P.O. Box 337
                                          Poplar, WI 54864
                                   cbfarmpr@pressenter.com

THE DELIVERY

Chapter One

Joe Reynolds scanned the letters in his hands, making sure they all had stamps. More than once Mrs. Granlund had forgotten to pay that little "toll," and then complained to Joe when her letters were returned from the post office marked INSUFFICIENT POSTAGE. "I wish you had told me I forgot a stamp!" she would scold, then huff back into her house. She was a complaining, quarrelsome woman that Joe was happy to miss seeing on his route.

The three outgoing letters today all had stamps, so he slipped them into his mail satchel, adjusted the strap a little to make it more comfortable, and stepped off the porch, a porch he had stepped off at least a thousand times in the last ten years. He did so without really thinking about it. That was a mistake that he later hoped never to repeat.

Just as his feet hit the sidewalk leading from the porch, without a warning of any kind, a missile struck Joe's left side, catapulting him several feet to the right of the sidewalk with an ominous cracking sound. Joe landed mostly on his stomach, then rolled over and over before coming to an abrupt stop, thanks to a couple of garbage cans and some recycling bins.

Joe was confused. It had all happened so quickly and without warning. He had seen nothing, heard nothing. The peacefulness of the beautiful day was shattered, replaced with pain.

Who shot at me? he asked himself dully, not even trying to get up. *And why? Why didn't I see him?* He knew he should open his eyes and try to find some way to escape or get help, but he didn't have the energy.

Joe felt increasing pain in his chest. *I can't breathe! Please Jesus, I need to breathe! Help me!* His eyes opened and with blurred vision, he began scanning back and forth trying to find some way out of this madness.

As he did so, he looked at his left arm. The sleeve of the U.S. Postal Service shirt that his wife, Amy, had so painstakingly ironed last night, was a bloody, ripped-up mess. Tilting his head down a little Joe saw that his pants legs were torn and blood was starting to ooze through where his knees were.

A scream filled the air, from the direction of the porch. Joe braced himself for another missile he felt sure was going to hit. But nothing happened. Joe was able to breathe a little and his lungs tried desperately to suck in larger and larger volumes of air.

There was more noise from the porch direction and then Joe heard an excited voice shouting. "Cameron, are you hurt?"

Boy, I must be confused, Joe thought, weakly. *My name's not Cameron. At least I'm pretty sure it's not Cameron. No,* he decided with increasing confidence in his own mental ability, *I'm Joe.* That shouting voice, coming from a woman running toward him, was getting closer. Then it let out another scream. *Does she have to scream?* Joe's head was beginning to ache.

"Oh no! Oh! Oh no! It's Mr. Reynolds! Somebody! Hey, sommmeeeebbbody, help!" Joe turned his head to the right and immediately recognized the panic-stricken face of Mrs. Granlund. She kept calling for help, louder and louder, but instead of stopping to help, she moved quickly away from Joe. He couldn't see what she was running toward because he didn't feel like tilting his head back far enough to see.

THE DELIVERY

In a continuing answer to his prayer, Joe's mind cleared quickly. He was able to hear the muffled voice of a young boy, who was crying and groaning at the same time. "Are you all right, Cameron? Talk to me!" Mrs. Granlund shouted.

Joe could hear people running toward him. *I suspect the whole neighborhood heard Mrs. Granlund's scream!* He finally summoned the strength to tilt his head backward. Doing so, although it was indeed a painful thing to do, he saw Cameron lying next to a bent and twisted bicycle. Cameron's mother was leaning over him.

"Are you all right?" a man drawled, bending down to look at Joe. "Are you breathin' mister?"

Joe was breathing better now, and the pain in his chest was rapidly subsiding. *Thank You Lord*, he prayed. However, Joe felt it would be too much effort to try to speak to the man. So, he just nodded his head a little bit, instead.

"Hey, I think this guy is probably goin' to be okay," the man said, addressing a small crowd that was gathering to watch. "How's that youngun' over there?" he asked Mrs. Granlund.

Sobbing, Mrs. Granlund was able to get out a weak, "I think he's okay." Hugging her son closely, she repeated with a slow drawl, "Yeah, I think he's okay."

"Someone better call an ambulance," the man said to no one in particular.

"Are you sure that's necessary?" a lady's voice asked. "Hadn't we better ask the man if he needs one or not?" Then turning to someone else who had just rushed up to the scene, the lady continued, "Look, Marge, it's the postman. Looks like Cameron ran over him with his bicycle."

"You think you ought to go to the hospital?" the man asked Joe. "Want us to call an ambulance?"

Joe had never been in an ambulance before. He had always thought of them as only being for two classes of people: those very sick and dying, or for those severely injured. Joe really didn't feel that he was either. He realized now that he had simply had the breath knocked out of him when he landed on his stomach.

"No," he answered the man, surprising himself that the words actually made it out of his mouth. Joe slowly lifted himself to a sitting position. There was a group of maybe five or six people standing near him, with a few children running across the road in his direction. "My head and arm hurt," Joe explained to the older man who had a very worried look on his face. "I think my head feels the worst." He looked at the man carefully, but decided that he didn't recognize him from his route.

"Well, I reckon it should be hurtin'!" the man exclaimed. "You've already got a knot pert' near the size of a walnut on your forehead!"

Joe gingerly touched his forehead and found the man to be right.

"Must have landed at least partly on your head. That there's a pretty lousy way to break your fall."

Joe didn't respond. He began to feel a little weak and dizzy. Maybe sitting up had been a bad idea after all. He slumped back to the ground.

"I think you're supposed to lift his head," said one lady, offering the older man her advice.

"No, Amanda, I've always heard you're supposed to lift their feet when they get that look like . . ." another lady started, but then paused. Finally she continued, " . . . I mean, when they . . . when they get real white in the face." Joe felt his legs being raised and something placed under his feet. Soon he felt less dizzy and less like he was going to pass out, but it did cause his right leg to start hurting.

"Is the boy okay?" Joe asked. His mind had cleared almost totally, and he knew now that it was indeed Cameron Granlund, a boy of about fourteen years. Cameron was one of the more rambunctious boys on his route. Joe recalled some of the mail packages he had delivered with Cameron's name on them. One a few months ago had been from the "Estes Rocket Company," with a label that read, "Caution: Keep away from heat or flame!" Another, about three years ago, had been a C.O.D. from a company located in Los Angeles with the unusual name of "George's Great Big Surprises." A label on the package had read, "Watch out! When George comes to town, people notice!!"

"Hmm, I'd say that 'when Cameron comes to town, people notice'!" Joe said out loud.

"What'd you say?" the man asked. He had been looking at Cameron's cuts and only half-heard Joe.

"Nothing," Joe replied. He hadn't realized that his thoughts were getting relayed by his mouth. Perhaps he didn't have full use of his senses after all.

Someone brought water and cotton gauze, and an older lady, whom Joe recognized as Mrs. McCurry, was busy trying to clean up Joe's wounds and stop the bleeding. When she touched the left arm, Joe winced and involuntarily drew his arm back.

"Sorry," Mrs. McCurry apologized, wincing a little herself.

"Thanks, Mrs. McCurry," Joe said encouragingly. "I appreciate what you're doing. I really do."

Joe listened as someone related to a new onlooker what had happened. A child from across the street saw the whole thing. There was a row of tall bushes in the Granlund's yard. Apparently, when Joe was just stepping off the porch, Cameron was coming around the corner of the shrubs on his bike. Cameron had a reputation in the neighborhood as a daredevil and fast rider on his bike, and today was no exception. Unable to stop, he ran right into Joe's left side. "I saw Mr. Reynold's glasses go flying off and his body sort of doubled up like he was a rag doll or something. Yep, the bike hit him, and smack! . . . " the boy clapped his hands together loudly, ". . . there went the mailman flying through the air!" the boy offered graphically. "Then he bounced like a rubber ball and rolled into the garbage cans! Man, was he really moving!"

Joe winced as he again thought of the impact. *No wonder I thought I had been hit by a missile!*

After a few minutes, Joe felt like trying to sit up again. This time he didn't feel woozy, just sore. He started to get to his feet.

"Hold on there!" the man intervened. "Where do you think you're a goin'?"

Joe noticed the concerned look on the man's face. "I think I'm okay," he assured. "I have to finish my mail route. It's getting late."

"No sir. I believe you're through with your route for today. You've not seen yourself in the mirror, you know." The man couldn't help laughing. "You mail guys really must be serious about your job!" he noted. "Let's see. How does that saying go? 'Neither rain, nor snow, nor dead of night . . . nor Cameron running over you with his great big bike . . .'" The man laughed at his unexpected rhyme.

"It is my job," Joe offered, simply. But when he looked at his bloody and ripped pants and shirt Joe decided that he wasn't going to be able to finish the route

THE DELIVERY

after all. What would people think, seeing this bloody man walk up onto their porch? "Maybe I just better get back to the post office and let them finish my route," he decided.

"Are you sure you can you drive your truck? I'll be happy to give you a lift," the man volunteered.

"Yes, or I can call them from my house," Mrs. McCurry suggested. "I'm sure that someone could come and get your mail truck and mail. Then we could take you straight home."

"Thanks," Joe replied sincerely. "I may take one of you up on your offer. But first I think I'll see if I can drive back." Then looking at the man, he added, "Sir, I appreciate your help. I didn't get your name?"

"Aw, just call me Fop."

"Did you say, Fop?"

"Yeah, that stands for Friend of Postmen," the man laughed. "Name's actually Elmer Smith," he added cheerfully, automatically sticking out his hand to shake Joe's. However, he withdrew his hand quickly, not wanting to do anything that might hurt Joe's bruised hand.

"Well, I do thank you, Elmer. You too, Mrs. McCurry."

One of the children handed Joe his glasses, which miraculously hadn't been damaged even though they had gone sailing through the air. "They landed in the rose bushes," the boy grinned. "I think they're okay."

"Thanks," Joe smiled back, but then groaned, "Ohhh. Smiling isn't something I want to do too much of. It hurts to smile."

Joe walked over to Cameron, who had some cuts, but didn't look as bad as Joe felt. Mrs. Granlund was still trying to mother him, but Cameron looked like he just wanted her to leave him alone. "Is he all right? Is there anything I can do?"

Mrs. Granlund smiled through the tears in her eyes. "He's all right. Just shook him up, didn't it, Cameron?" Cameron didn't speak.

"I'm sorry, Cameron. I should have looked before I stepped off your porch."

Cameron still didn't respond. "Cameron, honey, I think you need to tell Mr. Reynolds that you're sorry for running into him," Mrs. Granlund pleaded. Still, Cameron didn't speak. Joe wasn't sure if the boy thought the accident was Joe's fault, or if he just had trouble admitting that he was wrong. Mrs. Granlund continued to try to talk Cameron into apologizing, but to no avail. Cameron's refusal to speak made everyone standing around uncomfortable. It was especially awkward for Mrs. Granlund and Joe.

"Oh, that's okay, Mrs. Granlund," Joe said, trying to break the ice. "I'm sure Cameron is sorry that the whole thing happened, too. I do hope you'll feel better soon, Cameron."

The scattered mail from the satchel had been gathered by some boys in the neighborhood and they had already delivered the mail to addresses on their street for Joe. Joe wasn't sure how the Post Office would react to that, but what could he do now? It was already done! They had crammed the rest of the mail back into his mail pouch. Naturally, it would need resorting before being delivered, but that was something that could be done back at the post office.

Joe walked to his truck parked at the end of the street, waving weakly to a few curious children who had followed him. He unlocked the door, slid it open, and then climbed in. Joe drove slowly toward the post office, wondering what his supervisor would think of his "new"

THE DELIVERY

uniform style. Then, a bigger dread hit him: what would Casey say?

Chapter Two

In contrast to the tragedy just experienced, Joe's day had certainly started out nicely. It was a lovely early April day in central Alabama, with a few scattered cumulus clouds lazily drifting by. The sun was warm, but not hot, as it would be in a few months. Birds were singing, flowers were blooming all over the place, there were no phone books to deliver, and he only had one C.O.D. to worry with! How could it get any better than that?

Joe wasn't one to whistle. At least not out loud. However, he was whistling "in his heart" as he pulled away from the loading ramp that morning. In his devotional before heading to work, he had read and meditated on Psalm 93:

> The Lord reigneth, He is clothed with majesty; the Lord is clothed with strength, wherewith He hath girded himself: the world also is stablished, that it cannot be moved. Thy throne is established of old: thou art from everlasting. The floods have lifted up, O Lord, the floods have lifted up their voices; the floods lift up their waves. The Lord on high is mightier than the noise of many waters, yea, than the mighty waves of the sea. Thy testimonies are very sure: holiness becometh thine house, O Lord, forever.

THE DELIVERY

That's really true, thought Joe. *I serve a magnificent God, the Creator of the heavens and earth!* He had looked at his surroundings as he drove to his route. Oh sure, man had built roads, bridges, buildings, and dams. Men often thought of them as permanent structures, as though they were going to last forever. Nothing is eternal except God. Joe thought back over a few tornados that had ripped through the area, about rushing flood waters he had experienced, about seeing the aftermath of a hurricane on a beach in Florida. No, his God, the only true God, was more powerful than even nature itself. "Thou art from everlasting," he prayed out loud.

Joe's zeal for God was something he hadn't always had. In fact, as recently as seven years ago he didn't call on the name of the Lord at all. As Joe drove to his first mail stop, he thought back over his spiritual journey.

Actually, for the first thirty-five years of his life, it could hardly be called a spiritual journey at all. Not if you have to actually be moving toward something in order to call it a "journey." Joe wasn't raised in a Christian home and had never had any interest in things that had to do with God. Then, after getting married, he was much too busy to be bothered with that stuff. Raising a large family, at least large from today's standards, took much of his time and energy. Skip, now age 17, was the oldest, followed by Meghan (15), Rob (10), Laura (6), and Pete (3).

Back then Joe felt like he needed to be concerned with more practical issues, like how to scrape together monthly house payments, how to please his wife when he couldn't afford new furniture, and how to win the occasional battles he had to wage with his children, especially with his oldest son, Skip. Skip was actually Joe, Jr. and Joe realized that he couldn't have been named more appropriately. As a young man, Joe had been trouble for his father, too.

No, Joe hadn't called on the name of Jesus back in those days. Although Amy, his wife, at times seemed to have some interest in churchy things, Joe had no inclination toward them. "They're all a bunch of hypocrites!" was Joe's consistent reply when his wife would ask him shouldn't they be going to church, "for the children's sake." Joe's attitude and lack of belief in God had also been his father's, and Joe had been determined to nurture the same thoughts in his own children.

"Forget it!" was Joe's response to people who pestered him, trying to get him to come to their church. "Look. I'm not blind, you know! I deliver the mail. I know what people get 'secretly' at their home. I recognize from the return address labels and even the wording on the outside of the packaging what is inside some of those letters and parcels. I don't let that kind of stuff in my house, and I don't even go to church. And some of those same people also get a bunch of religious kind of mail! No thanks."

One of the men on his route, Mr. Dithers, had the audacity to try telling Joe about Jesus once. Imagine! After the kinds of stuff that Ralph Dithers had gotten in the mail, it amazed Joe that the man would try to proselytize him. *What does he think I am? Blind?* Joe thought.

No, he wasn't interested in their hollow, fake religion. What did it offer him, except the opportunity to be a hypocrite himself? Joe couldn't stand the thought of having that title pinned on him. Especially after calling others hypocrites all of his life. Besides, Joe was a good man. He was faithful to his wife and tried to be a good father to his children. Joe gave to the United Way and volunteered sometimes in the community. He was a good man. Better than a lot of those churchy Christians.

THE DELIVERY

Then it had happened — Joe's conversion. No, it wasn't an earth shattering experience. No voice from heaven came booming down instructing him to repent. Joe would have probably welcomed something like that. Instead, Joe was humbled by God using a soft-spoken, shy Gideon to accomplish His will. This Gideon, one of a group of men dedicated to getting Bibles into the hands of the lost, was a meek little man about sixty-five years old who was standing on the corner of White Street and 21st Avenue one morning. He simply offered Joe a Bible as he walked down the sidewalk. Joe had seen these men on the streets before, and had always thought they looked very out of place in their Sunday dress-up clothes, trying to get someone, anyone, to take one of their Bibles. This little man, very shy, hadn't even said anything. He just reached out toward Joe with a small green book in his hand and raised eyebrows, as if to say, "Would you please take this?"

Joe felt kind of sorry for the little man. *I guess he has some kind of quota of Bibles he has to hand out or something. I'll take one just to help him out so he can get back home out of this heat. I can't believe they would make little old men like this stand out in the burning heat in a suit (of all things!) passing out books.* "Sure, I'll take one, fellow," Joe had said kindly. Actually, to Joe, taking the Bible from the poor little guy proved Joe's point that Joe was already a good man and didn't need anything extra like religion in his life.

"Thank you, sir," the Gideon replied, bowing his head. "May God bless you as you read His Word."

Read it? Joe thought. *Not likely! I've got no use for this silly little book. I'm just trying to help you out, little guy, by taking one!*

But what was Joe going to do with it now that he had it? He had seen people take these books before and then toss them behind some bushes or into a garbage can a little way down the sidewalk. *What a waste of money!* Joe had thought. He didn't feel as if he could just throw it away, even if he had gotten it free. His parents had taught him to be thrifty, not wasteful. Somehow throwing away a brand-new book seemed ridiculous.

I know. I'll sell it in a yard sale. Upon reflection, he realized that plan had a few flaws. *No, that won't work. You can get them everywhere for free. Why would someone pay for them?*

So Joe placed it into his pocket and when he got back in his truck, he tossed it on the dash. At the end of the day, he happened to see it there and felt embarrassed. He surely didn't want any of the guys at the post office to think he had been reading it. So he grabbed it and put it into his pocket again.

That night as he changed his clothes, he pulled the Bible from his pocket. Another decision to make: What to do with this unwanted and useless Bible? Laying it on his dresser, he glanced at it from time to time as he changed from his postal uniform into his "civilian clothes."

He couldn't help but remember the face of the little man who had handed him the Bible. Joe thought it was shyness he had seen there, but now that he reflected on it, the man had looked more hopeful than anything else. Was it hope that Joe would take the book, or hope that Joe would actually read it? At the time, Joe had been sure that it was the former. Now he wasn't so sure.

"Oh, what does it matter anyway?" he grumbled under his breath. "I'm sure not going to read it." Completing his change to civilian attire, he walked out of the room to eat supper.

Joe did eat supper. He talked with his family and learned about their day. Then he sat down to watch a

THE DELIVERY

little TV. Joe was one who prided himself on keeping up with what was happening in the world. He took *Newsweek*, read the daily paper from cover to cover, and watched the ABC nightly news on TV. But for some reason, he couldn't keep his mind on the news tonight.

One of the segments was filmed at the West Bank of Israel. As Joe watched, the reporter talked about yet-another bombing and pointed to some rubble behind him. As the reporter continued to tell the story of the bomb blast, a man wearing a business suit slowly walked behind the reporter and seemed to stare at the camera. Having a gawker in the background of a film was not new, but Joe couldn't stop staring at this one. *Now what about that guy looks familiar?* he asked himself. *Is he a terrorist? . . . No, now I know!*

"Hey, that guy looks almost exactly like that man handing out the Bibles today!" Joe exclaimed, pointing to the TV and sitting forward in his seat excitedly.

"What?" Amy asked, a little absently. She had been preoccupied with a *Ladies Home Journal* magazine that came in the day's mail, and didn't really hear what Joe said.

The man behind the reporter walked out of camera-view, and Joe suddenly felt silly. Amy still wasn't really paying any attention to the whole thing, so Joe just said, "Oh, it's nothing, honey." Amy settled back into her chair, totally engrossed once more in an article about the proper watering and feeding of indoor plants.

Joe was restless. Even though he usually looked forward to unwinding each day by watching the evening news, he couldn't seem to sit still. *Nothing interesting tonight anyway*, he thought, standing and stretching. "I think I'll go for a walk. Want to come?" he asked Amy.

Amy didn't hear his first request. This article was the clearest explanation she had ever read about how to keep indoor plants alive, something she had longed to do for years, but at which she had never been very successful. Based on this article, it looked like she had always been drowning them. "What?" she asked absently as she closed the magazine. Then glancing at the clock and realizing what he must have asked, she replied, "No, you go without me, dear. I'm a little tired after making supper."

Joe put on his Crimson Tide baseball hat and started for the door. Starting to sneeze, he reached for the handkerchief in his back pocket, but found none. *Better get one before I leave*, he thought, heading back to his bedroom. *I wonder if this is a cold I've picked up somewhere.*

As he reached for a handkerchief in a drawer, he couldn't help seeing the Bible again, lying right in front of him. "Hmmmpp," he grunted, picking up the book. The book looked a little cheap to him. He flipped it open. The words were small and the paper wasn't really top quality. There was nothing in its physical characteristics that attracted Joe or made him want to read it. Even the color of the cover was not to his taste. He looked at the page he had randomly opened to. At the top it said "Hebrews 11," whatever that meant. He read a few lines:

> By faith Enoch was translated that he should not see death; and was not found, because God had translated him: for before his translation he had this testimony, that he pleased God.

Joe stared at the words. "What in the world is that supposed to mean?" he wondered, laughing out loud. "You'd think that they could at least write these things in

THE DELIVERY

English." He really meant to drop the book and take his walk. But he read on.

> But without faith it is impossible to please Him: for he that cometh to God must believe that He is, and that He is a rewarder of them that diligently seek Him. By faith Noah, being warned of God of things not seen as yet, moved with fear, prepared an ark to the saving of his house; by the which he condemned the world, and became heir of the righteousness which is by faith. By faith, Abraham, which was called to go out into a place which he should after receive for an inheritance, obeyed; and he went out, not knowing whither he went. By faith he sojourned in the land of promise, as in a strange country, dwelling in tabernacles with Isaac and Jacob, the heirs with him of the same promise: For he looked for a city which hath foundations, whose builder and maker is God.

For some reason, Joe was intrigued by this writing. It went on to talk about the faith of Sarah, Isaac, Jacob, Moses, Rahab, Gideon, Barak, Samson, Jephthah, David, and Samuel. Some of the things didn't make any sense at all to him, but others did, because he had heard a few Bible stories like most everyone else had. As he got to Chapter 12, instead of stopping, he surprised himself and kept on reading.

> Wherefore seeing we also are compassed about with so great a cloud of witnesses,

> let us lay aside every weight, and the sin which doth so easily beset us, and let us run with patience the race that is set before us, looking unto Jesus the author and finisher of our faith; who for the joy that was set before Him endured the cross, despising the shame, and is set down at the right hand of the throne of God.

Racing. Now that was something that really interested Joe. At the time, he was a long-distance runner and had even entered a few marathons. *I didn't know the Bible talked about races*, he thought. He sat on the edge of his bed and flipped through the Bible some more, hoping to find something about racing.

He would read a few words on a page, and then turn to another page. The topics seemed to be endless and randomly discussed: "purify thyself with them," "having then gifts differing according to the grace that is given to us," "thou shalt not muzzle the ox that treadeth out the corn," "be sober, and hope to the end for the grace that is to be brought unto you at the revelation of Jesus Christ," "he that hath the Son hath life; and he that hath not the Son of God hath not life," "and I saw the dead, small and great, stand before God; and the books were opened, which is the book of life: and the dead were judged out of those things which were written in the books, according to their works," "Peace be unto you: as my Father hath sent me, even so send I you."

Needless to say, Joe was somewhat confused by these passages. They didn't seem connected. It was the first time Joe could remember ever having actually read the Bible himself.

"Looks like you have to be a college professor to understand it!" he remarked a little angrily as he tossed

THE DELIVERY

it back onto the dresser. Turning, he was completely surprised to find his wife standing there looking at him. *How long has she been there?* he wondered, sheepishly. *And why is she spying on me anyway?* Joe could feel his cheeks turning red with embarrassment. *I hope she didn't notice I was reading that.*

"What's that you're reading, Joe?" Amy asked, picking up the book. "The Bible? Where did you get it?" When Joe didn't answer, she flipped through it casually. "I didn't know you cared about stuff like this."

Joe knew that Amy wasn't going to let the matter rest. That's just the way she was. He might as well confess all. "A man gave it to me today. You've seen those guys who stand on the sidewalk handing out Bibles? Well, I felt sorry for this little old man so I took one. I just happened to open it and see what was inside. Aw, it's a mess, though! Looks impossible to understand, and doesn't seem like it would be worth it even if you could. I'm not interested in religion or in being a hypocrite. You know that!"

Amy was flipping through the book. "Some of these words and phrases do seem ancient," she agreed. "I wonder why they still have things like, 'verily, verily,' and 'but withal prepare me also a lodging.' No wonder it's confusing to you. Probably would be to anyone!"

"It's not just that," Joe added, enjoying this opportunity to criticize the Bible, and thankful that Amy was on his side this time. He needed to reestablish his disdain for spiritual things before she got some strange ideas that he was the least bit interested in them. "There doesn't seem to be a story or anything."

"Hmmm," Amy replied, still flipping pages, and pausing from time to time to read a sentence or two. "Did you start from the beginning?"

Joe felt his face get red again. *So, she wants to argue, huh?* he thought. *Oh boy, not again!* Verbally he replied, "No. I mean I didn't want to take the time, you know. I just sort of looked at different places. But I can tell you, there's not a story line there," he concluded confidently.

Amy laughed. "How can you tell if you just flip from place to place?" She held up her magazine. "If I just read a magazine the way you read this Bible, I doubt if it would make sense either!" She tossed the Bible on the dresser. "Ready to take that walk? I changed my mind. I would like to go with you."

Joe was relieved that Amy was dropping the subject of the Bible. Yet, he was also a little angry with himself. *Why am I embarrassed about her seeing me read that book? Can't I look at and read whatever I want to without worrying about what my wife thinks about it?* he asked himself. Then, addressing her question, he said, "Sure, let's go. It'll be getting dark soon. Want to take the dog?"

As they walked, Joe tried to enjoy the evening. Here he was, walking with his lovely wife. The temperature had cooled down to a comfortable 75 degrees. There were some neighbors and friends out in their yards and he usually enjoyed greeting people as he walked. But tonight he couldn't get that silly Bible out of his mind. "Jesus the author and finisher of our faith" was a phrase that kept pulsing through his mind, though he didn't have a clue what that meant.

That had been just seven years ago. As Joe turned the corner of Oak and 18th, he continued to think back to those days. After their walk that night, Joe found himself longing to peek at the Bible again. Over the next several weeks Joe actually started reading it in earnest. He took

THE DELIVERY

Amy's admonition to heart and started at the beginning of the book, which was Matthew 1. He almost gave up, working through all of the "begat's" in Chapter 1. He didn't quit, however. Tears came to Joe's eyes as he remembered how God had worked in a mighty way and allowed Joe to understand much of what he was reading. It was through the Holy Spirit and the simple reading of God's word that Joe was convicted of his sin, and then his need for the blood of Jesus to pay the price for his sin. Quietly, in his bedroom seven years ago, he had confessed his sins to God and thanked him for what Jesus had done. [If you would like to learn more about how a person becomes a Christian, we would encourage you to please turn to the section at the end of this book entitled 'What Is a Christian.']

Over time, he started attending a church, even though he was sure there were still hypocrites there. That had been a very hard, but important step for Joe. To his surprise he found that many Christians were sincere, not hypocrites. He took his family along to church, and Amy also became a Christian rather quickly. Over the last several years, Meghan and Rob had both accepted Christ. Laura was asking questions and certainly seemed interested in Jesus.

Skip, Joe's oldest, however, had shown no sign of interest in the things of God. To this day, Skip still was not interested. That led Joe to offer up a prayer for Skip, even while Joe walked on his route, something he had done countless times over the last few years.

Joe knew that his own spiritual journey wasn't over. Not by a long shot! He still had struggles and questions that he was dealing with. Yet with the power of the Holy Spirit he approached them boldly.

The reading in Psalms this morning had renewed and energized Joe. Yes, the day had started out perfectly. In fact, the entire day had gone well until he and Cameron's bike had . . . how should he phrase it? . . . "connected."

Now he was driving to the post office looking like someone who had wrestled with a grizzly bear, and lost! Turning into the parking lot, Joe wondered what his fellow employees would say. Especially Casey. Joe hoped that Casey wouldn't be there. As he backed up to the dock, Joe saw that his hopes weren't going to be fulfilled. For there on the dock, arms folded, cigarette hanging out of his mouth, was Casey, looking more smug and spiteful than usual.

Joe set the parking break, took a deep breath, opened the door, and stepped down. Casey flicked his cigarette to the ground and started walking toward him.

Chapter Three

"Hi, Casey," Joe greeted just as politely as he could while Casey walked up to him.

"Well!" Casey exploded. "Just look at what the dogs done drug in!" He laughed before continuing, while Joe walked toward the door of the building. "Joe, I declare you look . . . awful! What'd you do, go home for lunch and have a fight with the missus?" Casey let out another loud laugh. "Yep, I can see it all now. You forgot to bring the half-gallon of mint chocolate chip ice cream she asked you for and she tore into you! Come on now, Joe. You can confess all to me. You know **I** won't tell nobody!"

Joe continued to walk toward the building, trying his best to control his temper. *Help me, Lord*, Joe prayed. Then, answering Casey, "No, a boy ran over me with a bicycle. But I'm okay."

"Yeah, I'm sure you are. The kid's mother called up the office here and told Larry all about it. Larry told me to be here waiting on you in case you needed help unloading or anything." However, Casey had yet to look in the truck or to volunteer to help Joe carry his satchel. Instead he followed Joe right into the building.

"Lay off, Casey. I'm going to go talk to Larry now," Joe responded. "There is some incoming mail in the back, if you want to get it. Plus, there's still the rest of my route that needs to be delivered. Any idea who is going to finish it?"

Casey didn't remove any of the mail. "No, I ain't sure. Could be that new kid from Mobile. I wouldn't want him driving my truck, though. No sir. I wouldn't trust him as far as I could spit! I think he hits the bottle on the job," he concluded. Casey gave a demonstration of what he suspected by pretending to take a long drink from a bottle, wiping his mouth with his arm, and then looking around to make sure no one had noticed. Casey laughed as he finished this little bit of acting.

By now Joe had reached the office of his supervisor, Larry. Looking in, however, there was no Larry to be seen. Joe was sore and tired. All he wanted to do was report to Larry and then head home. *Why won't Casey just leave me alone? Can't he see I feel terrible?*

But Casey didn't leave him alone. As Joe walked through the office, trying to find Larry, Casey was right behind him. Most of the employees were shocked by Joe's condition and asked if there was anything they could do to help. Casey usually responded before Joe could, often saying something like, "Yeah, you can call off his wife! Or was it someone else's wife, Joe?" followed by mean laughter.

Joe, in studying scripture, had always been intrigued by what Paul referred to as his "thorn in the flesh." Well, if Joe had such a thing, Casey was sure to be it. Not only was Casey rude and uncaring, he also had a filthy mouth and a filthy mind to go with it. Casey was the person who was always telling crude jokes, creating and repeating gossip about the employees at the office, wanting to basically be a nuisance to all with whom he came in contact.

But Casey seemed to "have it in" for Joe more than the others for some reason. Although Joe wasn't sure, he felt like one of the reasons that Casey was so antagonistic toward him was Joe's faith in Jesus Christ. Oh, Casey had pretty much always been like he was now. But Joe could tell a difference in the way Casey treated him since

THE DELIVERY

his conversion. It was as though Casey thought it was his job to keep Joe from living a full and happy life.

Joe really struggled with Casey. *How can I love him, Lord?* he had asked over and over. *There's not anything to love. How can I do it?* Sometimes it was hard for Joe to even be civil to Casey. Like now.

There were opportunities from time to time when Joe had a chance to "get even" with Casey. Although he knew he shouldn't, at times he had fallen to the temptation. He always regretted it, however, as he was convicted by the Holy Spirit. God's Word was very clear on how he should respond to Casey. One passage that Joe had studied many times was the following:

> Love thy enemy. Do good to them which hate you, bless them that curse you, and pray for them which despitefully use you. And unto him that smiteth thee on the one cheek offer also the other; and him that taketh away thy cloak forbid not to take thy coat also. Give to every man that asketh of thee; and of him that taketh away thy goods ask them not again. And as ye would that men should do to you, do you also to them likewise. For if ye love them which love you, what thank have ye? For sinners also love those that love them. And if ye do good to them which do good to you, what thank have ye? For sinners also do even the same. And if ye lend to them of whom ye hope to receive, what thank have ye? For sinners also lend to sinners, to receive as much again. But love ye your enemies, and do good, and lend, hoping for nothing again; and your reward shall be great, and

> ye shall be the children of the Highest; for He is kind unto the unthankful and to the evil. Be ye therefore merciful, as your Father also is merciful. Luke 6:27-36.

Then there was that other passage, the one in Romans, that caused Joe much guilt and sorrow as he reflected on his life:

> Therefore if thine enemy hunger, feed him; if he thirst, give him drink: for in so doing thou shalt heap coals of fire on his head. Be not overcome of evil, but overcome evil with good. Romans 12:20-21.

Sure, Joe knew what he was supposed to do. But doing it was so much harder than just knowing what to do. Today, he was fully aware that he hadn't conquered his "thorn in the flesh."

"Hey, Joe! There you are!" It was Larry, walking in from an outside door.

Thank you Lord, Joe said to himself. *Now maybe Casey will leave me alone.* Sure enough, seeing Larry resulted in Casey walking quickly into the sorting area, pretending that was just where he had been headed.

"Larry, I've pulled the truck in," Joe said. "I hope you can find someone to finish my route for me today. I need to get home, get cleaned up, and take something for this pain." His headache was starting to get worse.

"Sure, no problem," Larry agreed quickly. "I'm going to let Rod finish your route for you. He had a slow day and is already back in. I'm sure we can figure out where you got to and what needs to be done. You go home and take care of yourself. Here," he said, handing Joe a few pieces of paper. "You'll need to fill this out before too long."

THE DELIVERY

Joe looked at the papers. There was a Form 169 Accident Report, for non-automobile accidents, as well as a Form CA-1 Federal Employee's Notice of Traumatic Injury and Claim for Continuation of Pay/Compensation.

Paperwork. A necessary evil. *I wonder how many other forms this accident will require that I fill out?* Joe thought. *Oh well, there's always another day to do that. For now I'm heading home!*

As Joe was walking out of the building, Casey took one final shot at him. "Say, if your wife is upset with you for messing up your clothes, let me give you a piece of friendly advice, buddy. Climb the nearest tree!" Following a crude remark, Casey added, "Women can't climb too fast." Casey laughed as he walked away.

"Goodbye, Casey," Joe managed to say civilly. However, he wasn't doing as well in his heart as he was with his words.

*Who knows? Maybe I'll have to be off a few days and won't have to deal with **him**!* That was about the only potential bright side of the accident, as far as Joe could tell.

Joe's headache had intensified even more, and all he wanted to do was to get home to Amy's tender loving care. He didn't have long to wait.

Before his car had come to a stop in his driveway, Amy was quickly walking out of the house in the direction of the car. "Oh, honey, they called me from the post office. Are you all right? Are you sure that nothing's broken? Do you need to go to a doctor? Here, how can I help? . . . No, don't worry about carrying that in, we can do it later."

Amy helped Joe walk into the house. In the living room, most of the children were lined up in front of the couch, staring at him as though he had just stepped out of a spaceship from Mars. Laura's mouth was wide open, but she didn't say a thing. Probably Amy had warned the children what Dad might look like and had instructed them very carefully not to make a sound when he got home.

Within fifteen minutes, Joe had taken some aspirin for the pain, had been helped to change from his clothing, had bandages on his cuts, and was lying in his bed with the curtains drawn shut.

"I think you'll feel better if you can get some sleep," Amy suggested. "I'll put this bell here and if you need anything at all you just ring it. I'm going to make sure everyone keeps the noise level down so you can rest. Can I get you anything else right now?"

Joe shook his head and tried to smile. "Thanks, Amy. It feels so much better just to be home where I'm loved and cared for. Don't worry. I really am okay."

"I know you're okay," she said sweetly. "My job is to make you 'super okay.' Even 'well' wouldn't be bad. Now you try to rest. Even get some sleep if you can. And don't worry about a thing."

The aspirin seemed to help and even though Joe still had a headache, he finally dropped off to sleep.

Sleep may have helped his body to heal, but it didn't do much for his mind. Joe had several nightmares that left him feeling more anxious and keyed up. In one nightmare, Cameron was behind him holding a double-barreled twelve-gauge shotgun. Cameron repeatedly pulled the trigger and then laughed wickedly when it didn't go off. Joe knew that sometime it would go off and that Joe wouldn't fare well when it did.

The other nightmare starred Casey in the leading role, driving Joe's mail truck on Joe's route. All of the customers on Joe's route were solemnly lined up along

THE DELIVERY

the sidewalks, mail in their left hand, their right hand raised, holding up a little red flag. Casey kept shouting out the window to people on the street that Joe had troubles at home. "You should have seen him this morning, folks. Looked like a mountain lion grabbed him! Wouldn't have believed it, if I hadn't seen it myself. Christian marriages are just like all the rest — mostly more trouble than they're worth!" This was followed by laughter and cursing by Casey.

This nightmare had several versions with Casey sometimes using a megaphone, and sometimes using a loudspeaker attached to the top of the truck. Regardless of the version, it was frustrating for Joe. Joe had a wonderful marriage to Amy. Besides, he hated the way that the institution of marriage, something that God Himself ordained, was being slammed by Casey.

It was during this restless phase, that something woke Joe up. He wasn't sure what it was at first, but he had the sensation that someone was in the room, quietly sneaking around. Could it be Casey? Not seeing anyone, Joe felt silly. That is, until he turned to look at the door. Joe realized it was partly cracked open, but was closing very, very slowly. The handle turned, almost like slow-motion, as the door neared the frame. When the door was finally pulled completely shut, he watched mesmerized as the handle slowly turned back in the other direction.

Joe started to call out to whomever was on the other side of the door. Then he remembered the bell. He could ring the bell and not have to shout. That would be a better plan, at least as far as his headache was concerned. He reached for the bell and saw a note beside it.

Picking up the note, he at once recognized the handwriting of his six-year-old daughter, Laura. Joe's eyes misted as he read:

Daddy,
I'm sorre you got hert. Mommy and us prade. A LOT!! This is flower. I hope you feel gooder soon. God knows your hert. So your not alone. The dog threw up today.
Love, Laura.

Next to the card was a smashed flower that made Joe's heart melt. How thankful he was for the family that God had blessed him with!

"You have been good to me," Joe prayed. "Thank You that I wasn't hurt any worse than I was. Please help me to recover as quickly as possible within Your will. Help me not to complain but to endure the pain I may have. Help me to learn any lessons You want to teach me now. In Jesus' name. Amen."

Chapter Four

Joe slept off and on the rest of that day and night. In the morning, he woke up automatically at 6:30, like always. Reaching over to turn off his alarm clock before it went off, he let out a low groan, and remembered the accident of yesterday.

"Honey, why don't you stay home today?" Amy offered drowsily, turning to face him. She, more than anyone else, knew what kind of night's sleep Joe had. "I'm afraid you might try to overdo it today if you go in."

Joe lay on his back and thought about her advice. "I'm sure that nothing is broken. I thank God for that," he replied. "Even though I would have to move slowly, I think I can make it."

"I'm sure you can **make** it," Amy smiled, propping up on one elbow to look down into his face, "but is there any real reason why you must go in? I'm sure if any of the other workers got hurt the way you did, they would take a day off. Maybe several days. Why not take a day and let your cuts heal a little bit?" She was honestly trying to suggest what was best for Joe, but she doubted if her advice would be heeded. Joe had only missed a handful of days in all the years he had worked for the post office.

"I know you want what's best for me," Joe smiled up at his wife. He let out a big sigh. "But I can almost see those letters and packages, and can almost hear my supervisor calling to me, 'Joe, Joe, come and deliver.'" He laughed a little, trying to reassure Amy he was okay. "Besides, . . ."

A loud knock at their door startled Joe and halted his conversation. "Yes? . . . You can come in," Joe stated as Skip peeked around the door.

Skip was fully dressed, but that wasn't unusual. He had a habit of getting up before anyone else and watching the sunrise or reading a book. "Dad, I was wondering if it would be okay with you if I went camping with Larry and Brian tonight. They're going to camp at the county park and they invited me to come along."

"Skip, you said you weren't going to bring this up until breakfast," Amy said, perturbed at her oldest son. "Couldn't you wait to ask your dad?"

"You said I had to wait until Dad got up," Skip replied, defensively. "I heard you guys talking so I knew that he must be awake. What do you say, Dad?"

Joe looked at Skip, then at Amy. "What do you think, Amy?"

"I said he had to ask you."

"Who are these guys? Is Brian that boy that lives down the road in the red house?" Joe asked his son.

"Yes, he is. He's a good kid, too. He isn't home schooled, but he is okay. You can trust me on that one."

"Well, who's Larry?"

"Larry Mellon. He goes to our church," Skip offered, hopefully. "And his parents home school him, too."

"Mellon . . . Mellon. For some reason, I don't recognize that name," Joe replied, thinking hard.

"His dad doesn't come to church," Skip said. "But you can't blame that on his son, can you?" he added quickly. "His mom is there a lot."

"But I can't picture this Larry," Joe said matter-of-factly. "Do you know him, honey?"

THE DELIVERY

"Yes, I think I've seen him once or twice when I was talking with his mother after church," Amy answered. "But that's all."

"He doesn't go to church a lot," Skip said hesitantly. "But he would like to. It's just that his dad usually wants to go fishing on Sundays and he wants Larry to go with him. I guess Larry is just being submissive to his dad." Skip hoped that last statement would help his case.

"I'll have to think about it," Joe answered. He had a policy of not making spur-of-the-moment decisions that he often regretted later.

"But, Dad! I need to know right away. The guys are going tonight. If I don't know soon, they might invite someone else. Come on, Dad, you can trust me."

"I'll let you know this morning sometime," Joe said with finality in his voice.

Joe did decide to go into work. He had a number of bandages covering some cuts, but the real pain he felt was in his back and legs, which were bruised. His boss and coworkers were sympathetic, with the exception of Casey, of course. Joe took his time and didn't try to overdo it.

In midmorning, he called home and talked to Skip. "I've decided to let you go on that camping trip tonight," he said. "But I want you to know that I am doing it because I assume I can trust you. Don't let me down, okay, pal?"

Skip was ecstatic. "No, Dad. I won't let you down! Thanks." With that Joe heard Skip's phone hang up. *Probably afraid I would change my mind,* Joe thought.

Even as Joe was hanging up his phone, he wondered, *Did I do the right thing?* Having children grow up into their later teen years had created some new challenges for Joe and Amy. When do you let go? And under what circumstances? When do you start letting children make decisions, and mistakes?

He had prayed about whether to let Skip go on the trip. But his decision today had been greatly influenced by a speaker on a Christian radio program he was listening to as he drove to an earlier stop. He hadn't heard the whole program and didn't even know who the speaker was. The man had reported on studies done by Christian psychologists. Their findings had shown that children adjust better as adults if they are given measured amounts of freedom and decision-making authority when older teens.

But how much is "measured?" Joe wished that he had been raised in a godly home. He wished he had more direction on how to raise children for Christ. Up to this point, he had pretty much said "No," anytime Skip had asked to do something away from the family. After all, Joe knew what kinds of trouble boys got into when not supervised by adults. But he knew he couldn't go on doing that forever. Sooner or later, he would have to cut loose the strings and let Skip make some decisions for himself, and pay for the consequences of those decisions, too.

Back home, Skip busily packed for his overnight camping trip. Ten-year-old Rob was a little pouty and upset that he wasn't going to get to camp with his seventeen-year-old brother. "I wouldn't be any trouble," he pleaded.

"Sure, but this is for older boys." Skip tried to reason with his younger brother. "Look, we can camp sometime in our back yard. Okay?"

"That won't be the same as sleeping by a lake," Rob replied, walking away with his head low.

THE DELIVERY

Meghan and Laura were happy for Skip, however, and helped him pack food. Laura even put a surprise in his pack when Skip wasn't looking. The surprise was a caramel she had been saving for some time, wrapped in a note she had written which said, "I love you Skip!" She placed this package in a pair of socks, hoping that he would have to change socks while on this short trip.

Three-year-old Pete was very excited by the trip his brother was going to take, but didn't seem to understand that the whole family wasn't going to go along. After all, just about everything the family did, they did together. He jumped up and down on Skip's bed, watching Skip pack. "Are we going to swim?" he asked excitedly.

"Yes, I'm probably going to swim, if it's not too cold," Skip answered, without correcting Pete's miscalculation of who was going on the trip.

"Goody!" Pete exclaimed. "I hope there aren't any bears in the woods. I don't like bears. Well, actually, I do like bears," he corrected himself. "But only the ones in books."

Skip laughed. "I'm not afraid of bears, Pete." Pete was awed by Skip's bravery.

Mom seemed apprehensive about the whole thing, but smiled and told Skip she hoped he had fun. He agreed to take the raincoat she placed on his bed, trying to make her feel okay about the whole thing, but he didn't really intend to use it.

Late in the afternoon, Larry stopped by and picked Skip up. "Boy, this is going to be fun," Skip said enthusiastically.

"Yeah," Larry agreed. After picking up Brian and getting all of their gear stowed away, the boys headed toward the county park. At first as they drove the boys talked about what they would do. After a while, though, the boys grew silent, each in his own world of thought. Skip noticed some clouds building in the east, but tried not to think about the threat of thundershowers he had heard mentioned on the weather radio at home.

At the campsite the boys worked quickly, pitching the tent and generally getting set up. "I'll scout around and find us some more firewood," Skip offered, as Larry and Brian set up a small lean-to by the fire pit. He was having fun.

But there was almost nothing to use for firewood around the campsite. *I guess all of the former campers must have used it all up*, he thought. That required him to venture quite a ways from the camping area into deeper woods. He traveled through a number of dips and hills and had to make several turns to avoid impenetrable undergrowth.

As he walked, his mind flitted from topic to topic. *What if we get a bad thunderstorm tonight? I wonder what the hot dogs will taste like since we forgot to bring buns or mustard. What if one of the guys isn't safe with the fire . . . should I try and correct him, or just act like I don't notice?*

Boy, it sure is dark in here, Skip thought. The trees were so large and fully-leaved that little sunlight reached the floor of the forest. Plus it was getting late and clouds were definitely building up darker. Looked like rain for sure tonight.

Skip gathered a big armful of sticks and turned to head back to camp. He walked for a few minutes, but suddenly got the sense that he was heading in the wrong direction. *Silly me!* he thought. Turning, he walked toward a knoll that he thought he recognized. *Now I really wish I had paid more attention to how I got here.* He wasn't afraid. Just a little concerned. It was a good

THE DELIVERY

ways back to the campsite, that much he knew. But exactly how far, and in what direction?

Skip sat down on a log and thought about something his father had taught him a few years back. Anytime you feel you are lost in the woods, first, sit down and think. Don't panic. If you can keep from panicking, chances are you will get out okay. Skip took a long breath and tried to think positively.

Next, Joe had instructed his children to pray if they were lost, that God would give them wisdom and peace. Skip didn't really see any need to do that. After all, he was sure he could get back by himself. But the years of Joe's instruction were a little too much for him, so he mouthed a quick prayer, with very little of it coming from his heart. "God, if you want to help me find my way back to the camp, that's okay with me. I sure won't begrudge your help! Thanks." For some reason this made him feel better. He didn't think it would do any good, but he knew that his dad would be happy if he could claim that he had in fact prayed to God about it, if asked.

*Okay, now what **practical** things did Dad say to do?* he asked himself, not considering prayer to be in that category. Joe had said to remember that water always seeks lower ground. So, all you have to do is find natural watersheds and follow them. Eventually you should end up at a stream or brook that will lead you to a river, pond, or lake. Joe said that you would usually find people living near rivers or lakes and that you would no longer be lost and helpless.

"But I'm not lost," Skip reassured himself. Sitting on the log, he surveyed what he could see of the landscape. To the left, the ground definitely sloped downward, so he decided to follow that path. *Now I'm onto something,* he thought cheerfully, following a sort of ditch for a ways. Soon, however, it was nothing but a tangled mass of briars and shrubs and Skip couldn't follow it further. So, he left the ditch and went to higher ground to circumvent the obstruction. He had to do this a number of times before it led him out of the really thick forest into a more cleared woodland.

In about five minutes, he saw glimpses of the lake through the trees and then got his bearings again. One thing he didn't want to do was admit to the guys that he had gotten lost, even for a few minutes. He began to think of things he could say as he entered the camp that would take their minds off how long he had been gone. As it turned out, however, he shouldn't have bothered.

Larry and Brian were sitting by the campfire watching a few twigs and some pine needles burning. Even at this range, Skip could make out what Brian was saying. "Wow, you mean he makes $40 just for carrying a package to the building?"

"Yep," Larry replied. "Just for carrying a measly little old package a few miles. I call that pretty good money. Cash, too. Two crisp $20 bills!"

"Me too!" Brian agreed. "But what's in those packages?"

Skip walked into the campsite. "Here's some firewood, guys. Looks like we might get some rain tonight." He placed a few of the smaller sticks on the fire and put the rest under the lean-to to keep them dry in case it rained. Neither of the boys acted like they even heard what he had said nor that he was even there.

"I don't know what's in the packages, but why care?" Larry answered Brian's question. "Forty bucks is forty bucks, that's what I say. If a man wants to pay me that kind of money, I'm not going to ask any questions."

THE DELIVERY

Skip felt left out and wanted to be a part of this conversation. "What packages?" he asked. "What are you guys talking about?"

Larry looked at Brian in a sideways glance before answering. It seemed as if the boys were trying to decide whether to tell Skip about what they were discussing. "Oh, go ahead and tell him," Brian suggested.

Larry stood up and kicked a burning stick with his boot to push it further into the fire. "Oh, it's nothing, Skip. I was just telling Brian about how Jeremy is making a little cash, that's all." Skip didn't know anyone named Jeremy, but didn't want to admit it.

"I heard something about $40," Skip suggested, trying to get more details about the conversation. After all, if you can't be a party to a conversation, you're not really good friends, are you?

Larry laughed a little. "He just delivers these little packages for a man he knows. The man pays him for his trouble. It's not a big deal."

Brian wasn't convinced of that. "You may not think so, but I'm going to see if I can get ahold of some of that business myself," he proclaimed. "I could use some money."

"So could I," Skip offered. He was hoping to buy a car soon after turning eighteen and he knew the immense value of cash in such a transaction. "Any chance that all of us can get in on that deal?"

"Maybe," Larry said. "Just maybe. But don't you guys go talking to Jeremy, you hear? Let me talk to him. I'm not sure he wants the whole world to know how he lives his life."

There was something odd about this conversation to Skip, but he couldn't quite put his finger on it. Before he could say anything else, the boys turned and watched as a car drove slowly down the campsite roadway. The driver seemed to be trying to find someone. Finally, the car stopped in front of their campsite and Skip's dad got out.

"Hi, guys!" Joe greeted, stepping out of his car. Skip was afraid his dad would embarrass him by doing something like reminding him to brush his teeth before going to bed. But Joe didn't do or say anything embarrassing. In fact, Larry and Brian seemed to think Skip's dad was okay.

After talking a few minutes, Joe said, "I thought you guys might want to have some of this venison to cook. There's nothing like venison over an open campfire."

"Say, thanks!" Larry said. "I've never had venison before. How do you cook it?"

Joe laughed. "Just like beef. I suggest you make a few skewers out of sticks and then cut the venison into little cubes and place them on the skewer. Then, stick it over the fire until well done, and you'll have yourself a pretty tasty treat."

"It sure was nice of you to come and bring it," Brian said, politely. "We were just going to eat some hot dogs."

Joe smiled and placed his hands over the fire. "Hot dogs might be good for a midnight snack. Well, it looks like you guys are all set up. I have to run. It will be supper soon at home. So long."

Joe was glad that he had stopped by, even if it might seem like he was interfering. He wanted a chance to meet the boys who were camping with Skip. After saying "yes," he had serious second thoughts that he had made a mistake. Even though you couldn't make a complete impression of boys just in a few minutes, Joe was pretty adept at sizing up a situation and figuring out

THE DELIVERY

what was going on. As best he could tell, things at the campsite were under control. The boys had not been smoking or drinking, and he didn't see anything else that might cause him concern. Larry and Brian seemed okay. Actually, his biggest concern was for the thunderclouds forming in the sky. Oh well, millions of campers, himself included, had lived through worse-looking storms than this one seemed to be building into.

As it turned out, Joe should have had more concerns than he realized at the time.

Chapter Five

Saturday morning broke clear, but the ground was soaked from the torrential thunderstorms the night before. Afraid of the storm, Pete had spent most of the night with his mom and dad, and was right now peacefully sleeping with one leg across Joe's chest.

Joe looked over at Amy. "Isn't he sweet?" Amy asked quietly.

"Y. . .e . . .s," Joe admitted slowly, taking his time to get the word out. "But I have to admit I wish he had been a little more still, like he is right now, last night!" Pete had been responsible for Joe's less-than-wonderful night of sleep, what with his hands and feet constantly pushing this way and that. "I never knew a three-year-old boy could be so active even when sound asleep!"

"How do you feel this morning?" Amy asked.

"A little sore," Joe admitted. "But I'm amazed at how well I do feel. When the accident happened, I was sure I would be in bed for a week."

"You said that someone even thought of calling an ambulance when you had your accident," Amy reminded him. "I'm glad you feel better. God has really blessed you." Changing the subject, she asked, "I wonder how Skip made it last night." The worry in her voice was hard to hide.

"I'm sure he did okay, Mrs. Mama Bear," Joe grinned at her. "Don't worry. He'll probably pull in here in a few hours, smelling like a campfire, soaked to the bone, but smiling like everything!"

THE DELIVERY

"I hope so," Amy replied, not so sure of Joe's prediction. "What do you have planned for today?"

Pete stirred, moved his leg from Joe's chest, and placed a fist in its place.

"I was going to work on Elaine's rotten fascia boards, but I'm not sure what I'll do after that rain we had last night."

Elaine Jackson was an older widow in their neighborhood who lived in a small white cottage. From the road, someone casually passing by would have described it as a quaint, well-maintained, charming home. On closer inspection, however, the person would note signs of neglect and decay. Some of the boards were rotting, and a few of the window panes needed replacing. Several trees had huge dead branches that needed to be pruned. As usual, the most serious problems were found inside the house. The plumbing was ancient and pipes were always getting clogged, the wiring needed updating, and the furnace looked like it was designed by a part-time engineer during the Civil War. Also, the foundation was warping and buckling.

However, the occupant of the house was well-loved by all who knew her. Seldom did anyone see Mrs. Jackson without a smile on her face. And that was true regardless of the pain she was enduring. She was always doing things for others, such as cooking meals for the sick, visiting people in nursing homes, and volunteering her time for activities at the church. Yes, Elaine was a jewel, that sparkled wherever she went.

Elaine couldn't do many things for herself, however. Mr. Jackson had always done the household repairs, and Elaine didn't even know where to begin. That's where Joe and his family stepped in and offered to help. Joe had taken Elaine as his family's own mission project. They had decided to help her in any way possible. Joe thought it would be nice if every Christian family did the same — took one widow as their own responsibility to look after.

Over the years, the children had helped in many ways. Today, what she needed most was to have some of her fascia boards replaced. Fascia is that part of the house where gutters, if you have them, are attached.

Elaine's gutters had fallen off the back of her house a few months ago, thanks to the rotten fascia. Joe had purchased some boards and was looking forward to getting them installed today. When the accident with Cameron Granlund's bicycle had occurred, Joe wasn't sure he would even be able to climb a ladder this weekend, much less work on a house. However, God had helped him to heal quickly, although he was still a little sore.

"I'm glad I didn't get to go camping last night," Rob admitted at the breakfast table a little while later. "That was some storm we had last night!"

"Yes it was. Dad, did you see the limbs that blew off our oak tree?" asked Laura, with wide eyes. "They are huge!"

Joe looked out the window. His yard was strewn with debris and limbs from the power of the storm. "Whew, that is a mess. I suppose we better clean up our own yard before heading over to Mrs. Jackson's. Then we'll need to pick up her yard, too."

"Can I cut her grass today?" asked Meghan. Skip usually did the honors, but Meghan wasn't sure he would be home from camping in time to do so today.

"We'll see," Joe answered.

"I know how. Honestly," Meghan assured him. "I've watched Skip do it many times. I would really like to."

THE DELIVERY

Like most parents, Joe couldn't remember exactly why using a gas-powered lawnmower would be thrilling to a child. "We'll just have to see," Joe repeated. "The grass may be too wet to cut, even this afternoon."

"I'm going over to Elaine's too," Amy noted. "I told her I would help her clean out two of her closets and go through some of Mr. Jackson's things. You know it's been five years since he passed away, and she still hasn't gotten rid of some of his clothing." Upon reflection, she added, "I guess that would be hard to do, though, if it were my husband."

"I'm glad you can help her," Joe nodded. "I'm sure it would be hard. Laura, can you pass the honey, please?"

"I want some honey!" Pete demanded in a loud voice.

Joe stopped spooning the honey onto his biscuit and reprimanded Pete. "Pete, that isn't nice. We don't shout, we talk in a quiet voice. Tell Laura you are sorry and ask for honey nicely."

"I sorry, Laura," Pete said more quietly.

"Here," said Laura, starting to put honey on Pete's biscuit.

"Don't want any," Pete decided out loud.

"Don't sulk, Pete," Joe told him.

"What's sulk?" Laura asked, tilting her head to the side, as if that would help her understand what the word meant.

"That just means to pout, or to try and show someone that you don't like what they just said or did. It's a way to get back at them or make them feel bad. We don't do that. That's not kind or loving."

Pete sat there staring at his biscuit. The room got very quiet, with all eyes on Pete. He looked like he was about to cry. Finally, he asked, "I have honey? Please?"

With that episode concluded, the conversation turned back to Skip's camping trip. "I wish I could have gone by and seen him last night, Dad, like you did," Rob asked. "What did the campsite look like?"

Joe laughed. "Like most campsites, Rob. A lot like the one we camped at last summer."

"Yes, but didn't it seem strange not to see our whole family there?" asked Laura.

Joe took a bite before answering. "Yes, it did, Laura. I have to admit that it is pretty hard to think that we won't always all be together. But that's the way God planned that it would eventually happen someday. Someday, probably all of you children will grow up, get married, and move away from home."

"I'm not going to!" exclaimed Laura. "I'm staying right here. I like Mommy's cooking. And your stories, Daddy."

"You don't *ever* have to leave," Amy quickly responded, reassuring Laura. "I'd love to cook for you the rest of your life."

"That's a fact," Joe nodded. "Your mom wouldn't have any problems with all of you staying here all your lives. It's going to be especially hard for her to see you go." Joe looked at Amy, who seemed to be getting misty-eyed.

"Children, you know that things are bound to change over the years, though. Skip just happens to be the oldest, and it won't be long until he is legally an adult. I guess you can expect that things will change over the next few years."

"How will things change?" Laura asked.

THE DELIVERY 47

"That I don't know," Joe said honestly. "All I do know is that things in our family will change. Some of you will probably get married and have a family of your own."

"I don't want things to change," Laura protested. "I like things just the way they are right now."

It was quiet for a few minutes. Then Joe began, "I understand what you mean, Laura. But if you think about it, things have always been changing, ever since you were born. If things never changed since you were born, we wouldn't have Pete. That wouldn't be fun, would it? And you would never have met your good friend, Karen. That would be sad, wouldn't it? You see, things are always changing. And things will always change. That's just the way life is. But one thing I'm grateful for is that God never changes. He is always the same. Malachi 3:6 says "For I am the Lord, I change not." And James 1:17 says, "Every good gift and every perfect gift is from above, and cometh down from the Father of lights, with whom is no variableness, neither shadow of turning." So you see, even though things do change, sometimes for the good and sometimes seemingly for the bad, God is always there and He has never changed in all of that.

"It's also nice to know that God knows the future and is in control of it. So we don't have to worry, do we? God will take care of us and will make sure that whatever He wants to allow to happen will happen. Isaiah 46:9-10 says, "Remember the former things of old: for I am God, and there is none else; I am God, and there is none like me, declaring the end from the beginning, and from ancient times the things that are not yet done, saying, My counsel shall stand, and I will do all my pleasure." It's our job to be thankful for whatever God chooses to do in our lives."

Later that day, while the family was working at Mrs. Jackson's house, Skip came home from camping. Not seeing anyone at home, he looked on the refrigerator door, and sure enough there was a note for him that read: We're at Mrs. Jackson's house working. There is leftover pizza in the refrigerator and some fresh cookies in the cookie jar. Come on over as soon as you can. Love, Mom.

Skip smiled. Mom was so faithful in her role as a mother. Although he had never experienced having any other mother, he still knew he had a great one from the times he had been at other people's houses.

He warmed up some pizza, had a handful of cookies, and then walked toward the front door. Spying a newspaper lying on the living room table, he glanced at it and scanned the headlines. One article was about a type of nuclear reactor being designed that used nuclear fusion instead of fission. Interested, he slumped down in Joe's easy chair and began to read.

"Hold it steady there, son," Joe called to Rob, while balancing a level on top of a long board. "That's good. Nope, a little higher. There you go. Now try your best to hold it right there." Joe pounded in a few nails. "Good, now you hammer in a few nails there, Rob. Try to make sure they hit the 2x4. Okay, good. Yes, we can go down now." Joe and Rob, descending from a pair of ladders, were happy as they surveyed the work they had accomplished. Rob especially was excited because it was the first time he had been able to be "the big boy." Joe couldn't have accomplished all of this without Rob's help, and Rob knew it. It made him feel more like a man.

"What else do we need to do?" Rob asked, with a lower pitch in his voice than usual.

THE DELIVERY

"I think we need to round up the girls and take a little break," Joe grinned at him, placing his hammer in its holder on his tool belt.

"But I'm not tired, Dad," Rob informed, honestly.

"Good," Joe laughed. "But I am. Let's see what Mrs. Jackson has for us in the way of refreshment."

When they went inside, they found the girls helping Amy shove some men's clothing into large white plastic bags. "We're making good progress in here," Amy said cheerily, yet tired.

"Great! We've replaced all the fascia board," Joe reported. "Now, we're ready to take a break. At least, *I'm* ready," he concluded, slapping Rob on the shoulder.

Elaine Jackson came into the room with a tray of lemonade and cookies. "Let's see if anyone can help me get these things to disappear," she said pleasantly, winking at Rob. "You've all worked so hard for me. I know you must have many things you need to do at your own house. How can I ever thank you enough?"

"Just by letting us help you," Joe told her honestly. "All we ask is that you let us help you. We really enjoy it, don't we crew?"

There was an odd assortment of affirmations as children tried to agree, but still eat cookies at the same time. Pete just smiled, held up a cookie, and nodded his head emphatically.

"But where's Skip today?" asked Elaine. "I miss him."

"So do I," Amy admitted, looking over at Joe. "I wonder where he could be."

Joe noted the concern in her voice. "Maybe he's having a lunch to end all lunches," Joe suggested. "Don't worry, honey, I'm sure he's okay. I know he would be here helping if he could." Then, addressing

Elaine's question, he continued, "Skip went camping last night with some friends and wasn't home when we left to come here."

About thirty minutes later, the family gathered their tools and walked back to their own house. Rob raced ahead of everyone else, and then came running back to give them a status report.

"Skip's sound asleep in Dad's chair!" he announced happily. "He's okay."

"I guess he was just tired," Laura offered. "Still, I wish he would have come with us to Mrs. Jackson's."

Right before supper, Joe asked Skip how the camping trip had gone. "It was all right," Skip said, in a noncommital manner. "We had fun. Didn't get a lot of sleep, though! Boy, that storm was pretty bad. And we talked, of course." That's all he said.

Even though Joe asked several more questions, Skip didn't seem to want to say much about the camping trip. *That's strange*, thought Joe. *I wonder why he's not saying much? Is he just tired or does he have something on his mind?*

Before he could spend any more time thinking about it, however, Laura came into the room and announced authoritatively, "Daddy, you had better come into the bathroom. Pete was playing with the soap and it dropped into the potty. Now, he is saying that he wasn't playing with it. He says that it just fell in by itself. But *I* saw him playing with it. Daddy, you need to . . ."

"I'm coming," Joe sighed. With that, the subject of the camping trip was closed. It would, however, be discussed again a few months later by a trio consisting of Joe, Skip, and a police officer.

THE DELIVERY

Chapter Six

"Rob, are you not dressed *yet*?" Joe asked, a little exasperated the next morning. "You know we have to leave for church in about five minutes. What have you been doing?"

"I'll make it, Dad. I can get dressed in no time." Rob spoke hurriedly, unbuttoning his pj top quickly. He had learned how to read his dad's tone of voice, and knew this was no time to fool around any more.

Joe didn't often lose his temper, but this morning he seemed to have a short fuse. First, six-year-old Laura had stopped up the kitchen sink by pouring some leftovers into the drain. While Joe was plunging that little problem away, Pete came flying into the kitchen to watch, and accidently ran into Joe's sore leg with the toy fire engine he was driving.

And that's not all. Joe had a misunderstanding with Amy about breakfast. When he came down for breakfast, he saw Amy was making eggs, and commented, "Eggs?" Amy, preoccupied with cooking, had replied that they were out of eggs and would he please put it on the grocery list that was held onto the refrigerator with a little frying pan magnet. Joe took that to mean that she wanted him to eat something other than eggs. Since Amy seemed engrossed making the eggs, Joe quietly got himself a bowl and a spoon.

Just about five seconds after Joe had poured milk on a big bowl of cereal, Amy had turned from the stove and said, "Eggs are ready, Joe. Do you have a plate or . . . ?

Why, Joe, why are you eating cereal? You knew I was making you eggs. Don't you want these eggs?"

Joe had replied that he would just as soon have cereal, especially since he had already poured the milk.

"But the children and I saved two eggs just for you!" she said, sounding hurt. "And I never said you couldn't have eggs."

"Well, you didn't make it clear," Joe responded, a little perturbed. After all, just a few minutes ago he hadn't made a big deal out of Amy's apparent lack of planning which resulted in running out of eggs. In fact he felt a little like a martyr to be eating cereal because Amy knew how much he liked eggs for breakfast. And for that, he was now in trouble? It made no sense to Joe.

"What more could I say?" Amy had asked. "I can't read your mind and know what you think I said or didn't say." Her neck and face were getting red, a sure sign of irritation for Amy. But in a few minutes, she apologized. "I'm sorry."

"I'm sorry too, honey," Joe replied. He realized once again that she was the one who usually made the first attempts at reconciliation. Being the first to say he was sorry was hard for Joe, and something he knew he needed to work on. "I'm really sorry. It's okay."

But it wasn't okay. There was a friction between the two that persisted to this minute.

"Pete, have you been to the potty?" Joe asked, reaching down to straighten the little three year-old's collar.

"Yes," Pete answered.

"I mean recently," Joe clarified. "Who helped you to go?"

THE DELIVERY 53

Pete acted like he didn't understand the question, but Joe knew better. Pete reached down and picked up a toy car he had been playing with.

"Who took you to the potty?" Joe repeated.

"Laura did it," Pete said finally, and then turned back to his car.

"Amy, we're ready to load up!" Joe called loudly in order to be heard through the house. "Let's load up, everyone!" Not seeing everyone moving quickly, he added a little more sternly, "Right now!"

Children trickled down the hallway toward the side door, which led to the garage. Meghan was dressed very nicely, and had her Bible and a special bookmark she had made for the preacher that week in home school. Then, Rob came running from his bedroom, still trying to tuck his shirttail in. Skip appeared in the hallway and walked toward the door.

"Where's your Bible?" Joe asked Skip.

"Oh, I guess I forgot it," Skip said, slowly turning and walking back toward the bedroom.

"Hurry, son!" Joe prodded. "We're going to be late! ... Amy! Amy, are you somewhere in this house? Are you about ready?" he asked, his voice growing louder with each word.

But no sooner had he said the word "ready" than she appeared walking down the hallway quickly. "I'm sorry, but it couldn't be helped," she said curtly. "Has no one gotten Pete ready?"

"I thought he was ready," Joe replied. "I asked him and he said that he had recently been taken potty by Laura."

"His idea of 'recently' isn't the same as mine. Come on big guy, let's change your shirt and take you one more time." Amy picked up Pete and walked briskly toward the bathroom.

Finally, five minutes later, the car backed out of the driveway and headed for Solid Rock Christian Academy. The church that the Reynolds attended had been renting the auditorium from Solid Rock for about five years. Some of the influential members in the church didn't really want to go into debt to build a church building. Others did. Some of the conveniences of many churches, like padded pews, were missing. The church family had to set up the chairs, distribute song books, and then undo it all again after the service was over each week. A few families in the congregation were pushing to get a church building, but so far the members had decided that their offerings could be better spent on the mission field, and in helping local needs. The issue wasn't exactly divisive, yet there had been some pretty heated debates in the last few months.

Joe was supposed to hand out bulletins today, but when he got there, he saw that Marv Johnson was doing it. "I'm sorry we're running late today," Joe apologized.

"Not a problem!" Marv replied. "Gives me a good excuse for stretching my legs before services. I did want to talk to you, after church, about the Grovers. Seems like we're going to need to get over there and help them some this week." The Grovers were a family in the church who were going through tough times. Members of the congregation took it upon themselves to go by during the week and help where possible.

"What's up?" Joe asked.

"I'll tell you after church," Marv said. "I think they're going to start soon."

Joe had lost track of the time. He too noticed that the services were about to begin. "Sorry," he whispered. "Let's take our seats," he instructed his family, who

THE DELIVERY

quietly followed Joe down the aisle to the section in which they normally sat.

The music and prayers were pretty much like always. Usually they helped Joe focus on God and what He had done for Joe. But today, Joe was preoccupied with a myriad of thoughts. He was still a little grumpy, too.

After the offering was collected, the preacher stood to preach. "As you will recall, we've spent the last several weeks talking about holiness. I want to continue that theme today, but with a slightly different twist. You all know that God has revealed His holy will to us through the teaching, commandments, and examples of scripture. I think we could pretty much agree on what 'the rules' are. We know what is right and what is wrong.

"Furthermore, I know that most of you are striving to obey the commands of God. For example, I doubt if any of you would kill, or steal, or bow down and worship wooden idols. Today, however, I want to focus on the borders. How are you doing with the borders?"

Joe, whose mind had been wandering (actually, he was thinking about the Grover family), clicked on when the preacher said the word "borders." Joe looked at the minister, who had paused for effect. *Is he looking at me?* Joe winced. *Did he ask me a question and the whole church is waiting for me to answer? I wish I had been listening!* Joe could feel the sweat suddenly bead on his forehead.

Thankfully, the preacher continued. "That's right. The borders. How are you doing with the borders? Are you staying away from them?"

Joe was still confused, but not for long. The preacher explained, "A border is the dividing line between two things. Borders separate one thing from another thing. For example, my sister owns a house in Alabama, which is very near the border with Georgia. In fact, her next door neighbor lives in Georgia. The border is the invisible line that separates the two states. It's not too big a deal. My sister can walk across the border to her neighbor's house without any trouble and nothing happens to her. We also have borders between countries. They are a little more of a big deal. A few years ago, I went to Mexico and had to cross the border. I was asked questions, and was given permission to visit Mexico for only a short period of time. Then when I came back across to the U.S., I had another series of questions I had to answer before I could cross the border. Anyway, you all know what I mean by borders. Right?

"Today I want to talk about the border between sin and not sinning. And I want to encourage you to not only avoid crossing the border into sin, but also to stay as far away from that border as you possibly can.

"Let me illustrate the idea with an old parable. There was a king who needed to take a trip across a dangerous mountain range. Naturally, he wanted to make the trip in one piece, with no accidents. So he brought together three of his top chariot drivers and asked them this question: 'We're going to have to drive near some cliffs. How close can you get to the edge without driving your chariot off the cliff?'

"The first chariot driver replied, 'Oh, King, I am a very skilled chariot driver. I assure you that I can get within one foot of the cliff's edge and not drive over the edge!' The king seemed impressed.

"The second chariot driver walked forward quickly. 'Listen to me, O most high King. I am the most skilled chariot driver in all the kingdom. I can drive within one inch, yes, just one inch, and not drive over the edge! You would be safe with me.'

THE DELIVERY

"The king was even more impressed, yet asked for the third chariot driver's credentials, who replied, 'You are a great king. I love you very much and would want nothing to happen to you. I will stay as far away from the edge as I possibly can!'

"Which of those chariot drivers would you choose if you were the king?" The preacher paused. "The king chose the third man. Why? Because he stayed as far away from the edge, the border, as possible. I'm afraid that often we are like the first two chariot drivers when it comes to the borders of sin. We claim, 'I can get this close to sin, and yet not fall into sin! Aren't I great!'"

The preacher adjusted his glasses, then continued. "The truth is that the way we approach any border shows how much we respect the person who made that border. Let me give you an example. As most of you know, I live on a dirt road out in the country. I know that some of you think I'm a little bit crazy, but I like it there. Anyway, last week a young boy came driving down the road on a dirt bike. That boy was out to have a good time and he didn't care about anyone else. He raced that dirt bike up and down our road, throwing a ton of dust into the air. His machine was practically screaming, he was riding it so fast."

Joe happened to look down the row at his family at this time, and caught the expression in Rob's eyes. Rob had a look of glee and excitement in his face. *Well, at least I know he's listening to the sermon*, Joe thought.

"After a while, I guess it got boring staying on the road, so the young man started driving in the ditches. The ditch in front of my house seemed to provide him with the greatest amount of thrill, probably because it is so steep. He would start from a distance, pick up speed, jump over part of my ditch, climb to the top of the ditch, and then turn sharply, throwing a cloud of dust onto my fence. The *white* picket fence that I made especially for my wife, Doris. Then, he would circle back around and do it again. And again. And again.

"Now, here's the thing to keep in mind. In no way did he trespass on my property. No, sir. He never crossed my boundary. But the way he approached my border demonstrated to me that he had no respect for me. He didn't care what happened to any dirt he might throw up in the air. Legally, I suppose he was in the clear. He didn't actually cross my border and trespass on my property. But he showed me no respect.

"You can probably think of lots of examples of living right up to the limit of our borders. For example, when the speed limit says 55 MPH, do you drive right up to that limit, no matter what? No matter how bad the weather is, just because you can? What about folks who charge their credit cards right up to the limit? They are living right at the boundary. What about the student who asks 'What do I have to make on this exam to still get a C in the course?' That student is living right up to the limit. He's not showing respect for the teacher or for learning. He just wants to do the least he can get away with and still be okay. In our culture I'm afraid we like to live near the limits. And that includes the borders near sin, too.

"Now, let me ask you a question. How do you feel when someone gets close to the limits you have set? Mothers, have you ever made a pan of cookies for company and set them on the counter to cool? What do you tell your children? 'Don't eat them!' In a few minutes, you walk back into the room and a child is carrying one of the cookies around. You get angry, because you feel the child has disobeyed you. But the child replies, 'You said not to eat them. You didn't say I couldn't hold one!' Or a child touches them or sticks

THE DELIVERY

their face into the pile of cookies. 'Stay away from those cookies!' you command. 'But Mom, you didn't say we had to stay away from them, you just said we couldn't eat them.' Why are you angry, mother? Because you don't like the fact that your child got so close to the borders you had set. It seemed disrespectful to you. It probably made you think that any minute they might cross the boundary. At the very least, it demonstrated that they wouldn't mind being on the other side of the boundary, eating those cookies!

"Fathers, have you ever told your children, 'Now, don't get into the pool until I get back.'"? What happens if you return and they are throwing things in, or lying on their tummies and splashing with their hands, or putting their feet into the water? What do you think? How do you feel? You probably get angry. Your children, however, will remind you that you didn't say they couldn't throw things in, or splash, or put their feet in. They're obeying, technically, but they are right on the border of disobeying. Do you want your children to always be going right up to the border of your instructions? No! Neither does God.

"In fact, there are many times where God gave commands and then later clarified because men were living right up next to the border in some way. For example, God commanded men not to commit adultery. Yet, men kept coming right up to the borders on that one. So much so, that Jesus clarified the command in Matthew 5:28 and said not to even look on a woman with lust. He did the same thing with the commandment not to kill, and said not to even be angry or call your brother a fool (Matthew 5:22). Throughout history, God had revealed that he was pleased when men prayed to Him, yet in Matthew 6:6 He had to instruct us to be sincere, and not pray long prayers just for show. God was pleased that men would bring offerings to Him, yet in Matthew 6:3 He had to instruct men to do so in secret. In so many places in scripture we see that God gave a command, yet man tried to live on just this side of the line of breaking that commandment.

"Yes, God cares about boundaries and borders and landmarks. In Deuteronomy 19:14, Deuteronomy 27:17, Proverbs 2:28, and Proverbs 23:10 we read that God instructed men not to move landmarks and that any man who did move a landmark was cursed. If God cares so much about physical landmarks, how much more does he care about spiritual ones!"

The preacher looked over his congregation, a serious look on his face. "What is the practical application of this? It's simple really. If you want to be holy, if you want to be pleasing to God, stay as far away from the borders of sin as you can. The first things 'to go' are what we would probably call 'fringe' areas. Let me run through some examples for you. The Bible clearly teaches that we are to be humble. Are you humble? Perhaps just because you don't post a 3 x 5 card next to everything you do, announcing 'I did this myself! Aren't I great!' you think you are okay with this command. But what about making sure that the other party finds out what you did. See, even though you didn't come right out and say 'I made this pie from scratch! It took most of the afternoon! Didn't I sacrifice for you?!' if you make sure that the other person learns about your sacrifice, then you've still accomplished your goal. In so doing, you're failing the humility test.

"Or think about the fact that you're not supposed to gossip. So, instead of calling and asking your neighbor, 'Why do you think neighbor Fred came home so late last night?" you find some 'valid' excuse for calling and say something like 'Yes, I was up late last night. Couldn't

THE DELIVERY

sleep. I'm sure there was more traffic than usual.' Your hope is that the other party will offer you the information (gossip) you so desperately want. Then you might turn around and call a different neighbor and say something like, "I don't want to gossip, but we do need to keep Fred's family in our prayers. I don't know if you know or not, and I wouldn't want to say anything about it except that I know you will pray for him, but when he came in last night, he was drunk! And we don't think it's the first time.'

"Want another example of living close to the border of sin? The Bible clearly teaches us not to judge one another. So, to make sure you aren't 'judging,' you carry on a conversation with your wife that you think is on this side of that line. It goes something like this: "You know that new lady who has been attending our church? Her name is Naomi. Well, I don't want to judge her, but I'm glad we don't let our children watch the TV by themselves on Saturday mornings. I'm glad that we care about the bad influence that TV can have on our children!" What has this man done? He's come close to the border of judging Naomi. But he has pretended that the only reason he even brought it up to his wife was to solidify their own stance on the issue. I'm afraid it happens all too often.

"In closing, I am reminded that sometimes you might not know exactly where the borders are. What do you do in that case? Well, let's look at a secular example first. Let's say you're planning on building a house, but you aren't sure where the borders are. What would you do? You would find those borders by hiring a survey to be done, and then you would clearly mark them. You might even want to show your neighbor honor and back off from the borders a little before building, even though you know for sure where the borders are. The same holds true with God. If you're not sure where the borders of sin are, in other words if you're not sure if this act is sinful, then find the boundaries by reading and studying God's word. Then, to show God honor, back off a good piece from those borders. Don't try to live as close to sin as you possibly can.

"I'm convinced that we live near the borders way too much. Ask God to help you see where you're trying to live right up next to the borders of sin. Then back off."

Joe took a deep breath. He knew there were many gems of truth in the pastor's sermon and intended to spend the day reflecting and meditating upon them.

Chapter Seven

"That was a very thought provoking sermon this morning," Joe commented at lunch.

"Wasn't it?!" Amy exclaimed. "I don't believe I've ever heard anyone preach on living near the border of sin before."

"Yes, and his examples were so clear," Joe added. "That one about the kid on a motorcycle got my blood boiling. I can picture — oh so clearly! — someone treating my property line with disrespect."

Laura had large eyes and she stopped eating her cold turkey and cheese sandwich. "Really, Daddy? Your blood boiled?"

Joe laughed. "That's just a figure of speech, Laura. It means that I got pretty angry just thinking about someone riding their motorcycle up to my property line the way the preacher described it. I was putting myself in the preacher's place and feeling what he must have been feeling."

"That was neat about the motorcycle," Rob said, a little dreamily. He hadn't been listening much to the conversation, intent on eating his third bagel instead. "That guy was driving fast and throwing dust all over the place. I can just see it . . . zzzzooooooommmmmmm! rrrreeeeeeeekkkkkk! . . . zzzzzzoooooooommmmm!"

Pete, giggling, was listening and watching his brother drive the imaginary motorcycle around his plate. Almost instantly, he began zooming an imaginary motorcycle around his bowl of applesauce. On the second trip around, Pete's "motorcycle" upset the bowl of applesauce and it rolled toward the edge of the table.

Amy grabbed it just before it fell over the edge. "Whoa, boys," she said. "Please respect the border of your place at the table, okay? That includes not only your space at the table, but the airwaves as well."

"Ma'am?" asked Rob, not understanding anything but the command to "whoa."

"I just mean that you can make loud sounds like motorcycles after lunch. Outside!"

"Yes, ma'am," Rob agreed.

Pete had stopped when Amy was talking, but now started up his "motorcycle" again. "Zzzzzzooooommm."

Amy reached over and held his hand still. "Pete, I said to stop doing that. Do you understand?"

Pete didn't respond, and just looked down at his bowl with a pouty face.

"Mommy will have to punish you if you do it again," she said, turning his face with her hand so he would be looking into her eyes. Pete didn't say anything, but he did pick up his spoon like he was going to eat.

Joe was troubled by Pete's attitude but he didn't say anything.

"Hey, Dad," Rob started. "When are we going to take a camping trip again? It's plenty warm enough."

Joe looked at Amy, then scooped up some applesauce before answering. "I don't know, son. I'm not sure we all enjoy camping that much."

"I do!" Rob exclaimed. "It's great fun to eat outside, and build campfires, and sleep on the ground, and not have to take a bath or wash your hands all the time!"

"They are fun!" agreed Laura. "Can we, Daddy?"

"Can we, Daddy?" echoed Pete. He probably hadn't been listening carefully to the conversation, but almost always put in his two cents' worth anyway.

Joe noticed that Meghan hadn't displayed any enthusiasm for camping. Yet, that was sort of like her. "The quiet one" she was often termed by Amy.

"Like I say, I'm not sure we all enjoy it," Joe repeated. "And I like to do things that we all enjoy together."

"Sometimes we go fishing, and Mom doesn't do it," Skip put in, hoping that this piece of information would help their case for going camping.

"I know," Joe said. "And I don't think she really enjoys camping either." He looked at Amy who didn't say anything. She smiled, however. "I would like us to do things together as a family that everyone enjoys."

That statement seemed to be just what Skip wanted to hear, because he suddenly offered another suggestion.

"I know what every one of us would enjoy doing," he stated enthusiastically. "Let's plan a trip to the Wet & Wild Water Park. It's been years since we've been there. I even remember Mom saying one time when we were coming home, that she didn't remember having more fun."

Joe's expression was sad. This was not the first time Skip had made the suggestion and it had been discussed before. The fact that Skip brought it up now indicated that either he hadn't really been listening before or he didn't really care for the conclusions of previous discussions. Both thoughts made Joe sad, as well as a little angry.

"I think you remember that we've talked about that before, Skip," Joe reprimanded.

"What's a water park?" Laura asked, with a quizzical look on her face as though she ought to remember, yet couldn't.

"It's a really neat place that has all kinds of slides, pools of water, and stuff like that," offered Rob. "You put on your bathing suit and swim and have fun. One slide is about three stories high and it takes you at least three minutes to get to the bottom! Other slides are like a corkscrew, where you go around and around, very fast, and then you drop into a pool of water."

"Oh yes, now I remember you talking about it before! It does sound like fun. But didn't Daddy say we didn't need to go there?"

Joe was pleased with Laura. "Yes, I did." Why couldn't seventeen-year-old Skip accept what little six-year-old Laura accepted? "It is a lot of fun, I freely admit that," Joe stated. "The problem is that there are many, many people who go there who aren't dressed modestly. Even though we have very modest bathing suits for all of you to wear, others there don't seem to care about modesty."

"Keep in mind that some of those people are very aware of the idea of modesty. And their goal is to make sure that they are immodest in what they wear!" Meghan offered.

"But, Dad," Skip countered, "You've said a whole bunch of times before that we can't make people live the way we do. That's between them and the Lord. We just have to worry about how we live. Right? Well, we'd be living right because we would be dressed modestly. In fact, we could be a witness and a testimony to those who are dressed immodestly at the water park." He stopped, seemingly pleased with his last statement, which he was sure his father hadn't considered.

Rob had stopped eating and was looking at Skip. Skip's reasoning made plenty of sense to him.

Joe caught Rob's expression and knew how much Rob would enjoy the water park. Turning to Skip, he began to explain an important concept. "Skip, we do need to be a testimony to the world. The Bible in Luke 11:33 says that we are not to put our faith 'under a bushel,' but that we are to let it shine for all the world to see. But there have to be limits. Those limits have to do with the potential harm that can be done to the Christian by exposing himself to such a situation. Sure, we would be dressed modestly. But the fact that others are dressed immodestly might cause some of us to sin in our hearts. I'm talking about lust. I'm also talking about some of us maybe being envious about how another person looks. Both lust and covetousness are sins that God wants us to avoid. Avoiding the water park seems a small price to pay to avoid those sins."

Joe paused, and when he started to speak again, both he and Amy started at the same time.

"I'm sorry, you go ahead, honey," Amy offered graciously.

"No, you go ahead," Joe suggested, grateful for any additional light she could put on the issue.

"It's like the preacher was talking about today," Amy explained. "He cautioned us not to go right up to the borders of sin. Well, if we went to the water park, knowing before we go that people are going to be dressed immodestly, and that it might affect some of us, isn't that just what we would be doing? We wouldn't go with the intent of sinning. But we would kind of be saying to God, "Look, I know that some people who go there are going to sin. And I know that it is possible that by going we might sin ourselves. But, I'm not worried. I'm not going to sin. I'm just going to stay right on this side of the line of sin."

"Good point," Joe agreed. "By staying at home, and not going to the water park, we're doing what the preacher suggested. We're backing off from the border! We're saying to God, 'I love you, Heavenly Father. I want to show you how much I respect you by staying as far away from sin as I possibly can.'"

The lesson was obviously absorbed by Meghan, Rob and Laura. Pete didn't seem to care for the discussion, but that was to be expected of a three-year-old. However, Skip, who didn't have age as an excuse, also didn't seem to agree. But he didn't say so.

Joe didn't want to leave it there. "You don't agree, do you, Skip? I wish there was some way I could explain it to you that would help you see the issues more clearly."

"I'm not going to argue about it," Skip responded. "I know what you believe. I just don't believe it myself, that's all. But I won't disobey you."

It was a little somber at the table for a few minutes. There was definitely tension in the air, until Pete turned over his cup of milk for the second time. Meghan rushed to get something to clean it up with, while Amy held Pete's hands to keep him from playing in it.

Around two o'clock, the phone rang. Rob rushed toward the phone, asking loudly, "Can I answer it?"

Rounding the corner to the kitchen, however, he saw his dad pick up the receiver. "Hello."

"Hi, is Skip there?" a voice asked.

"Yes, may I ask who's calling, please?" Joe responded.

"Just tell him it's JoBo."

THE DELIVERY

"Skip! . . . Skip, the phone's for you," Joe called. "Rob, go see if you can find Skip anywhere."

"He'll be here in a minute," Joe notified JoBo. *Who's JoBo anyway?* thought Joe while waiting on Skip to arrive. Joe listened to the background noise on JoBo's end of the line. It was some kind of rock music playing, and JoBo was humming along.

"Who is it?" Skip asked as he came close to the phone.

"Somebody named JoBo."

"JoBo?" repeated Skip to Joe, indicating with his facial expressions that he had never heard of the person. Taking the receiver, he started, "Hello." Joe walked out of the room.

"Hello, is this Skip?"

"Yes, who's this?"

"You don't know me, but Jeremy told me to give you a call. He said you might be interested in making a little money. My name's JoBo."

"Oh sure," Skip replied, talking a little more quietly. It wasn't like he was doing anything wrong. He was just talking to this guy. But for some reason he lowered his voice.

"Well?" JoBo asked.

"Well, what?" Skip asked.

"Well, do you want to make some money?"

"Sure. I mean, who doesn't want to make a little cash? What do you have in mind?"

"Sometimes I need some packages delivered for me. Sometimes I need someone to make a phone call. Things like that. From what I hear you have an honest-looking face and you're pretty clean-cut. Right?"

"You can trust me, if that's what you mean. I wouldn't steal from you."

"Hardly!" JoBo laughed in a crude sort of way. "Nobody steals from JoBo. Well, are you interested?"

"What exactly would I be delivering? And when would I be doing it? I'm home schooled, so my schedule is more flexible than lots of other guys. Still, I don't want to have to work crazy hours, or anything like that."

"Home schooled, huh? Yeah, that should work out fine. You could do some of my delivering during the day. Say 2:30 or 3:00. How does that sound?"

"That should be great!" enthused Skip. "But, what exactly would I be delivering?"

"Packages!" repeated JoBo. "Just packages. And don't worry, they aren't bombs or drugs or anything you have to worry about. So, what do you say? You don't have to ask your Mommy or Daddy, do you?" JoBo added in a taunting tone of voice.

Skip had a bad feeling about this. Why wouldn't JoBo be more specific than just saying "packages?" Without even realizing it, he turned to look around the room, making sure no one was listening to his end of the conversation. They weren't. *What should I do?*

"Look, if you're not interested, I can find lots of guys to do it . . ." JoBo stated, sounding like he was going to hang up.

"No wait! I would be interested to try. I could use some money."

"Now that's more like it," JoBo stated slowly. "Come by tomorrow at 2:30 and we'll get acquainted. I'm at 2310 N. 13th Street. Small white house. Big dog in the yard, but he won't hurt you. Not unless I tell him to, that is!" JoBo laughed, then started coughing. "See you tomorrow." The phone went dead.

THE DELIVERY

Skip hung up the phone and stood there thinking. This sounded a little too good to be true. *Oh well, I don't suppose it can hurt to find out, can it?*

Joe lay awake that night, tossing and turning. For some reason he couldn't go to sleep. Maybe it was the smell of fresh baked banana bread. It was one of his favorites, and Amy had made one right before bedtime so he could take it in his lunch tomorrow. That was like Amy. Always thinking of Joe. Only trouble was that it was a long time until tomorrow at lunch, and Joe's stomach had already started getting the gastric juices ready to digest that treat. His stomach growled. "Oh, you be quiet!" he said to his stomach.

"Mmm?" asked Amy, who had been asleep.

"Nothing," Joe reassured her. "Sorry I woke you up. Go back to sleep." He patted his wife's shoulder and took a deep breath. That was a mistake, because he got another noseful of wonderful banana nut bread aroma. *I need to just go to sleep*, he thought. *Joe Reynolds, you go to sleep! You know that in the morning you will give anything for a few more minutes of sleep. Here's your chance.* But few of us can reason ourselves to sleep, regardless of what well-constructed arguments we pose to our brains. And that was true for Joe tonight.

Several things kept pulsing through his thoughts. First, was Pete. What a blessing he was to the family. Joe loved all of his children, but Pete was special somehow. Was it because Amy almost lost him in the first trimester of her pregnancy? Was it because he was the youngest, and right now, the cutest? Was it because he adored his dad and was always giving him big hugs? Joe didn't know.

But Pete was three. Three and a half, actually, although sometimes he acted more like a two-year-old.

Joe and Amy had talked about it on occasion, and had agreed that they simply weren't holding Pete to the same standards as they had their other children at the same age. All too often Joe or Amy would excuse some kind of behavior that they would have never allowed from Laura or Rob.

But he's still a toddler, Joe thought. He thought of that innocent little face, and the smiling eyes looking up at him. *What a cutie! We shouldn't expect him to act like Laura does. That's not fair. On the other hand, didn't we expect Laura to behave better than Pete is acting sometimes? Sure we did.* The more Joe thought, the more he was convinced that the only difference between Pete and the other children was his and Amy's expectations. He resolved to discuss the issue with Amy tomorrow and, with the Lord's help, try to be more consistent with their discipline.

If I ate a small piece, it might help me sleep. Besides, I don't think I ate enough supper tonight. Joe's thoughts kept coming back to that silly banana nut bread downstairs. He calculated that it would probably only take about five minutes to get up, cut the bread, have a piece, clean up the mess, and get back into bed. Why, he had already been awake at least an hour thinking about it!

But he didn't get up. The adult in him wouldn't let him. He had to be in control of his appetite. That's what adults are supposed to be able to do. An adult shouldn't be swayed by food! Wouldn't to do so be gluttony?

For some reason, his mind turned to the pastor's sermon of today. He had been turning it over in his mind all day and had resolved, with the help of the Holy Spirit, to stay away from the borders of sin. One thing he wanted to work on was in the area of honoring his parents. True, his parents weren't Christians and didn't have a lot to offer in terms of spiritual food. Yet, they

THE DELIVERY

were his parents and the Bible said he was to honor them. Even though he couldn't remember ever blatantly dishonoring them, still he had oftentimes come close to the border. At times, he would tell stories to his children and he would say things about his parents that he knew came close to being dishonoring. He would try to stop doing so.

Another area he was going to work on, was something the pastor mentioned explicitly: judging others. Since they had become Christians later in their lives, Joe and Amy had to make some pretty radical changes. If they did it, why couldn't others make radical changes? They simply couldn't understand why other Christians, especially those who had been Christians most of their lives, couldn't also make right decisions, even if they were hard or even if the world called them "radical." Joe and Amy often talked about other couples and families, coming close to judging them for their behavior. No, they didn't actually condemn others, but their tone of voice and raised eyebrows and statements of "we would never do it that way!" were very close to judging other Christians. And it needed to stop. With the Holy Spirit's help, Joe was going to try to stop.

Joe's thoughts turned to Skip. So often lately, he had been irritated or downright angry at Skip's attitude or behavior. He and Amy prayed so often for Skip. *He's at a very vulnerable age*, Joe thought. *He thinks he is practically a man, yet he has so much to learn in life. He's going to have to make more and more decisions for himself as time goes on. And without the Savior, it will be easy for him to make a wrong turn.* Joe thought back to his own life, when he was Skip's age. Yes, Joe had made some bad decisions back then, some that he still regretted even to this day. Joe spent some time thinking about how he could help Skip through this time. However, in some ways it seemed hopeless. *If he doesn't have Christ as the foundation of his life, there's not that bedrock to judge things against.*

Joe looked over at the clock. 12:21. The same number forward or backward. He remembered something he heard at work. Some guys were giving examples of words, phrases and sentences that are the same spelled forward or backward. Like "sue us," "ma is as selfless as I am," and "wow." Thinking harder, he finally remembered a longer passage that was the same in either direction: "Doc, note. I dissent. A fast never prevents a fatness. I diet on cod." Then Joe looked back at the clock and spent several minutes thinking of combinations that are the same forward or backward, like 10:01 and 03:30, until he realized the whole exercise was a total waste of time.

How could someone call it gluttony if I didn't actually get enough to eat at supper? Joe thought again of the banana nut bread. He looked over at his wife who was snoring peacefully. Slowly, carefully, he pulled back the covers and stood up. Joe tiptoed to the door and then turned down the hall.

Just as he was about to start down the stairs to the kitchen, Pete cried out in his sleep, "No, that hurts!" Then Pete started crying.

Joe hurried to Pete's bed and took him in his arms. "You're all right, big guy. Daddy's got you." Joe carried him to the bathroom and then back to bed. Covering him up, he stroked Pete's silky hair. "Good night little Pete."

Joe walked out of the room into the dark hallway. He sighed, trying to decide what to do now. He remembered a Robert Frost poem that started, "Two roads diverged in a yellow wood, . . ." Which "road" would Joe take? The one to bed or the one to the banana nut bread in the kitchen? Decisions!

Chapter Eight

"Well, it's good to see the whole crew up bright and early this morning," Joe said at breakfast on Monday. Sometimes all of the children weren't up before Joe had to go to work. "How did you sleep last night?"

An assortment of dreams, and 'I heard this noise' were shared by various children. Little Pete claimed, "I didn't sleep."

"Now that sure is something there, Pete," Joe grinned at his youngest son. "Not all night long?"

"I didn't sleep," Pete repeated, confident in his assertion.

"You sure could have fooled me, when I checked on you during the night," Amy offered. "Was I just dreaming or did Pete cry out last night?" she asked Joe.

"Yes, but I was already up and took care of him," Joe answered.

"Had trouble sleeping again, huh? I'm sorry," Amy sympathized. "I hope I didn't keep you awake. And I'll always be glad to get the children if they call out. All you have to do is wake me up."

"Thanks. I know you will. I just couldn't sleep."

"I hope the banana nut bread helped," Amy added with a grin.

"Well, yes and no," Joe laughed. "The smell certainly helped keep me awake. But then I did go to sleep after . . . well, a little later."

"Uh huh," Amy laughed too.

"So what are you children going to do in home schooling today?" Joe inquired.

"I'm working on phonics," Laura said. "I'm working on the sounds of 'e'. It's fun!"

"Mom has me doing long division," Rob groaned. "It's hard."

Skip laughed.

"Don't laugh, Skip," Amy corrected. "I remember it was pretty hard for another boy in our family at one time." Then turning to Joe, she said, "Actually, Rob is doing very well on his math. Now his compositions are quite another thing."

"Need some help in writing compositions, huh?" asked Joe in a friendly tone of voice. "Maybe it would help to have a good topic."

"Last time, I let him choose," Amy offered. "Rob chose to do a composition on The Battle of the Little Big Horn. It was quite exciting."

"I see," said Joe. "So, it's not for lack of an interesting topic. Mmm. Maybe it would help if I got involved." Joe knew that many times, it was a great help for him to take a very active role in the younger children's home schooling activities. For some reason, perhaps it was his leadership or his personality, when he got involved Amy said that they did seem to do better.

"That's fine with me," Amy agreed.

Joe thought for a minute, while he buttered his toast. "Okay, how about this? Rob, I want you to write a composition today while I'm at work. The topic is 'What is Courtship?' When I get home, I'll look over it and then we can work on corrections that are needed. How about that?"

"Yes, sir," Rob agreed.

THE DELIVERY

"Meghan, that would be a good topic for you also," Joe added.

"How about me, Daddy?" Laura asked, not wanting to be left out.

"Well, since you can't really write much yet, why don't you think about the topic I've assigned, and you can give me an oral report when I get home."

"What's an oral report?" Laura asked, puzzled.

Joe laughed. "It just means you can tell me with your words by speaking your report."

Looking at Pete reminded Joe of his thoughts the night before. "Amy, remind me when I get home that we need to have a talk. About . . ." Without saying anything he glanced at Pete. Amy nodded.

Before long, Joe left for work. It was a rainy morning, and just a little chilly. A cold front had come in from the north last night and was responsible for lingering showers. The weatherman had said it should start clearing in the afternoon. A man whose job involves outdoor work tends to keep a pretty close eye on the weather and listens carefully to forecasts.

As one red light changed to green, Joe stepped on the accelerator, but instead of going forward, the car just died. It was "rush hour" and someone behind him honked his horn. "I'm trying," Joe said out loud to himself. But try as he might, the car just wouldn't turn over. Cars behind him started trying to switch lanes to maneuver around him. There was almost a wreck when a blue Honda behind Joe pulled right in front of a speeding minivan.

"Get that thing off the road!" an angry motorist shouted as he passed Joe. Joe just threw up his hands as if to say, "I'm doing everything I can. I'm sorry!"

Finally, the car started and Joe was able to drive to work. That wasn't the first time the car had acted up and probably wouldn't be the last. Joe knew he needed a newer car, but where was the money going to come from? He also needed a bigger house, Meghan needed braces, and Amy had postponed elective knee surgery, waiting for more money in the family budget first. Plus, Joe had dreamed of taking his family on a good vacation, maybe to Washington, D.C. or St. Louis. But where would the money come from? Sometimes Joe had feelings of failure as a father. *If I just had some more money*, he would think, *everything would be okay*.

However, he knew in his heart that money would not bring instant happiness and might even come with some negatives as well. Someone had suggested last year that Joe apply for a supervisor's job which would have given him more money. However, in talking it over with Amy he had decided that it wouldn't be a good move. Joe wasn't the "supervisor type." He didn't really care for conflict and the position that was open would have thrown him directly into conflict with a couple of older employees who, seemingly, could not be coaxed to give an honest day's work.

Joe breathed a sigh of relief when he pulled into the post office. Upon entering the building he made eye contact with Casey, who sort of sneered at Joe. *If the car was my only problem, I would be a happy man*, Joe thought. Much to his surprise, however, Casey didn't say anything to him. He didn't even come near Joe.

The route was a wet one today, and Joe, thankful for his waterproof jacket, buttoned it tightly around his neck. Even with the rain, he was feeling better. Somehow getting outside in the fresh air was good for Joe. That's another reason he had avoided the supervisor's job.

THE DELIVERY

His left arm was still sore, and his leg was stiff where Pete had run into it yesterday with the toy car, but he was making good time on his route. 'Regulate travel to arrive at the boxes at about the same time each day' was the direction in his Carrier Duties and Responsibilities Manual. Well, he was trying.

Often, he prayed silently as he walked the sidewalks, and drove his mail truck. Today was no exception. *Lord, I want to be careful about the boundaries You have set for me. Help me to know them and respect them. Help me to stay far, far away from them out of respect and love for You. I can't do it myself. I ask for the power of the Holy Spirit to accomplish what You want me to do. Amen.*

As Joe approached 33rd Street, something he saw made him a little sad. There, playing in the yard of 3819 33rd Street, were little six-year-old Julia and four-year-old Keith. It was raining, and with umbrellas in their little hands, they were trying to build something with pieces of wood.

"There's Joe!" Julia shouted, observing him walking toward their house.

Keith dropped his hammer and ran toward Joe. "Hello, Joe! We're trying to build a playhouse. Want to see it? Please come and see it!"

Joe stepped aside and looked at the mess of lumber nailed into a contorted shape. "Going to build a playhouse, are you? Well, that's fine. Where'd you get the wood?"

"Mr. Schmidt gave it to us. It was an old crate that he got when his refrigerator was delivered."

"Well, I might never have guessed that was at one time a crate," Joe remarked, smiling down at the children. "How are you going to set it up?"

"This is supposed to be a wall, but it's not working very well," said Julia gloomily. "We can't seem to make it work."

"Here, let me help you . . . is that what you were trying to do?" Joe asked kindly.

"Yes. Oh yes, that's it!" shouted Keith in pleasure. "Now, can you help us put the back on it too?"

"I would love to help you, but you see I have a lot of letters to deliver today. I think you've got a good start, though. I'll see what you've gotten done tomorrow when I come by, okay?"

Although the children were a little disappointed that Joe couldn't stay, they were happy for his help. Joe delivered the mail to their house, some addressed to Lance Norton, their father, and some addressed to their mother, Ellen, and picked up an outgoing letter. As he walked back down the Nortons' sidewalk, Keith ran over and hugged Joe. He did it almost every day. It broke Joe's heart.

You see, the children had a father. He had a good job and provided for all of their needs. He didn't appear to harm them in any way, but he never had time for them. Never. At least that is what Julia and Keith had told Joe many times, although Joe had never asked. Once, their mother had even commented to Joe that she wished her husband would spend time with their children.

"He loves them, I know he does, but he doesn't really like to be around them," Ellen had volunteered. "Says they aren't as much fun as other things he can do. The children sure do appreciate you, Mr. Reynolds. Why, I guess you're kind of like the father they don't have!"

How sad. To have children and then not want to be around them. Perhaps if they had been bad children or

THE DELIVERY

unruly or loud one could understand, but not condone, their father's attitude. But they weren't. No, someday, Joe was sure that Mr. Norton was going to regret not spending more time with his children. And then it would be too late.

Joe crossed the street and delivered the mail on that side. As he did so, he thought about the lessons that God was teaching him. Joe was excited when he thought about how much he had matured in the Lord over the last few years. He was also excited about the possibility of doing even more for Christ in the future. He spent some time thinking about the work he and some other men were going to do at the Grovers this week. It made his heart leap for joy to think about helping a fellow believer in need. Joe knew that joy was a gift from God, a graciousness to be treasured.

After finishing 33rd Street, he walked one block over to 34th Street. This was a pretty street, with not much traffic, and with large comfortable-looking houses. It was one of the most peaceful streets on his route. One would almost describe it as secluded, although it was very near the heart of town. It was rare for Joe to see any pedestrians and today was no exception. In fact, there was no sign of life, except for a small collie named Lady nosing around a garbage can. Joe made his deliveries and started thinking about that banana bread in his lunch bag.

He delivered to house numbers 3418, 3420, 3422, and then walked up the sidewalk to number 3424. Joe noticed that the front door was wide open. When he reached the porch, he sorted through the mail in his hand to make sure all of it was addressed to the Webbers. As he did so, he could hear the sound of gently swaying music inside and smell the scent of fresh orange blossoms, probably from some perfume.

"Hello, Joe," a soft voice called from inside.

Joe turned to look, and there was Mrs. Webber, lying on the couch. She had a woman's magazine in her hand, but she wasn't looking at it. No. She was looking right at Joe. With an inviting expression on her face. Joe stared at her.

Chapter Nine

How long he looked at her, he later couldn't be sure. It was more than a glance, though. He took a deep breath and turned back to his task. Placing the mail in the box, he quickly walked off the porch. He thought he heard her call "Joe!" but he wasn't sure. It wouldn't have mattered anyway.

It wasn't the first time that Mrs. Webber had tried, directly or indirectly, to seduce Joe. Why she would try, he had no idea. He knew she was married, and apparently to a very wealthy man. Also, Mrs. Webber knew that Joe was married. In fact, he had made it a practice to talk of his wife often when out on his route, to hopefully avoid something like this. But that didn't seem to make any difference to some folks nowadays.

Joe was angry with himself as he walked down the street delivering the mail. *Why does she do that to me? It's not fair to be tempted that way.*

It wasn't fair that she would do what she had done. Then, he thought about the fact that he had turned his head to look when she called him. *Well, it's not my fault,* he reasoned with himself. *I had no idea that she would be like that.*

Or did he? As he continued mulling it over in his mind, and started being more honest with himself, he admitted that he should have known better. That is if history is any indication of the future. And with Mrs. Webber that sure seemed to be the case!

Now he was really angry. But his anger was directed toward himself. *Why did I look? Why did I keep look-*

ing!? Even though he knew the answer, he wished he didn't. Silently he prayed:

Lord, I want to be a pure and holy vessel for Your service. Help me, when I am tempted, to remain pure and holy. You've made us a people to be separated for honoring and worshiping You. Help me to do that with the way I handle situations like I was just in. Then he thought about the pastor's sermon again. *God, please help me to stay away from the borders. Please forgive me, because I just got very close to them. Give me the power to stay far, far away from them. In Jesus' name, Amen.*

Joe continued to work his route. Entering a portion of fraternity row, he parked his truck next to the dumpster of one of the larger college fraternities that was on his route. Joe was often saddened to see what went on at some of the fraternities. Some of it was pretty bad. The newspapers occasionally reported on the happenings at the frat houses, but Joe could have written some things that would have shocked the community. *I wonder why parents would send their children to college, give them lots of hard-earned money, give them total freedom to spend their time however they want to, with whomever they want to, with no accountability of any kind, have them taught by some teachers who would like to poison their minds, and do all of this when these students are at one of the most vulnerable times of their lives?* It just didn't make sense to Joe. He knew a few stories of students who had been raised in godly homes, only to have all of the parents' influence and values erased in a few years at college. And the parents paid to have that happen! Amazing! Absolutely amazing! Joe knew that many professions required college education, but surely students didn't have to attend some of the kinds of functions that Joe had witnessed.

THE DELIVERY

Getting back into his truck, Joe drove to his next stop. His mind kept coming back to Mrs. Webber. *Why can't I forget her? Why does she keep coming back in my mind?* He realized it was a problem he was going to have to deal with.

Joe began to think of his options. An obvious solution would be to confront Mrs. Webber directly. Tell her he didn't appreciate what she did. Ask her to please stop. Joe generally liked the direct approach. It lets people know where you stand in no uncertain terms. Yes, that seemed like a good plan.

But the more he thought about it, the less optimum that option seemed. *What if she denies doing anything? Or what if she then uses my confrontation as an opportunity to seduce me again?* To be honest, he didn't feel it was wise to have more contact with her than was absolutely necessary. As strong as his convictions were, he just didn't know what might happen. That thought terrified him.

Okay, what are my other options? I could report the situation to my boss. I could file a formal complaint about the situation. Yes, that does have merit, especially if sometime in the future she asserts for some reason that I am the one seducing her! As crazy as that sounds, it could happen. A woman who is spurned might try all kinds of things for revenge. And what if she claims not to have seduced me? I sure don't have any evidence. It would be my word against hers. I'm not sure the postal service would back me, especially for fear that it might be sued by Mrs. Webber for some reason. Yeah, and what will Casey say or do if he hears about it? Boy, I sure don't want to go through all of that! The more Joe thought, the less comfortable he was in filing a formal complaint. However, he did decide to write a confidential memo to his boss, outlining what all had happened.

It wouldn't be a formal complaint, but it would be evidence if someone were to question it later.

But just writing a memo sure isn't going to help me with lust, or prevent me from being exposed to it again. I should probably tell Amy. That way she could help hold me accountable. Joe squirmed in his seat. *But I do hate to tell her. I hate for her to know that someone is doing this to me while she's at home, working hard, home schooling and mothering our children. She will say "It's not fair! I'm doing the right thing, but you're out there in the world being seduced!" And she's right, of course. But what can I do about it?*

Thinking of telling Amy brought to mind that he could also tell another man about the situation. A godly man, to whom he could be accountable. Yes, that might help. If Joe knew that someone else knew, and was praying about it, it would help him fight any temptations he might have.

But what if he still wasn't strong enough to do the right thing? What if he lied to his friend or Amy or whoever he promised to be accountable to? They would have no real way of checking up on his story.

Joe was beginning to see the seriousness of the predicament. *Maybe I should just ask for a different route? That way I won't be exposed to Mrs. Webber. Yes, but what's the probability that I won't have a woman like her on my next route? Or several like her? What if someone on the new route is even more aggressive in her attempts to seduce?* Joe shuddered. *No, changing routes probably wouldn't help*, he concluded sadly.

Would I be willing to quit my job in order to protect my wife, family, and my own purity? Why had that thought come to him? Surely it wouldn't help. Surely all jobs have their temptations and opportunities to commit sin. And besides, would it be wise to give up the retirement benefits, health care benefits, and job security that the Post Office provided? Joe had built up a good bit of seniority and that would be very hard to leave. Should he throw it all away just because of Mrs. Webber?

Joe didn't think that quitting his job would be the ultimate answer. Yet he knew that he had to be **willing** to do anything for the sake of Christ. Even if it meant quitting his job. *Am I willing to do that?* Joe reflected.

Obviously, this issue needed more prayer and reflection. Joe decided that he should tell Amy and seek a godly man to be accountable to. He also realized the need for prayer before and when a situation like today came up again. In terms of other long-term solutions, well, he would have to give that more thought and prayer.

As the work day came closer to an end, Joe headed back to the post office. He recorded his return time; disposed of the collected mail (after affixing postage to some letters); took care of the registered, certified, insured, and special delivery mail; and processed the express and postage-due mail. He then checked his box for any messages or notices. *What's this?* he mumbled, pulling a magazine article out of his box. It had been torn from a popular magazine that Joe didn't subscribe to. A graphic of a handcuffed man wearing a large cross prominently filled half of the first page. The headline read, "Ministers: For God? Or for Money?" Joe skimmed the article and realized that it exposed the many ministers and preachers who had been caught stealing money from their congregations. It was a blight on the Christian community, but it was true. Joe had heard of some of the cases mentioned in the article but he was surprised and incensed at what some had done.

After skimming the first few pages, Joe had enough. He got ready to toss it into the garbage can, but then wondered who might have placed it into his box. Flipping through the pages, he found his answer. On the last page, in bright red ink, it read:

Thought you might like to know where your hard-earned money is going!   Like they say, there's a sucker born every minute.
Yours truly, Casey

Chapter Ten

As Joe drove home, he wondered about several things. First, was his old car going to even get him there? Second, what problems or issues would he have to deal with at home? He decided that something relaxing might improve his spirits, and found some gentle classical music on a radio station. As he turned onto his street, he was feeling a little more calm.

Pulling into the garage, he was greeted almost at once by Laura, wildly waving some math sheets and saying something about "borrowing."

While he was trying to understand what she was saying, Pete ran up and tugged at his pant's leg. "Come see! Come see!"

Rob walked out and announced, almost casually, "I got that composition written. And Cathy died today. We think it might be food poisoning."

Pete continued to shout, "Come see, Daddy. Come see!"

Somewhat bewildered, Joe looked toward the house to see Meghan standing there, smiling, with a math book in her hand. "Here's the mail, Dad. You and Mom got another letter from that man in Texas. Mom read it at lunch. His wife still has the cancer and they are asking for more help. Also, we got a UPS package today. The outside says that it contains lamp oil, but we didn't open it. We thought you should look at it first. Mom said she sure didn't order any oil like that. And," she hesitated a little, seeing the tired look in Joe's eyes, "I'm afraid I need some help with ratios, Dad. But it can wait."

"Here it is," Rob said, holding the composition up to Joe's face. "I need some help on a few words. Mom said it is pretty good. But I don't know what you'll think."

"Wow!" Joe exclaimed, overwhelmed by this verbal barrage from his children. "Let's go inside. I need to talk to Mom first. Then, let me sit down, and you can all start over again." The children seemed to vanish.

Joe walked into the kitchen and kissed his wife on the cheek. Amy was stirring something in a big pot. "Good day?" he asked, pleasantly.

"Pretty good," Amy replied. "I hate to tell you, but I don't think the water heater is working right. Skip looked at it and tried to see if he could figure out what was wrong. He thought maybe it was a loose electrical connection. While he was working on it, he accidently backed into our shelf of honey and knocked a few off. It was a pretty sticky mess, but it's all cleaned up now."

"Did we lose much?" asked Joe, sighing.

"About three quarts," Amy replied, hesitantly. She knew how much honey cost and hated to tell him of the loss.

"Oh well, at least Skip didn't get hurt working with the electricity," Joe said, walking numbly toward the living room. "He didn't, did he?" Amy shook her head. "I think I'm going to sit down in the living room and rest before supper."

Joe walked to his favorite reclining chair, leaned back, and rested his hands on his stomach. The living room was empty and quiet. Taking a deep breath, he closed his eyes.

About that time, Pete walked in. "Come see, Daddy!" Following close behind him were the other children with their assortment of questions and papers.

THE DELIVERY

Joe remembered what a speaker had once said about men coming home from work: "Most wives and children think that when Dad walks through the door, he's home. No, actually he's not home. Oh sure, his body is there, but his mind isn't there yet. It's still on what happened at work, and on what he was thinking about while driving home. Usually, it takes about thirty minutes for the average man's mind to catch up with his body. Families might be wise to take that into account, whenever possible. You know, maybe give him a few minutes right when he gets home to relax and get ready to take on the role of Dad. I know one wife who has a rule for her children not to 'bother' Dad for ten minutes after he comes home. It's not thirty minutes, but it's more than most men get."

Joe loved his family and started trying to decipher all of the messages they were sending to him. First, he went to see what Pete just had to show him right away. Turns out it was just a piece of bright yellow cellophane paper that had blown into their yard, and that Pete had picked up as a treasure. Then he learned about Laura's progress in school that day. He was particularly curious to know who this Cathy was who had died.

"She was the Joyner's cat," Rob informed his father sadly. "We think she was poisoned, too."

"Why do you say that?" asked Joe, interested to know where his children might have developed their forensic medicine ability. "How do you know it was food poisoning? You didn't cut it open, did you?" he questioned. He could just picture his neighbor George Joyner coming home to find that his cat was not only dead, but had been dissected by the neighbor's children.

"No, Dad, we didn't even touch her. Mom wouldn't let us. The cat just looked like it had been poisoned," Rob answered, matter-of-factly. "I don't know how you can know for sure, but that's what I would say happened to it. Its eyes were open."

"Okay, we'll go with your diagnosis, until and unless we learn something different," Joe replied. He had learned long ago not to argue or do battle about issues which make absolutely no difference. "What about that composition? How did it go?"

"Here it is," Rob said with enthusiasm.

Joe read over the report carefully. "That's a pretty good job there, Rob," Joe grinned. "After supper we can go over it and talk about any corrections or changes we both think should be made." Rob was beaming.

Meghan walked into the living room. "Ready to tackle that math problem you were having?" Joe asked her.

"Let's just do it after supper," Meghan suggested. "I'm helping Mom right now. But here's the mail. The letter from the man in Texas is on top."

Joe sat back in his chair and looked at the stack of mail. First, he went through it quickly, throwing away anything that looked like junk mail. He had once said, "I'm sure that junk mail helps me to keep my job as a mailman. Without it there wouldn't be half as much mail to deliver. Yet, that doesn't mean I have to read it!" Anything with a bulk rate stamp was a suspect and often went sailing into the garbage can without being opened. After sorting his mail, he first looked at personal letters.

Joe read the letter from Texas with a heavy heart. It was actually from a family that one of Joe's friends knew. The mother of the family of six children had been diagnosed with cancer just a few months ago. It had looked bad at first, and now it sounded hopeless. He made a note to pray for them at the family's devotion time tonight. *It's only by the grace of God that it isn't our family*, he thought soberly. *What would that do to the peace and serenity of our home?* He shuddered as he thought, and said a prayer for them right then.

The rest of the mail was not very exciting, so he leaned back in his chair again and closed his eyes. Within a few minutes the call went forth, "Supper's ready!" Joe struggled to get out of his easy chair, then the smell of something good helped his legs to get moving a little faster.

"We got a letter from the IRS," Joe said as he passed a basket of crackers to Meghan. "They recalculated our taxes."

"Well?" Amy asked anxiously.

"We owe $300 more than I had calculated. Had something to do with some medical deductions I took. I just can't seem to keep on top of the continuous changes in the tax laws."

"What will that do to us?"

"Oh, it's okay," Joe assured her. "We'll still get a refund. It just won't be as big as it was going to be."

Rob had been listening to this conversation, not fully understanding it. However, he did understand the word "refund." "Did you buy something you didn't like?" he asked innocently. The only refunds he had ever seen were when his parents had returned something that didn't work, or they decided not to keep.

Joe and Amy laughed, then Joe explained the concept of a tax refund. Then he added, "Now if you are asking am I happy the way the government spends all of my money, that's another matter entirely. The answer would have to be a resounding 'No!'"

"Did you get a chance to read the children's compositions?" Amy asked Joe.

"I read Rob's," he said, pulling it from his pocket. "I thought maybe we could talk about it. First, though, I think Laura was going to give us a short oral composition on courtship."

Joe looked at Laura, who suddenly froze. "It's okay, honey. You're not in trouble. I would just like to know what you know about courtship. What does 'courtship' mean to you?"

Laura relaxed a little. "Well," she began in a sing-song sort of way, "courtship is when you don't date." With that she took up her spoon and started eating again.

"Good," Joe said. "Do you know what 'date' means?"

Laura shook her head.

Joe was a little surprised. After all, his family had been discussing courtship for years.

"Thank you for that oral report, Laura. I'll read Rob's composition now. Don't worry, Rob, I won't talk about your grammatical errors right now. I just want to talk about courtship. Joe read Rob's entry:

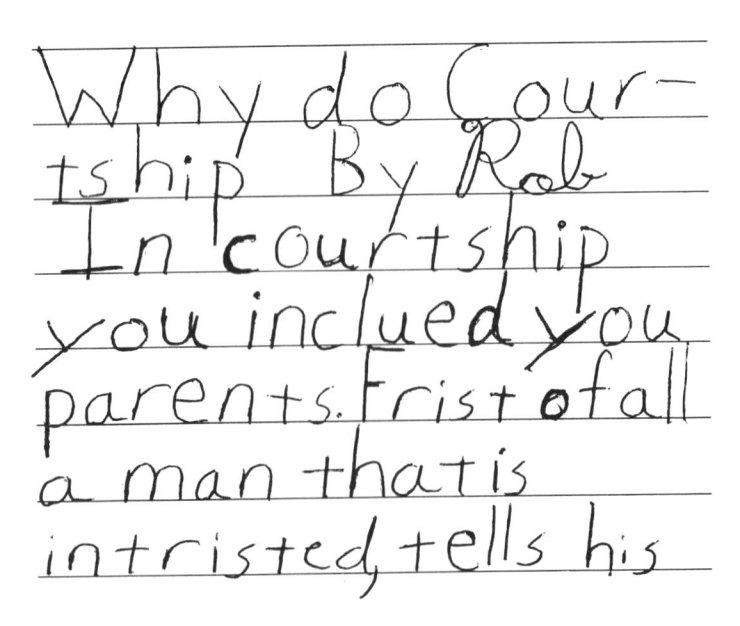

> Why do Cour-
> tship By Rob
> In courtship
> you inclued you
> parents. Frist of all
> a man that is
> intristed, tells his

THE DELIVERY

mom and dad. He asks his dad and mom for advice. Do they like the young lady? If so have the family over. After you get to know them better, then you go and talk with the young lady's parents and ask to marry her. Why do coutship? Because your parents are inclued. And so is the girls parents.

"Another good job," Joe praised Rob. "It is important for the parents to get involved as much as possible. After all, they have more experience and can help the young couple make wise decisions. Parents would help the young couple think of issues and character traits that the couple might not think of on their own.

"And it is different from dating, as Laura pointed out. Dating is much more casual, with the goal often being just to have a good time. The problem is that sometimes young people do things to have a good time and later regret it. Also, since dating isn't a serious thing, especially for some young men, it can help create what is referred to as a "dating spirit."

"What's that?" asked Rob.

"A dating spirit just means that a person falls into the habit of interacting with members of the opposite sex on a casual level. Not serious. Just for fun. And often just for variety's sake. Let me give you an example. This week I'll date Susie, next week I'll date Cathy because it will be fun to date someone different. The week after that I'll date Ginger, again because it'll be fun to be with someone totally new and different. And all of that can create problems when the person gets married. When married, the person should no longer date. But if they have the dating spirit, they may still have a desire to date, because they're tired of their spouse. That's wrong. Does that make sense?"

Rob nodded his head. "It's kind of like when we go bike riding. We usually go to the same park every time. And we have a lot of fun. But sometimes you take us to a new place. If you do that a couple of times in a row, I get to where I just want to go someplace new. The old places aren't that fun to me anymore. I guess that would be called a 'biking-at-new-places spirit.'"

"I suppose so," Joe agreed.

"But you said that one thing about dating is that it's fun," Skip commented. "How much fun can courting be if all you're doing is meeting with parents and stuff?"

"Courtship should be fun, too," Joe noted. "In fact, I'd be surprised if it weren't fun! But that's not its primary function. Its goal is to help two people find the right mate for their entire life. Once you do that, you will have fun the rest of your life together."

"Yeah, but you and Mom didn't court, and you turned out all right," Skip reminded. It was a statement he had made before.

"I'm glad you think we turned out all right," Joe said. "What we are today is very different from what we were when we started dating. As you know, we weren't even Christians back then. I'm so thankful that God blessed me even as a non-Christian, and allowed me to marry your mom. She has become a very godly woman. But I have to tell you that there are things I regret about dating."

"Me too," Amy agreed. "Just because we came out all right sure doesn't mean it was the best way. And we know lots of friends who didn't 'come out all right.' Like Dad said, it is a gift from our gracious Lord that we are different today."

"I would like to make another point," Joe said. "Rob, in your composition, you clearly listed some steps that a young couple go through. The steps you mentioned are certainly a great way to do courtship. But they aren't necessarily the only way to do courtship. We'll have to see how the Lord unfolds each of your courtships, assuming each of you do get married. I guess all I want to say is that I think there can be different paths and steps that a young couple might take."

After supper, the family met in the living room for their nightly time of devotions. At one time, they had them right before bed. However, recently Joe had changed the time to right after supper. Children, especially the younger ones, were more awake and alert then. He opened the Bible to read. They were reading through the Bible, a chapter each night.

"Tonight I think we're up to 1 Timothy 2. Right?" A few older heads nodded. Joe read the passage and then started discussing it. He spent a good bit of time talking about prayer, and the importance of making sure it wasn't just a laundry list of things you wanted. "Remember to praise God, to give thanks also, and to offer intercessions for others. When we pray, we're talking to God. We never want to be guilty of being selfish and thinking of our own needs first, and that certainly holds true when we pray to God."

Then Joe discussed the truth that "there is one God, and one mediator between God and men, the man Christ Jesus" (verse 5). "There aren't a lot of different mediators, a lot of ways to get to God. All religions don't take you to the same place. There is only one way to God: Jesus Christ. Don't ever let anyone fool you into thinking anything different. As you know, I deliver mail to some university housing areas, and I overhear conversations sometimes. It is clear to me that some professors and some leaders there are teaching something directly opposed to what I just said. They teach that you can get to God many different ways. That all ways are equally valued and none should be given higher weight or prestige. They claim they are just being tolerant. I call it false teaching. Don't fall for it."

"I won't," Rob said seriously.

"I trust that you won't," Joe replied. "And as long as I am teaching you and discipling you, I think there is less risk of that happening. But some day you'll be on your own. You'll be exposed to all kinds of teaching and doctrine. At that time you will be responsible for what you let yourself get exposed to, and for what you let yourself get foolishly led to believe. That's when I will have the least influence on you and the most concern for you. Build the foundation right now. Study the scripture and know what you believe and why you believe it. Then when times of doubt or false teaching come your way, you will be able to stand up under it."

Joe made a few more comments about the rest of the verses in the chapter, which deal with the place and dress of women, and was about to call for a time of prayer, when Meghan quietly lifted her hand. "What is it, Meghan?"

"Dad, I know the verses you just read said that we should dress modestly. Let's see, what did it say exactly in verse nine? 'In like manner also, that women adorn themselves in modest apparel, with shamefacedness and sobriety . . . '" She paused and looked at Joe.

"That's right," Joe nodded. "We've talked about that many times before, so I didn't go over it again in any depth. Do you have a question?"

"Not really," Meghan replied. "It's just that . . . well, last week Melinda had some friends over to her house. I went over to visit Melinda and her friends kind of made fun of the long dress I was wearing. I know that dressing modestly is the right thing to do. I also know that Christians disagree as to what is modest and what is not modest. I think our standards are right." She stopped again. Joe didn't say anything but smiled to encourage her to continue.

"Sometimes Dad, I don't know if you know how hard it is to be different," Meghan finally blurted out. "I mean, the clothes you ought to wear aren't that much different from what other men wear, even very worldly men."

Joe smiled and nodded. "I think I understand. Believe me, I know that sometimes you and Laura and Mom stick out like sore thumbs in this neighborhood in terms of what you wear. I know you do receive curious glances, and wouldn't be surprised if you sometimes even got rude remarks. I'm sorry. I'm sorry that you have to put up with things like that. But it seems to me that what is even more important than that is what God calls you to do. And God has clearly called women to dress modestly."

"I know all of that," Meghan said. "It's just hard sometimes, that's all."

Joe was sober. "What can we do about Meghan's problem?" he asked his family. "Does anyone have any suggestions?"

"We could move," Skip said.

"We could," Joe replied. "And in some situations the Bible tells us to flee persecution. I'm not sure that is what we should do in this case, however. Any other ideas?"

"We could pray," Laura said quickly.

"That's right," Joe praised. "Pray for what?"

"We could pray that Meghan would be able to stand the junk that other girls say or do to her," Rob offered.

"Good, what else?"

"We could pray that the other girls would be led to our Savior and learn the importance of modesty themselves," Amy suggested.

"Good, what else?"

"What you said tonight made sense. I suppose I should be prepared to give an answer to anyone who asks me why I do something. I never really thought about that

THE DELIVERY

much before," Meghan said. "I should study scripture myself and then be able to explain why I do what I do."

"Good, any more ideas?" Joe asked.

"I suppose she could just stay home?" Laura said, half as a statement, half as a question.

"Sometimes that is good advice," Joe agreed. "Sometimes it is best to just stay home. Let's pray that Meghan would have wisdom as she deals with this situation. Let's also pray for the family in Texas. They need to know of our love for them." Turning to Amy, he added, "Who is the Christmas card from tonight?"

The Reynolds family received a lot of Christmas cards each year, and a few years ago Joe decided to start a new tradition. They would take all of the Christmas cards they received and put them in a pile. Each night, they drew the one on top and prayed for that family or individual. Then they put it in the back of the pile. This method insured that they prayed for each family many times throughout the year. It was a blessing for both the Reynolds and the families they prayed for. Several families commented on how blessed they felt to have another family praying specifically for them so often.

"This card is from Uncle Timothy," Amy said. She passed the card around the room so that everyone could see it again. There was even a picture of Uncle Timothy and Aunt Ruth attached to the inside of the card. "We need to remember to pray for Aunt Ruth's hands. The last time I talked to her, the doctor had said they might have to do surgery again soon."

"Yes," Joe agreed. "And remember to pray for Uncle Timothy's job. Logging is a very dangerous job and he has had some near-accidents in the last year. Most importantly, let's pray for their salvation. Is there anything else we should pray for?" Since no one mentioned anything, the family bowed their heads and prayed, Joe first, then Amy, then each of the children in birth order. Amy helped Pete voice a prayer.

After prayer, Joe reached for a book of hymns and asked if anyone had a song they wanted to sing. "How about 'O for a Thousand Tongues to Sing'?" Meghan suggested.

"Sounds good to me. This song was written by Charles Wesley on May 21, 1749," Dad commented, turning to a page in the book he held in his hands. "He wrote it to celebrate his conversion of eleven years earlier. Apparently the theme came from a Moravian missionary, Peter Bohler, who stated that if he had a thousand tongues, he would praise Christ Jesus with all of them. Each of us only has one tongue. But we can use it to praise our Lord and Savior. Let's sing!"

The family sang:

O for a thousand tongues to sing, my Great Redeemer's praise, The glories of my God and King, the triumphs of His grace.
My gracious Master and my God, assist me to proclaim, To spread through all the earth abroad the honors of Thy name.
Jesus! The name that charms our fears, that bids our sorrows cease, 'Tis music in the sinner's ears, 'tis life and health and peace.
He breaks the power of cancelled sin, He sets the prisoner free; His blood can make the foulest clean, His blood availed for me.
Hear him ye deaf; His praise ye dumb, your loosened tongues employ; Ye blind, behold your Savior come; and leap, ye lame, for joy!

THE DELIVERY

After singing, Joe dismissed his crew to enjoy the rest of the evening. "Please remember to bring in all of the bikes before you come in for the night," Joe requested. "This morning I found three bikes left outside in the rain. And Skip, when are you planning to get on that grass? It's starting to look a little bushy."

"I can do it right now if you want me to," Skip offered, cheerfully.

"Sounds good to me," Joe agreed.

Pete walked over and clung to Joe's legs. "Daddy, my socks are tired."

Joe laughed. "I guess you could say that my socks are tired, too. Why don't we take them off and relax? Where should we put tired socks?"

Pete shrugged, then had an inspiration. "Mom knows!"

Joe scooped Pete up, and tickling him as he went, carried him to get a bath.

Chapter Eleven

Joe flopped on the hotel bed without even taking off his shoes. To say he was exhausted was the biggest understatement of the year. What a day! What was supposed to be a "short" three hour flight, turned into a nine-hour nightmare of bad weather, missed connections, and lots of time sitting on the runway, waiting for takeoff clearance. Then, to top it off, Gerald wasn't at the airport when Joe walked through the gates. He had to wait thirty minutes before his old high school friend showed up.

Why am I here anyway? Joe thought with closed eyes, fumbling to take his shoes off without sitting up. A phone call last week from Gerald was responsible for this day. It seems that Gerald was in some kind of trouble and needed Joe's help. Gerald had promised to reimburse Joe if he would fly, right away, to Boston.

"Then what?" Joe had asked his old friend.

"I'll meet you at the airport and take care of everything," Gerald had promised. "Look, I wouldn't ask if it weren't important!"

"But where will I stay?" Joe had asked. The Reynolds didn't have a stack of cash set aside for friends' emergencies like these.

"I'll get you a hotel room and everything," Gerald had promised. "It won't cost you a nickel. Look, I wouldn't ask you if I thought there was any other way, would I? You said a few years ago that I could call you if I ever needed anything. Right? Well, now's the time I need you, buddy!"

THE DELIVERY

Joe lay on that hotel bed, thinking of three things: food, sleep, and how nice it would be back home with his own family.

Joe's near-slumber was interrupted by the phone in the room. "Why do they set the ringers so loud on hotel phones?" he said groggily, reaching for the receiver.

"Joe, are you ready?" a voice almost whispered on the other end of the phone. After a second it repeated, "Joe . . . Joe! Are you there?"

"Ready for what? Who is this . . . " Joe began to ask. Apparently he had gone to sleep, at least for a few minutes, and was very disoriented.

"Don't be crazy, Joe. I'll be there in a few minutes," the voice said. Joe finally recognized it as Gerald's. "And you probably want to change into some nicer clothes. Your's looked pretty rumpled, old boy! It's important for you to look . . . how should I say it . . . presentable?"

"Sure, I'll be ready in a few minutes," Joe volunteered. "But, what's going on? I mean . . ."

"I'll meet you in the lobby of your hotel," Gerald interrupted, then abruptly hung up.

Joe struggled into some fresher clothes, then stumbled toward the elevator. When the elevator door closed, he looked at the buttons. None were marked as "lobby." In addition to the nineteen floors, the buttons included a "G", "M", "D", and "S."

"What's a man to choose?" he thought out loud. The elevator doors closed automatically while Joe was trying to decide. In panic, for fear that the elevator might go up instead of down, he pushed "S" just to have somewhere to go. He knew that Gerald was probably pacing the floor, looking at his watch.

As the elevator descended, Joe leaned against the mirrored wall and closed his eyes. *Boy, wouldn't sleep feel good about now. Well, it would if I just had some food in my stomach first.*

No one else got on the elevator as it made its descent. Joe was jolted awake by the elevator coming to an abrupt stop. The doors opened, and Joe mechanically walked out. The elevator closed behind him. To say that he was a little mixed up is quite true. Without doing much thinking, he walked toward an emergency *Exit* sign.

Opening that strong metal door, he stepped into a long hallway and kept walking. Thanks to cooler air in the hallway he started to regain his mental ability. "Wait a minute! What's wrong with me!" he said out loud. "I'm supposed to meet Gerald in the lobby and this is certainly no lobby." Laughing to himself, he turned to go back the way he came, but the door he had just walked through clicked shut.

Joe turned the knob, but it wouldn't open. Apparently it was some kind of a fire exit door that would allow people to leave the hotel, but not return. "Great!"

Joe didn't know what else to do, so he continued walking down the long hallway. It was one of those stark hallways not meant for people to see except in an emergency. His shoes sounded loudly on the painted concrete floors and the noise echoed on the gloomy concrete block walls. Bare light bulbs, spaced about twelve feet apart, lit the way.

Joe didn't know what else he could do, so he just kept walking down the hallway. *It has to come out somewhere*, he thought.

Around a corner, he came to another heavy, fireproof door. He opened it and noticed that it led to a set of stairs going up to some unknown place. He checked the

THE DELIVERY

lock and noticed that it too would lock behind him. Now he was in a quandary. Where would these stairs lead? What if he got trapped somehow? *Yeah, but what's my option?* he thought.

Joe walked through the door and cringed a little as it shut, and locked, so loudly behind him. Committed to his course of action, he was determined to find a way out. He walked up several flights of stairs and again came to a strong door. Opening it cautiously, he found that he was at street level in a dark, secluded place.

Not sure which way to go, but realizing the futility of retracing his steps into the tunnel, he started walking. He felt that he couldn't be far from the hotel entrance, probably just around the corner.

He started to walk to the right, but there were several questionable men leaning against a wall, looking at him. The last thing he wanted was trouble, so he decided to go to the left. Even though it might take more time, he was sure he would eventually end up at the hotel's entrance.

But, after walking down the sidewalk and around the corner, Joe was surprised to find the sidewalk blocked due to construction. Besides, it didn't look like there was a hotel down that street anyway.

"Uh-oh!" he exclaimed. "That tunnel must have caused me to lose my bearings. Maybe it went under a street or something." Joe crossed the street and walked north against the traffic on the one-way street. Why? Later, he would have trouble remembering exactly why he did so, but it may be that he saw a neon sign up the road that looked like a restaurant. He was terribly hungry, and as he walked, he thought a lot about food.

"First, I'll start with a big juicy steak and a tall glass of iced tea," he decided. "Then I'll order a large, cool salad and finish off with a piece of pecan pie, if they have it." He continued in this train of thought for some time, walking toward the restaurant. He even knew what he would say when he walked in: Nonsmoking, a party of one, and yes, I'm ready to place my order!

But the building wasn't a restaurant. It was the headquarters building for a labor union: the neon sign read "Labor Temple AFL-CIO." Joe walked away in disgust.

Now he was really lost. How many blocks had he walked? Which direction was the hotel?

"I know," he said happily as he thought of his next move. "I'll just find a phone book and look up the hotel. Now let's see, what was the name of that hotel?" He fumbled through his pockets, looking for the key. At first, he was afraid he had left it in the room, but he finally found it in his T-shirt pocket. "Whew!" he was relieved.

He pulled it out, but like many modern hotels today, it was a magnetic little doo-dad with no mention of the hotel name or the room number.

"That's no help," he decided. Try as he might, he could not remember the name of his hotel! Boy, he had sure been tired when he arrived at the hotel with Gerald. And Gerald had paid for the room, and had all of the receipts.

Joe was getting a little worried. He knew that Gerald didn't live in Boston and thus wouldn't be in the phone book. In fact, it was still a mystery why Gerald had wanted to meet Joe in Boston. Right now, he was still waiting in Joe's hotel lobby, probably wondering how long it was going to take Joe to change clothes. Joe laughed at this ridiculous thought.

Joe didn't laugh long. It was cold and Joe hadn't brought his heavy coat with him. He had assumed that Gerald would drive him wherever they were going, and

THE DELIVERY

Joe just assumed that they wouldn't be outside much. In fact, he had intended to ask Gerald if he needed to go back up to his room and get his heavy coat, when the two met in the lobby.

Although the city lights of Boston were fairly bright, and there were many cars on the streets, the sidewalks in this part of town were pretty deserted. The buildings were of the type that are used mostly during the day. Joe began to wonder about the crime and gangs that he had read about in large cities. He hadn't visited many cities, and this was his first trip to the northeast.

What should I do? Not knowing, he started walking west.

After a few blocks, he came to a section of town that had a restaurant, several bars, and a small ethnic grocery store. *Finally!* he thought. *At least I can get something to eat and then maybe I'll be able to think more clearly.*

He checked out the restaurant and decided that it looked a little too rough for him. He wasn't interested in the bars, so his only option was the grocery store. Walking in, he jumped a little bit as a bell, right by the door, sounded a warning to the owners that he had entered. A short foreign-looking lady walked from a back room and looked at Joe with unfriendly eyes. Joe tried to smile (as if to say, "I'm not here to rob you!") and walked toward the back of the store.

To Joe's way of eating, there was nothing but weird food in this store. Sure, he had heard of some of the items, but had never tasted them. You see, Joe pretty much just liked American food. However, as hungry as he was, and as dim as were his prospects for finding anywhere else to eat, he selected a few items and headed for the counter. *Maybe these rye crackers, this yellow-green cheese, and this puny bottle of ginger-root tea will tide me over until I know what to do.*

The lady was smiling now. *Maybe she has finally realized that I'm just a friendly customer*, thought Joe. The lady totaled the sale, and asked Joe for $9.44.

"Did you say $9.44?" The lady looked at the register and nodded. Joe couldn't believe it. That seemed like a lot, but he was in a mood for eating, not arguing.

Reaching for his wallet, he made a very sad discovery. It wasn't there. Red-faced, he fumbled in his pockets, hoping there would be some change or better yet, a few bills, but found nothing.

"I'm ... so ... sorry," he stumbled. "I can't imagine ..." Then he remembered that he had changed his pants in the hotel before leaving.

The lady's smile vanished as quickly as a pepperoni pizza did when Skip was hungry. Her eyes squinted a little, revealing her suspicious inclination. Suddenly, out of the back room a man with shoulders just about as wide as the doorframe emerged. He had a scowl on his face that seemed to go perfectly with the large scar that went from his left ear down to his neck. As the man began walking toward the cash register, Joe could feel the sweat trickle down his arm pit.

I wonder if she hit some kind of an alarm, Joe thought quickly. He then apologized and, leaving the goods on the counter, walked briskly out the door of the grocery store.

The cold air, and the hunger in his stomach helped clear his brain totally. *Let's see, I don't have any money, don't know where my hotel is, don't even know what my hotel's name is and probably couldn't even recognize it if I walked right past it. I haven't eaten for a while, and I'm cold. I have no way to contact Gerald. It's late at night in Boston, a town where I know no one, and there are probably gangs or crooks that don't know I have no money on me. Where should I go? What should I do?*

THE DELIVERY

"Did you really dream that?" asked Meghan in astonishment. When Joe nodded, all she could do was shudder. "What a nightmare!"

Joe grinned. "I can smile now, but I assure you I wasn't smiling in my dream."

"What did you do next?" Rob asked, with large eyes. "Did you ever find your hotel?"

"I woke up," Joe laughed. "So I need your help. What would you have done if you had been in my shoes?" he asked his family. "Chances are you won't be in that kind of a situation exactly, but you never know what you might learn now that can help you later."

Joe looked at Pete. "What would you do, Pete?"

Pete, enjoying his breakfast, had only heard bits and pieces of the conversation. "I eat Cheerios. I eat bread. Drink milk."

"Good plan," Joe agreed. "How about you, Laura? What would you do?"

Laura looked bewildered. Finally, she answered, "I would walk back into that store with the . . . bad food and ask them if they could help me."

"But they aren't friendly," Joe reminded her. "Do you think they would really help after they knew I didn't have any money, and thus couldn't pay them for their help?"

"Yes," Laura answered in her simple faith. "I think they would help. People want to help!"

"I wish that were always true, sweetie," Joe sighed. "Before you have me walking back into that store (and I'm not sure I painted a very accurate picture of what it felt like, standing there with that big man coming toward me), let's see what Rob would do. How about it, Rob?"

"I don't know," he answered, thinking through his options. "I don't think I would go back into that store, since they're mad at you. Dad, you should have had your wallet with you!"

"I know!" Joe agreed. "But it's a dream. Besides, things don't always go the way you want them to. So, what would you do?"

"Maybe go into the restaurant. That's all I can think of. I don't think you would want to go into the bars." He thought another minute. "Yes, I would go into the restaurant!"

"But Dad said it was kind of rough," Meghan reminded him.

"Okay, what do you suggest?" Joe asked Meghan.

"I know what I want to do. I just don't know how to go about it." She twisted off a piece of bread and slowly ate a bite. "I would want to get the police to help me."

"How?" encouraged Joe. "Remember I don't even have the money needed to use a phone."

"But it doesn't cost anything to call the police. You just dial 911. That's free, isn't it?"

"Yes, I believe it usually is," Joe agreed. "But what phone would you use?"

"That I don't know," Meghan admitted. "All of the businesses seem bad to me. And you don't want to walk all over the city."

"I think I would walk, at least for a block or so," Skip commented. "Surely there is a pay phone somewhere close by. I would choose the places I walked carefully, however. If possible, I would walk along with other people. There is safety in numbers. And I would make sure any places I walked were well lit. I wouldn't stray too far from the edge of the sidewalk nearest the street, either. You want to stay as far away from shadows as you can."

THE DELIVERY

"What would you tell the police when you finally got them, assuming of course that you could?"

"That I was lost and needed help finding my hotel?" Skip sounded unsure.

"What if they don't believe you?" Joe asked. "What if the lady at the ethnic grocery store had already called the police with your description as a suspicious character? If the police asked for identification, don't you think it would be a little odd to say you had nothing on you, proving you were who you said you were?"

Skip went into a deep thought mode. Finally, he shrugged his shoulders. "They would just have to believe me, I guess. I can't find Gerald, who would back up my story. I would hope they would believe me. I do look honest you know!"

Everyone laughed. "How about you, Amy?"

"I would never have gone to Boston by myself!" she exclaimed. "Pete needs me here."

"Yes, but what if you had gone? And these things had happened? What would you do?"

Amy poured Rob some more milk, got Laura another piece of toast, and buttered a piece of toast for herself. "I suppose if I **was** there, I would do pretty much what Skip suggested." Skip grinned.

"Yes, but how can you prove that you are honest?" Joe asked. "And how can it be resolved if you don't even know your hotel's name?"

"Well, "Amy answered slowly. "I think I would make a phone call from the police station."

"And who would you call?" Joe questioned, smiling.

"I would call my devoted spouse, who was back home keeping the home fires burning while I was helping some high school friend. I would simply ask my spouse to verify to the police who I was. My spouse could even wire me some money."

"Not bad," Joe said. Then addressing the family, he added. "Of course, the best way to "get out of trouble" is to avoid trouble in the first place. Don't make decisions when you're tired. Don't agree to do things that don't make sense for you to do them. Don't be led astray by people who seem well-meaning, but who actually, if you follow their advice or requests, can do you harm. Think, think, think!"

Joe didn't notice it, but had he been looking at his children closely, he would have seen an older boy that was doing some thinking right about that time. Some mighty serious thinking!

Chapter Twelve

"Where's Skip?" Joe asked Amy on a Saturday morning, several weeks later. "According to Rob, he was the last one to use my glue gun." Joe had been working in his shop, trying to repair Laura's tiny wooden shelf for her china set and he needed that hot glue gun to do so.

"Oh, you're going to fix Laura's china shelf? That's nice. I know she'll be excited," Amy answered.

"I would sure like to," Joe replied patiently, "but I can't find Skip. Any ideas?"

Amy furrowed her brow. "He didn't say anything to me. I assumed that he was working with you this morning."

"Nope." Joe turned to head back to the tiny "shop" in his garage. Actually, it was just one corner shelf, loaded down with nails, screws, tools, and junk. It was one dream of his: to have a real shop someday. But it didn't seem like that dream was going to be realized anytime soon. Finances had gotten tighter lately, thanks especially to an unexpected $212 bill from D.K's Auto Repair Shop.

"Hmpf," Joe said in disgust, looking at the disarray on his work table. "What a wreck! It could be down in all of that mess somewhere." Joe lifted up an empty box that, at one time, housed a brand-new battery charger. Now it was filled with some moldy grass and a few rocks. Some sort of treasure of his children, no doubt. He picked up the box to look underneath.

"Oh, look at this mess!" he exclaimed, in anger. "Who turned over this . . ." but Joe didn't finish his sentence. He knew it would do no good. The turned-over quart of oil, with the lid off and a resulting pool of sticky oil covering everything underneath, was probably due to someone carelessly tossing the empty box on top of the pile of junk. Instead of complaining, he methodically picked up the items and wiped them off with a paper towel. The items included, among other things, the following: his good 7/16 inch box wrench that he had been hunting for some time, some left over house numbers (the kit had come with four sets of all numerals and he couldn't bear to just throw the rest of the numbers away — what if he needed them for something?), a chain saw sharpening file, part of a bicycle pump, a very oily empty plastic bag, and a host of dead flies. Digging further into the pile, he found no glue gun, however.

"Oh well, maybe I can use regular glue and rig up something to hold it together until the glue dries," Joe thought out loud as he absently dug around in the pile of stuff.

"I got gue," Pete offered in his tiny three-year-old voice.

"I'm sure you do, partner," Joe said smiling. "Sometimes you're a pretty gooey person, that's a fact."

"I got gue," Pete repeated, emphasizing the word "gue."

"Okay," Joe agreed, somewhat weary with the task that was going to only take a few minutes, but that had already consumed twenty minutes of his busy Saturday. He was hoping to take the family to a park to go skating today, but that hope was dwindling as the minutes passed and jobs weren't being accomplished. "You show Daddy."

THE DELIVERY

Pete took his daddy's hand and walked him into his bedroom. Crawling under Rob's bed, he dug around a few minutes before reappearing. Pete's clothing and hair was covered with lots of dust and lint. Apparently, the carpet under the beds didn't get vacuumed very often, something Joe hoped to remember to tell Amy. But in his hands was the hot melt glue gun.

Joe was startled. "Now, how did that get under there?" he asked.

Pete just looked at Joe and smiled.

"Thanks, Pete. That was being Daddy's big helper," Joe praised.

"I got gue," Pete repeated, beaming at his importance. "I do!"

Joe made quick work of repairing Laura's toy and soon was looking at his long "to do" list for the day. It read:

- fix Laura's thingumajig
- check water heater temperature setting
- move brush to front ditch (Tue P/U?)
- fix Rob's back bike tire (check mine)
- change oil and filter (make sure have filter first!)
- wash car
- tighten Meghan's bed rails
- check on Elaine and get paint color for porch floor
- check for moisture in crawl space
- lime front yard
- have some fun?

Joe looked at his watch. 9:27. *Where has my morning gone?* he thought. *If we're going to go skating this morning, we'll have to leave soon, so we can be home in time for lunch.* Amy said she should be ready around 10:00. That left him with a little over thirty minutes to make some progress on the list.

Stuffing the list back into his pocket, he decided he had better check on the crawl space next. With all of the rain they had gotten lately, he was afraid that there might be too much moisture under there. Amy was having her allergy symptoms again; runny nose, sore throat, and draggy feeling. She thought it might be due to some mold or mildew in the crawl space.

Joe walked to the side of the house and started to open the tiny access door to his house's crawl space. He dreaded it. Joe wasn't fond of sliding on his belly on damp, clammy ground. It stunk under there. Also, he was always afraid that a snake would be under there. Wouldn't it just be great to come face to face with a poisonous snake, or even a large rat snake for that matter, when you're far away from the door?

"There you are, Joe!" a friendly voice called from around the corner. It was Peter Udeen, one of the Reynolds' next door neighbors. Peter, around twenty-five or twenty-six years old, was a doctoral student at the university, working on his degree in forestry management. He and his wife, Jane, had no children, but did have two well-trained black lab dogs. Beautiful dogs. Dogs that liked to bark at night, keeping Joe awake. Joe never could figure out why they barked so much. Anyway, Peter was really into pheasant hunting, and he probably had as much right to keep his dogs on his small lot as Joe had to "keep" five children on his lot.

"Howdy, Peter!" Joe greeted. "What are you up to today? You look like you're dressed up for some big trip." Usually on Saturday, Pete dressed in an old green pair of Army pants and a ragged T-shirt that said "New Jersey: For all the right reasons!" and played with his dogs or worked in his yard. He seemed to like to be

THE DELIVERY

outdoors as much as possible. Today, however, he was dressed in white pants and a Madras sport shirt. Joe was visibly impressed.

"What, these?" Peter said, touching his shirt and pants. "Yeah, we're leaving on our trip this morning. Going to see my folks. Next week is my mom's 60th birthday and Dad has planned this big surprise party for her. We were going to leave early," he said, looking nervously at his watch, "but we're having some trouble with our pipes. I was kind of hoping . . ." Peter hesitated, and turned to look across to his own house. His dogs, barking like crazy, were looking over at him, jumping high near the fence.

Joe waited for him to continue, but Peter didn't say anything. He looked at the dogs again, then looked at his watch. "You look pretty busy this morning," he finally said.

"I've got a 'to do' list a mile long," Joe admitted. "But that's not unusual," he added laughing. Joe knew that Peter was hinting that he could use some help. Yet, Joe had his own things that needed doing. *I can't help every person in every situation,* he argued with himself. *Peter can afford a plumber. If he can afford to keep those noisy, expensive dogs, he can easily afford to call a plumber. I know I can't afford dogs like those! Besides, Peter has never helped me with stuff I've been working on before. Not a single time!* In those few seconds, Joe developed a resentment that Peter would even suggest he come and help him. *He's made his choices. Let him live with them!* Joe felt justified in his decision.

"Yeah, I know how you're always busy over here," Peter said. "It looks like you know how to do just about everything. I've never much known how to do things.

I'll talk to you later. Jane is waiting on me." With that, Peter started walking away.

"I'll be glad to try and help you this afternoon," Joe offered, feeling a little guilty, but still annoyed that Peter would be asking for his help. And to be truthful, Joe hoped that Peter would sense his annoyance.

"Thanks," Peter said. "I think we can find some way to handle it."

"Hope you have a good day!" Joe called as Peter rounded his house. Peter didn't respond. "And have a good trip!"

Joe opened the crawl space door further and crawled in. "What's under there?" asked Laura, who with Pete was standing near, watching. Joe didn't let his children play under the house, which resulted in a certain fascination and curiosity about the place.

"Just a bunch of pipes and wires that go into the house. And the water heater," Joe said. "Now you children stay out there, please."

Joe crawled deep inside and looked things over. There was some moisture in the soil but nothing really to worry about. *At least that's good!* He looked up at the underside of the floor to see if there was any mildew. But it was dark under there and he had forgotten to bring his flashlight.

"Laura! Can you bring Daddy his flashlight, please?" Pause. No answer. "Laura!" Pause. Still, no answer. "Laura! Pete!" Pause. Still not a word from the two children who had been practically glued to him all morning.

Slowly, he inched back toward the door. Reaching fresh air again, he straightened up and headed toward the car for a flashlight. *Why is it that children are always hanging around you when you work, asking you "can't*

THE DELIVERY

you **please** think of something we can do to help?!" but then when you really and truly could use their help, they've disappeared for a few minutes? Of course, as soon as you've bloodied your hand trying to retrieve a bolt that has fallen into a small hole (a hole that their tiny hand could have reached oh, so easily); or you've taken the light fixture back apart, put it on the floor, and are walking toward your tool box to get the cutters (that your children would recognize instantly by sight) you needed to finish the job, they reappear. But it's too late. Such was the case now.

As he rounded the house, Laura saw him and came running. "Through already, Daddy? That was fast!"

"I needed a flashlight," Joe said.

"Let me get it for you, Daddy!" Laura beamed and in a flash she was handing her dad the object. "See, I'm a helper too, just like Rob, aren't I?"

"You're a helper all right," Joe agreed. "Thank you."

The underside of the floor was fine. Apparently, Amy's allergy symptoms were due to something else. Joe pulled out his list again. "Let's see, what should we tackle next?" he asked Laura and Pete. Knowing he wasn't going to get it all done, Joe tried to think about what really should be done today. The weather man had predicted rain tonight. In fact, the skies were already getting overcast. *Hope it holds off until we can go skating*, he thought. The entire family enjoyed in-line skating and there was a nearby park that had some wonderful trails for doing it. Pete couldn't skate, but Joe was good enough as a skater to be able to push a three-wheeled stroller in front of him that Pete rode in.

"I think we'll lime the front yard," Joe announced.

"What can we do to help?" Laura asked.

"Help you?" chimed in Pete.

"Do you know what my spreader is?" Joe asked.

Laura thought for a minute. "I think I do," she said with a cute grin.

"Can you get it for me?" Joe asked.

"Yes," and she went running off, followed by her younger brother, who was repeating, "Yes! Yes!" In a few minutes she returned, and said, "Is this it?" holding a garden trowel.

"No, but that's kind of close," Joe said. "We do use that to spread dirt around our rose bushes sometimes. I'll get it."

It took some time to get the spreader oiled, the lime loaded, and the chalk placed in the little marking canister on the side. Then Joe started spreading. The children thought it was neat the way the spreader laid down a thin line of chalk so the user could see what he had already covered.

As Joe worked, wiping beads of sweat off his forehead, he couldn't help looking over at Peter's house. *I wonder if they got their pipes fixed.* Guilt started eating at him. Couldn't he have at least taken five minutes to see what the situation was? Maybe all Peter wanted was an opinion as to what the problem was or a recommendation as to who to call. That wouldn't have taken much time.

Yeah, but Joe could also envision it turning into a half-day project on his part, that would have knocked out his family's planned outing. *You have to make priorities in life. My family is a higher priority than Peter's pipes.* The guilt came and went as Joe worked.

It took about forty-five minutes, but the liming job was finally finished. Joe had noticed that Peter and Jane still hadn't left on their trip and that no plumber had

THE DELIVERY

arrived. Clouds were building, and the air was getting more stuffy and humid. Joe was sweating heavily.

Taking out his list, he marked off "lime front yard." *Now what?* he thought. Again, his mind wandered to the Udeens'. Sensing that maybe God was directing him, Joe decided to see what was happening over there. He told Amy what was going on and urged her to get the water jugs filled with water since it was going to be a hot day to skate. Joe headed over to the Udeens'.

It took a while for Jane to answer the door. When she did, Joe noticed that she had been crying. "Hi," Joe said awkwardly. "Peter said that your pipes were messed up or something?"

Jane nodded, trying to hide her tears by looking back toward the kitchen.

"I thought maybe I could take a look at them for you," Joe offered.

"Is that the plumber?" Peter shouted from the kitchen. "Send him in!"

Jane motioned with her hand for Joe to go to the kitchen. Her facial expression seemed to say, "Go in there if you want to. But I'm not going to. And I wouldn't recommend it!"

Joe walked into the kitchen. It seemed smaller, somehow, than the last time he was in there. *How long since I've been in their house?* he wondered. Then almost with shame he realized that it had been over a year. *And here they are my next door neighbors.* From time to time Joe had prayed for Peter and Jane who were not Christians.

It was then that he noticed a table beside their kitchen table. *So that's why the kitchen seems smaller!* On it were a variety of things. Joe didn't recognize them all, but he did know them to be the kinds of things that

New Agers would have. There was a book on finding the god within yourself, an unusual deck of cards, and a collection of candles. He looked at the title of another book quickly — Feng Shui in Easy Steps. The subtitle read, How to Arrange Your Home to Be Healthy and Happy — Includes Personalized Astrological Charts. A catalog lying there announced products for sale ranging from ritual books and power wands to dream catchers and pyramids of power, whatever that meant. *It's terrible they've fallen for this,* he thought. *If they only knew the truth of Jesus Christ.*

"Hi there, Peter. Boy that sure looks familiar to me. You under that sink looks like something I do a lot!" Joe said happily, trying to lighten things up a bit. Peter didn't reply.

"Sorry it took me a while to get here, but I did have to get that lime down before the rain, you know." He was hoping that Peter could relate to the absolute necessity of liming before a rain, and how the season was already getting almost too late to do it. What else could he have done, but lime today? Surely Peter would understand.

"Uh huh," Peter mumbled, with his head still inside the sink cabinet. He was tinkering with a tool, apparently trying to tighten something.

"Can I help?"

"I don't know. I think I've really messed the thing up," Peter said, including some foul language that Joe had not heard Peter use before. "I don't know anything about this stuff and there isn't a plumber that can get here before late this morning. And now it looks like I'm going to be late for my mother's party. That is unless we drive a lot further tomorrow than we planned."

"Here, let me look," Joe pleaded. Peter finally crawled out and violently threw a cheap bright red

THE DELIVERY

plumbers' wrench into a new, but cheap tool box. The sound echoed through the house. Jane, who had been sheepishly standing at the edge of the kitchen doorway, fled to the back of the house.

Joe realized that Peter was in no mood to answer a bunch of questions, so he decided to try and figure out what had happened just by looking at the situation. Joe examined the pipes and saw what Peter meant. Probably, the only thing wrong originally was that the drain had come loose from the drain pipe. That would only have taken a few minutes to reposition and tighten. And that looked like what Peter had tried to do. However, he apparently had over-tightened it, stripping the threads on the sink. Now, it looked like Peter was trying to stop the leak and hopefully allow the two parts to tighten up by wrapping a rag around the threads. That wouldn't solve the problem, Joe knew. In fact, it wouldn't do anything but add frustration to the person attempting it.

"It looks like you're going to need some new strainer basket assemblies for your sink," Joe said softly.

Peter reacted angrily by slamming his fist on the counter top.

"I'm sorry, Peter, but the threads are stripped under your sink and there is no way to fix them. They're not expensive. But listen, really, there's no reason that you have to fix this before your trip. It's in the waste water system, not the water supply system."

Peter looked like he didn't understand.

"I mean that if it was your water supply, which is under pressure, you would have to fix it or it would keep leaking. The waste side, though, isn't under pressure. This won't leak as long as you don't use your sink."

"It leaked this morning!" Peter informed Joe. "All under that counter and all over the floor!"

"That's probably because you were using the sink for something. Trust me, if you don't use the sink, this can wait until you get back."

"But the plumber is coming. Now we have to wait on him to show up or be charged a second service call when he comes again. Maybe you have money to burn. We don't!"

Joe thought fast. *Should I volunteer to be here when the plumber comes? That way they can take their trip. But, we're supposed to go skating!* Joe was torn. He felt like Peter wouldn't be in this mess if he had just taken a few minutes this morning and looked at the problem. It would have been a good opportunity to display the servanthood of Christians and to share the love of Christ with him. Now, there seemed to be no easy way out.

Joe noticed several, ugly black stains on the back of Peter's nice, white pants, probably from lying on the shelf under the sink. He wondered if Peter knew his pants were ruined.

"If you'll leave a key with me," Joe finally said, "I'll let the plumber in when he comes. If I'm not home for some reason when he comes, I'll fix your sink myself. How's that?"

Peter looked at his watch, said something under his breath, then said, "No, we'll just hang around until he comes. It can't be much longer. Besides, we couldn't drive too far today anyway." Peter's mother lived in New Jersey, making it a many-day trip. Peter didn't want to have to pay for a hotel room after only a few hours of driving.

After talking about it a few more minutes, Joe walked back to his house. He felt bad that he hadn't been a better witness to the Udeens. But didn't Joe have the responsibility to take care of things at his home also? How would they get done otherwise? Wasn't the health

THE DELIVERY 127

and welfare of his family as important as that of the Udeens?

Maybe if he had taken more interest in the Udeens, however, over the last few years, they might not be so much into that New Age stuff. Of course, there was no guarantee of that, but Joe couldn't get that out of his mind. Joe was still, in many ways, a relatively new Christian and often didn't know what the best course of action should be. He was destined to struggle with the following issues the rest of the day: *What should I have done differently? What would Christ have done?*

Chapter Thirteen

Skip's hands were shaking a little as he pedaled down the narrow street on his trusty old blue bicycle. He kept looking back over his shoulder, at the sidewalks, and at cars that passed by. Skip was normally a very inquisitive person, always keeping his eyes open. But today, he seemed to be more so. It was as though he was expecting someone and didn't want to miss seeing them.

But nothing could be further from the truth. Skip had no desire to see anyone he knew at this moment. And that's what made it seem a little strange to him. Why not? What would be wrong with running into, say Mr. Bitten, or Mrs. Preston, or Eric, or Josh? He wasn't doing anything wrong. Just riding his bike. No law against that, is there?

If that's so, Skip thought, *then why do I sort of feel like I'm doing something wrong? Why didn't I tell Mom and Dad what I was doing this morning and where I was going?* Oh, he had already gone over that last question several times in his mind. He didn't tell them, because there really wasn't anything to tell. He was just going to go for a bike ride. While he was out, he was going to pick up a package and deliver it halfway across town. *Shouldn't take more than an hour. Nothing wrong about that, so why say anything? Besides, I'm going to make $40 for doing it. I don't want to tell them just yet that I have a job. I'll wait until I have $200 or $300 and then surprise them with what I've saved. I'm sure they will be*

THE DELIVERY

proud of my independence and ability to make money without interfering with our family's way of life.

Yes, that had seemed like the best approach. Skip had met with JoBo a few weeks ago and this was his first delivery. Skip could almost feel the two crisp twenty dollar bills in his left front pocket. Not bad for an hour's worth of work. And it wasn't even really work. Skip liked to ride his bike, and this was a way to kill two birds with one stone.

"It's real simple," JoBo had said at that meeting. "You pick up a package here from me. I'll tell you exactly where to take it. In fact, sometimes you won't even have to see the person you're delivering to because I'll just let you leave it under some stairs or in some place like that. I have several requirements for all the guys who work for me, though. First, when you leave my apartment, you must go straight to the place you're delivering to. Never, under any reason, stop to have a Coke, or do anything else. I'm paying you for a prompt delivery and I expect you to come through for me. You understand?"

Skip had said that he did.

"Good. Now the second thing is that I don't want you to go around blabbing about our arrangement. You're working for me. There is no reason for the rest of the world to know about it. So just clam up. You understand?"

Skip was unsure what to say. Why this secrecy? I mean, if you get a job at K-mart, it's certainly okay to tell someone where you work. So why couldn't he tell his friends, for example, how he was making some money? When he asked JoBo, Skip was surprised at JoBo's quick reaction.

"Look, kid. If you want the job, fine. If not, I don't care. But if you work for me, you'll play by my rules or no rules. Understand? If I needed advice, I would have asked you. I didn't. So just do what I say, or walk out that door right now and we're through. Can you understand that, Mr. Homeschooler?"

JoBo said all of that without raising his voice or anything. He was obviously angry, yet he was totally in control of his voice. It was a coolness that Skip hadn't seen before, and frankly, he was impressed by it. *I wish I could be in control of my emotions that much*, Skip had thought. *I'm going to learn from this guy!*

Although Skip had his driver's license, he thought it might be best to use his bicycle instead for the delivery. Why? Well, that way he wouldn't be using his parents' car and gasoline, he told himself. Besides, then he didn't have to really tell them where he was going. Not because it was bad, mind you. There was just no really good reason to tell them. Living at the edge of town, he often rode his bike to get around and his parents never objected. He enjoyed it, except when it got unbearably hot.

Now he was wondering if maybe he had made a mistake. It was getting really hot. Or was it just him? *Am I perspiring because of guilt and fear, or heat and humidity?* Skip wasn't sure. Looking up, he noticed that some darker clouds were rolling in. He hadn't remembered rain in the forecast, but then again, he didn't really pay much attention to things like that. Skip pedaled hard, just like he had been doing the entire time since he left JoBo's place. He had a sense that he wouldn't be relaxed again until this little job was over. And the best way to get the job over was to pedal as fast as he could. Skip's legs were trying to give his brain a message: *Go easy on us! We could use a break.*

4422 43rd Avenue West. That's where he was heading right now. "Just knock on the door twice and a man will open it right away," JoBo had instructed.

THE DELIVERY

"Hand him the package and you're done. And Skip, don't waste the man's time by trying to talk to him or anything. He's way too busy to talk to you. Understand?"

So far Skip hadn't seen anyone he recognized. Good. *But why is that good? I'm not doing anything wrong*, he continued to argue with himself. JoBo never did tell him what was in this little package, about the size of a football, but he had said once that it wasn't drugs or anything like that.

Past 41st Avenue. Then 42nd Avenue. There it is! 43rd Avenue. Skip steered his bike to the left after making sure no cars were coming up behind him. He could feel his heart start to race and his hands got so sweaty he was having a little trouble holding onto the handles. *This is ridiculous*, he thought. *Everything is under control!*

When JoBo had given him the street address to deliver to, Skip had been a little apprehensive. *What if it's a dangerous neighborhood? What if I stick out like a sore thumb because I'm not dressed like the people there, or am a different race, or whatever?* Now he was able to put all of those thoughts at ease. This looked to be a much nicer neighborhood than the one he lived in. It was lined with stately old oak trees and the houses and yards were immaculate. In fact, it was so nice that he settled down a little, and looked carefully at the house numbers. "4418 . . . 4420 . . . 4422 .. . there it is!" he said out loud, but softly. The house was nice, almost elegant. It was an old Victorian style house with a wide front porch and lots of detail.

Skip jumped off his bike and parked it at the curb. Before he started up the sidewalk, he looked in all directions. There was an older man washing his car three doors down, and some children were playing in the yard across the street, but that was all. *Is that older man watching me? Or is that just my silly imagination again?*

Skip walked to the front door. Before he knocked, however, the door opened and a man was standing there. How to describe the man? Just average in about every way. Didn't seem nice. Didn't seem mean. Average height. About thirty-five or forty years old.

"You the delivery boy?" he asked.

"Yes sir," Skip replied and handed the man the package. With that the man took the package, and closed the door. He didn't even say "thank you."

Skip quickly turned and walked back to his bicycle. The only thing he could think of was to get home. Jumping on his bicycle, he started pedaling back down the street. The man washing the car stopped and watched Skip carefully. That made Skip pedal even faster!

Rounding the corner, Skip pedaled as hard as he could. The wind in his face seemed to exhilarate him and with each passing mile he could feel his anxiety melting away. So much so that he stopped at a convenience store and bought himself a Coke and some chips. He sat out on the curb and ate them, enjoying the day. That Coke really tasted good. It was hot today! Now he knew it was humidity, not stress, that had caused him to sweat so much. Finishing his snack, he mounted his bike and rode slowly toward home.

Thirty minutes ago, he wondered if he would ever deliver another package for JoBo. Now that it was over, he was sure he would. Nothing bad had happened. And that forty dollars in his pocket felt good. Really good!

Late in the morning the family did get together all of their gear along with some coolers of water and snacks.

THE DELIVERY

"Looks like it will be a short skate," Joe said. "We need to get home before too long and have some lunch. I have a lot of things I would like to do this afternoon, too."

At mention of the word "lunch," Pete started begging for a snack. "In a little bit," Amy tried to postpone. "But not now."

Usually the family had so much fun when they did things together. In addition to in-line skating, they also enjoyed hiking, going to the ice cream parlor (especially Rob!), visiting the library, and going to community festivals that were held each spring and fall. Yes, the family had many good memories of their times together. It was doubtful, however, if today would live in that area of memory.

For one thing, it was becoming oppressively hot and humid. For another, Joe seemed preoccupied with something. He didn't talk much, tell jokes, or make sure everyone had a good time. He wasn't mean, he just didn't seem to be all there.

Then there was the fall that Rob took. It wasn't really a terrible fall, and his protective gear kept him from really getting hurt. But when he fell, he landed on his head and that shook up Amy a lot. She kept worrying that maybe he had done more serious damage, even though Rob kept promising that he was okay. And Pete had an accident in his pants, something he hadn't done for quite sometime. No, this excursion wouldn't go down in the history books. At least not in the ledger on the side of "what a great day it was!"

"I think it's about time to head home," Joe said, sooner than usual. "I know I could use some lunch and I imagine the rest of you are hungry, too." Amy agreed and the crew headed home.

In the middle of the afternoon, Joe noticed that the plumber's van was in the Udeens' driveway. *Should I go over?* he thought. After a minute he decided that it wouldn't really do any good. The plumber sure didn't need his help. To go over now, in fact, might look like he was only interested in learning more about plumbing, and less interested in actually helping Peter and Jane. He was sad that he hadn't gone over this morning when Peter had first come over. But that was history. There was nothing he could do about that now.

Joe's thoughts were interrupted by a siren going off. It was the weather radio, and the family members who heard it gathered around to see what was up. "This is the National Weather Service in Hastings City, Alabama. The National Weather Service, in conjunction with the Storm Prediction Center, has issued a severe thunderstorm watch for portions of eastern Mississippi, and almost all of Alabama for Saturday afternoon and evening from 2:00 P.M. Central Daylight Time until 11:00 P.M. Central Daylight Time. A severe thunderstorm watch means that conditions are favorable for thunderstorms. Severe thunderstorms can form quickly and can produce damaging winds in excess of 60 MPH, destructive hail, very heavy rain, and deadly lightning. Be prepared to move to an interior room on the lowest floor of your home or business if a severe thunderstorm forms in your area. Heavy rains can flood roads quickly, so don't drive into areas where water covers the road. Again, there is a severe thunderstorm watch for persons in the following counties . . ."

"Sounds like we may be in for a bit of rough weather," Joe said to Amy, thinking about the lime he had put down this morning. Fertilizing your lawn before a slow, soaking rain is smart. Doing so before a massive storm isn't. Heavy rains could wash practically all of your fertilizer away.

THE DELIVERY

Joe began to think about the things that needed to be done before a storm might hit. This was the first really severe storm of the season. It seemed early to Joe, but he knew it wasn't. It's just that one never quite gets used to the threat of severe weather. Joe had seen the destruction that storms could do. *Oh well, at least this is just a severe thunderstorm watch*, he reminded himself.

With Skip and Rob's help, Joe picked up things in the yard that shouldn't get wet or that might blow away in a storm. They checked to make sure everything was in good shape before Joe went back to working on his to-do list. Things went smoother with the help of his older boys, and he was able to get his oil changed. As they were working, Joe noticed the Udeens pulling out of their driveway.

Amy walked outside. "Honey, the weather radio alarm went off again a few minutes ago. There's heavy hail northwest of us. It's pretty far away, but they said we could get some here later. There's a tornado watch until midnight. Just thought you would like to know."

"Thanks," Joe said, walking to the house. "I'd like to hear what the weather man says." Turning his radio on, he listened to news of this latest threat:

"The National Weather Service, in conjunction with the Storm Prediction Center has issued a tornado watch for portions of east, central Mississippi, and western and central Alabama for Saturday afternoon and evening from 3:30 P.M. Central Daylight Time until 12:00 midnight Central Daylight Time. Tornados, large hail up to three inches in diameter, strong wind gusts up to eighty miles an hour, and dangerous lightning are possible in the following areas: in eastern and central Mississippi this would include the counties of Pine, Gates, and Fayetteville, which includes the cities of Albertville, Englewood, Mercer, Bergen, Nettletown, Pine City, and

Caswell. And in western and central Alabama, this tornado watch, number 381, includes the following counties: Coleman, Adams, Stark, Bowman, and Steele, including the following cities: Coleman, Truman, Northway, Morris, Williams, Edgecomb, Goshen, Burnt Hills, Lake George, and Oakes. Repeating, the National Weather Service, in conjunction with the Storm Prediction Center has issued a tornado watch effective this Saturday afternoon and evening from 3:30 P.M. until 12:00 Midnight Central Daylight Time. This tornado watch is number 381. A tornado watch means conditions are favorable for tornados and severe thunder storms in and close to the watch area. Persons in these areas should be on the lookout for threatening weather conditions and listen to later statements and possible warnings. Remember that severe thunderstorms occasionally produce tornadoes with little or no advance warning. Be alert, but remain calm. If you see damage or large hail, please call the National Weather Service or local law enforcement. This watch, number 381, does not include the cities of Irongate or Hastings City."

In the early afternoon, the clouds of the morning had disappeared, but now they were building up again. Instead of low clouds that blocked out all the sunlight however, they were billowing clouds that seemed to go straight up. Joe and the boys watched them grow.

"Look at how fast that thundercloud is building at the top!" exclaimed Skip. "It's really boiling and churning." Thunderclouds weren't new to the Reynolds. Yet they were still a phenomenon that awed them. Joe always said that they displayed the majesty and power of God.

"I guess we better hurry and get this brush moved," Joe suggested. There were no lightning bolts and it looked like a while before any would even possibly start.

THE DELIVERY

The three worked hard. Sweat rolled off their faces due to the humidity and heat.

"That's good enough," Joe said finally. "We can work on this next week after I get off from work. Surely it will be cooler then." They walked into the house.

"I was just coming out," Amy said. "The weather radio just reported that a tornado was spotted about seventy-five miles from here. It hasn't touched down, but there is a tornado warning now posted there. For us, it's still just a tornado watch."

"Dad, can we turn up the air conditioning?" Meghan asked. "It's awfully hot in here."

"I know," Joe said. "We could, but I think it will cool down very rapidly just as soon as this storm passes."

The family was now interested in one thing: the approaching storm or storms that might come their way. It was still pretty sunny, but they all knew that would change rapidly. And this was a fast-moving storm system. Joe decided it would be good to have their devotional time right away. The whole family congregated in the living room with Bibles and song books. Rob, more preoccupied with the coming storm, had gathered just about every candle and flashlight in the house and was looking anxiously out the windows.

It got darker. Then peals of distant thunder shook the windows. Flickers of lightning danced off the walls.

"I had better make sure the windows are closed almost all the way," Joe remarked, standing up, and laying his open Bible on the coffee table.

Right then the weather radio alarm blasted again. Everyone jumped. Joe hurried to cut the noisy alarm off and listen to the message. All Reynolds huddled close.

"This is the National Weather Service in Hastings City, Alabama. The National Weather Service in conjunction with the Storm Prediction Center has issued a tornado warning, number 124, effective this Saturday afternoon and evening from 4:45 P.M. until 8:00 P.M. Central Daylight Time. This warning is for persons in the following area: from 35 statutory miles East and West of a line that reaches from thirteen miles south, southwest of Truman, Alabama to thirty-two miles north, northeast of Gratings, Alabama. This tornado warning includes people in the following cities: Coleman, Northway, Truman, Morris and Everdell in the southern half of Coleman County and people in the cities of Wake, Gulliford, Schroon Lake, and North Creek in the northern half of Adams county. This tornado warning is in effect from 4:45 P.M. until 8:00 P.M. Central Daylight Time. A state trooper near Dodgeville reported a funnel cloud. Also, at 4:35 P.M., Central Daylight Time, National Weather Doppler Radar indicated a tornado two miles west of Buhl. This tornado is on the ground and causing damage. It is moving east, southeast at 45 MPH. Some locations in or near the path of the tornado include the cities of Pendelton and Coleman. The tornado could reach Pendelton by 4:55 P.M., and Coleman by 5:03 P.M.. This is a life threatening situation. Persons in the track of the storm are urged to seek emergency shelter immediately. Go inside a sturdy building and stay away from windows. The safest place to be during a tornado is in a basement. Get under a workbench or other piece of sturdy furniture. If no basement is available, seek shelter on the lowest floor of the building in an interior hallway or room such as a closet. Use blankets or pillows to cover your body and always stay away from windows. Large hail has also been reported with this storm. This is a very dangerous storm situation. Again, move immediately to a shelter below ground or to a small interior room on the lowest floor."

THE DELIVERY

"Everyone go to the hallway," Joe commanded decisively, yet calmly. "I'm going to close the windows and the doors and will be there in just a second. Skip, take the weather radio with you. Amy, get the blankets from the linen closet. Rob, take those flashlights with you."

Joe ran to the back bedroom and closed the window. Looking out, he saw that there was an ugly look to the sky. Lightning was striking from cloud to cloud. The wind had picked up. Yet, there was still no rain. It looked eerie. Quickly, he shut the mini-blinds also, and then ran to the other rooms, shutting windows, pulling down blinds, closing doors.

In less than three minutes, he was safely with his family in the hall. It was stuffy and close. Peals of thunder shook the house. The light in the hall went out; then, as Rob was turning on the flashlights, it came back on.

Joe could see alarm and concern written on every face. "Let's pray," he said. He took Amy's hand, on his right, and reached over and grabbed Rob's hand, on his left. Others held hands to form a circle.

"Dear Heavenly Father, thank You for this house, our shelter from the storm that is building outside. Thank You that our house is strong and well-built and that it has weathered many, many storms in the past. Thank You for the way You have protected us in the past in the storms we've been in. You have been so good to us and we pray that You would protect us once again.

"As we think of this earthly shelter, we're reminded that You, the Creator, Lord and Master of the universe, are our shelter from the 'storms of life,' from sin and Satan and evil and the things that would destroy us. Help us to seek Your shelter from those things, just like we sought the shelter of this house during this storm. Help us never to think that we can take on the 'storms of life' alone, just like we wouldn't think of standing out in the street right now. Father, forgive us for the many times we have tried to do battle against the powers of darkness alone and without Your help, because of the pride or ignorance in our hearts.

"I thank You for my family and the love we have for each other. I thank You for the love You have helped us to have for You. Your mercies are everlasting.

"Help us to remain calm. Help us to have wisdom to know what we should do. Teach us, even as we are sitting here right now, the lessons You would have us to learn.

"We pray for those who aren't in a shelter right now, that You also would protect them. We ask, if it's Your will, that no one would get hurt during this storm. Please let this be a time when men, women, and children see Your awesome power and seek You in prayer. Above all things, dear Father, we want Your will to be done. In Jesus' name. Amen."

As Joe was finishing his prayer, there was a loud pop on the roof. In a few seconds there was another. Then another. Then it sounded like hundreds of people were hammering on the Reynolds' roof at the same time.

"What's that?" asked Laura, fear in her voice. Pete was already sobbing in Amy's arms.

"That's hail," Joe answered.

"Hell?!" Laura repeated, in disbelief.

"Hail is frozen rain that comes down from the clouds. It's just a small ball of ice. Sounds like that hail is pretty large. Wouldn't it be fun to go out and pick up a bunch of the hail, put it in a glass and use it as ice for our iced tea?" Joe was trying to lighten the moment so Laura wouldn't be so scared.

THE DELIVERY

It didn't work. Laura looked at Joe like maybe he was crazy. She sure didn't want to go outside right now.

Joe had Laura come and sit in his lap. "I've been in lots of hail storms in my life, little sweetheart," Joe comforted, hugging her tightly. "It's no fun being outside when they hit, but we're plenty safe in here."

While Joe was saying this, the hail changed over to torrential rain. Joe gave Laura a strong hug and tried to continue over the loud noise. "See, now it's just rain. We've seen some pretty strong rain storms before. Do you remember that one we had last summer, right after the fourth of July? And the beautiful rainbow that we all enjoyed? Why, I remember . . ."

But before Joe could finish his sentence, the lights went out. Rob fumbled with a flashlight, then succeeded in getting one to come on. Shining it toward the ceiling gave everyone's face a strange, scary hue. Joe was about to finish his thought when Meghan asked, "What's that?" Everyone listened carefully.

The new popping sound was impossible to miss. "Sounds like power lines shorting out to me," Skip volunteered. "You can almost hear a fizzle in the background. I wonder if the electrical lines are going down, or are just lashing against each other." For a minute the family listened to the sound, saying nothing more. Then the popping sound stopped as suddenly as it had begun.

It was replaced with something that sounded much more menacing. A terrible roaring, growing in intensity with each second, seemed to be moving right toward their house. *The tornado!* Joe thought, with a fear and helplessness like he had never felt before. *And it's coming right toward us!*

Chapter Fourteen

The sound got louder and louder. Pete was sobbing and Laura started as well. Rob's eyes were big as saucers. Joe prayed out loud for safety and courage. The sound was even louder now.

The noise level increased. In addition to the roaring of wind, they could hear glass breaking, large objects hitting the house, trees snapping with the force of shotguns, and something that sounded like several animals screaming. Joe hoped it wasn't Peter's dogs.

Rain was lashing against the house. You could hear trees crunching, sounding like something huge was walking over them like they were grass.

Joe was most concerned right now about the structural integrity of his house. *Will it hold up?* Joe wondered. *Can it withstand all this wind and rain?* Somehow he just knew that if the tornado or tornadoes touched down really near his house that it would not. His house was like most houses built in less-expensive subdivisions since the 1960's — they were designed to be built quickly and cheaply, not built with the intent to last hundreds of years.

The wind and rain and lightning increased. *How can it get any stronger?* Joe was amazed that he hadn't heard his roof blowing away, that water wasn't pouring down the walls or from the ceiling. And then, above the roar, he did hear what sounded like shingles slapping up and down in the wind, followed by the sound of ripping and tearing.

THE DELIVERY

"The floor, Joe!" Amy half-whispered in terror. Joe felt it too. The floor seemed to be moving, shaking violently.

We're going to be lost, Joe was sure. There was no hope now. With the floor and walls swaying and moving, he knew that it couldn't be more than half a minute before the tornado swept through their house. The air pressure was tremendous.

Then, even though the family couldn't dream that the noise could get louder, it did. It sounded like a freight train was about to run over the house.

"Father, we place our trust in You," Joe said loudly, over and over. Very large debris was hitting the house now. A kitchen window popped and the sound of glass shattering somewhere else was quite audible.

Just when it seemed absolutely hopeless, the sound of the train moved away and died down. "It's going!" Amy shouted with tears of joy. "It's going away. Thank You Jesus!"

True, the sound of the tornado seemed to be diminishing, but the rain seemed to be increasing in strength. Joe could hear water running into the house somewhere. *Is that in the kitchen?* he wondered. That would make sense, since the window sounded like it had been broken. However, it sounded more like it was coming from the living room.

"Can I go see what it looks like?" Skip asked. "I hear water."

"No," Joe answered. "We don't know what's ahead. Sometimes there are several tornados close together. We need to . . ." He was interrupted by the weather radio.

"The National Weather Office in Hastings City reports that a tornado has been spotted in the town of Coleman. It is moving . . ."

"Is that a new one, or the one we just heard?" Amy asked, with worry in her voice.

"I don't know," Joe answered. "It could be either. We'd best stay right here until the weather service tells us there is no longer any threat of tornados." Easy to say. Hard to do. Especially with the sound of water running into the house and the desire to survey the damage to his house. But Joe knew he had to be wise, not hasty.

Thankfully there were no more sounds like freight trains rumbling near by. Amy led the family in several songs. Pete went to sleep in Amy's arms, exhausted from crying and worry. Laura seemed to be very tired also, although it wasn't late.

Joe stood up and walked to one of the doors leading to a bedroom. Before he could open it, Rob called out, "Dad, don't go in there. What if a tornado comes through?"

"I'm okay," Joe reassured him. "I'm not going anywhere. I just want to see what kind of damage I can see while staying here in the hall. I'm just going to peek." Joe had been thinking of his homeowner's insurance and exactly what coverage he had. *What's the deductible?* he thought. *And what items aren't covered?* He just couldn't remember.

Joe looked in all the rooms that led off the hallway. No water was pouring in and none of the windows were broken. "Amazing," he sighed in relief. "How could they still be intact?"

The sound of sirens filled the air. Returning to his place in the hall, Joe suggested, "Let's turn on the weather radio and see what's happening." Doing so, they found that the tornado warning had been canceled.

THE DELIVERY

"It's safe to leave the hall," Joe reassured his family. "But before we do, let's have a prayer of thanksgiving that God protected us."

"And let's pray for others in the path of the storm," Amy quickly put in.

"Exactly what I was going to say next." Joe smiled at her. Bowing their heads, Joe led them in a prayer.

Skip, rushing out of the hall with one of the flashlights, was the first into the kitchen. "Be careful in here!" he shouted. "Broken glass all over the floor!" The kitchen was a mess. With the glass broken out, the wind and rain had poured into the room. Puddles of water had tiny ripples from the wind coming in the opening where the window had been. Dishes that had been on the counter were broken on the floor. Amy's favorite iced tea pitcher was lying against the wall, handle broken off and a large slit down its front. The cookie jar was on the floor and cookies that just a few hours ago were coveted by all the children, were soggy, gooey messes.

Joe was surveying the living room with his flashlight. Sure enough, the ceiling had large dark water stains and water was still running down the front wall of the room. *It must have blown off some of the shingles.* He began to try and prioritize what he should do next. Clearly he needed to protect as much of his property as possible from further water damage. He considered going outside to assess the damage, but it was raining very hard and was quite dark. Occasional flashes of lightning streaked across the sky and thunder rumbled.

How much could I see with a flashlight anyway, he thought. So instead, he walked from room to room with Skip, looking for damage. Except for the kitchen and living room, it looked surprisingly good.

Amy put Pete to bed and was helping Laura change. "I'm going to stay here with them so they can settle down," she said softly as Joe entered the room. "Do you need me for anything?"

"No, I don't think so," Joe answered. "I wonder when the power will be back on? Quite a while, I imagine. I would think that the lines are down in lots of places." Then it dawned on Joe that perhaps his neighbors hadn't fared as well as he had.

"Maybe I should go and see if the Christensens and Joyners are all right. And dear Elaine. She must be terrified!" Joe was about to walk out of the room, when Amy caught his arm.

"I know you want to help," she told him. "So do I. But what if the power lines are on the ground and you come in contact with them? Please be careful."

Joe thought that was wise advice. "You're right. It's so dark it would be hard to see where they are, if in fact the lines are down." He paced back and forth. "I feel so helpless! I can't survey the damage outside my house, I can't help my neighbors, what can I do?"

Amy didn't say anything. She continued to gently rub Laura's back and sing softly. She shrugged her shoulders as if to say 'I don't know what to tell you.'

"I guess I'll try to clean up the kitchen and living room," Joe said finally. Amy nodded, still stroking Laura's back.

Joe did what he could. A police car, lights flashing but moving slowly, came cruising down the road, shining its bright spot light on the houses and roadway. The sound of sirens continued throughout the night. Electricity was still nonexistent. Even the phones were dead.

In a few hours the rain slowed and the older children headed to bed. After midnight, Joe finally lay down to

THE DELIVERY

sleep. Expecting to lie awake a long time, he was, instead, asleep in less than ten minutes.

In the morning, Joe and Skip surveyed the damage. There were no power lines down on their street although the electricity still wasn't back on. It was still raining steadily, and the wind was gusty from time to time. Puddles were everywhere and people were out looking things over.

"Looks like we're going to need to replace some shingles," Skip commented. A section of roofing about ten feet by twelve had been blown away. Other shingles were standing up and might need replacing or maybe they just needed to be re-nailed. The house seemed to be structurally in good shape.

"It's going to need a paint job," Joe decided, looking at the results of the many 'missiles' hurled at the house the night before. "It's amazing what flying sticks and rocks and hail can do to a paint job!" He looked across at the Udeens' house. "Let's go and see what kind of damage they had."

Skip and Joe surveyed the storm damage in their neighborhood, especially their close neighbors. The Udeens needed some roofing repaired. With them gone on the trip, Joe especially felt like he needed to help them out. It looked like they might have some leaks inside the house. The fencing needed fixing to make sure the dogs stayed in. Thankfully, the dogs were okay.

Isaac Christensen was already on his roof, nailing down some loose shingles. Isaac and his wife, Marlene, had lived in the neighborhood for years, even before the Reynolds had moved in. A professor at the university, Isaac was a committed follower of Jesus Christ. The Christensens had two children: John, twenty-eight, who was a contractor, married and living in Baton Rouge,

Louisiana; and Kenneth, twenty-three, who still lived at home and worked at a nearby paper mill.

"Hello, Joe!" Isaac called. "How did you fare?"

"We have some damage," Joe replied. "A window, a section of shingles, and water damage in several rooms. Plus, a ton of minor things to patch, repair, and paint. How about you?"

"Loose shingles, a few broken windows, and a big sweet gum tree down in the back yard," Isaac shouted down. "And it blew away the roof of our little shed in the back. And oh yeah, Marlene's bike is missing. We were just outside the path of the tornado. Have you been over to the Foxboro subdivision?"

"No. What's it look like over there?"

"Haven't seen it," Isaac said. "But I heard it got hit very hard. About five houses were pretty much destroyed, ten houses had a lot of damage, and the whole area is full of debris blown in from all over the place. A man on the radio said there was even half of a billboard from about three miles away over there! I hear there are TV crews and relief workers practically tripping over each other this morning."

Joe hadn't heard the radio that morning. All of his radios were run by electricity and he had decided to buy one that operated on batteries just as soon as he could.

"Do they need help?" Joe asked.

"No," Isaac replied. "Radio man said to please stay away. The last thing they need is gawkers."

"I wouldn't be looking, I'd be there to help."

"I know," Isaac nodded, coming down his ladder. "But they already have a ton of emergency folks there, cleaning up, helping the families, doing that kind of stuff."

THE DELIVERY

"I'm just heading over to Elaine's house," Joe said. "Have you been over?"

"No," Isaac answered, a little embarrassed. "I guess I didn't even think about it. Too busy worrying about my own place."

Joe and Skip found Elaine Jackson's house to have experienced about as much damage as their own house. Her roof needed repair, and she had buckets and bowls placed throughout the house to catch the water coming in.

Her yard was also littered with debris. Joe struggled to pick up a large piece of twisted metal that was about five feet long and two feet across. "I wonder what that is from?" He and Skip inspected it for a while, but couldn't figure the mystery out. Given the strength and longevity of the tornado path it could have blown in from ten miles away, or maybe even more.

Joe looked at the sky. "We've got our work cut out for us. Every minute we wait to patch up these roofs, the more water damage the houses will get from the rain."

Elaine was in good spirits, having been calm during the storm. "I will never leave thee nor forsake thee," she quoted from the scriptures. "I know that it is God's grace that has allowed me to see this day."

When Skip and Joe returned home, Amy stuck her head out the front door. "What about church?" she asked.

"I totally forgot this was Sunday!" Joe exclaimed. He thought about the work that needed to be done, especially at Elaine's house and the Udeens' place. "I'm afraid we're going to have to miss," he finally concluded. "These roofs have to be patched, even if only temporarily, right away."

"Okay," Amy nodded. "I'll have breakfast ready soon."

Rob had joined the men by that time and exclaimed, "How can we miss church, Dad? You always say how important it is to go."

"If Dad doesn't think we should go, that's good enough for me," Skip jumped in, with a condescending tone to Rob. "We're supposed to obey Dad, not question him."

Joe looked at Skip. "I'm glad you want to obey, Skip, but Rob has raised an important question. Yes, Rob, I do think we should try our best to go to church. It's where we can fellowship with other believers, sing praises to God, and learn from His word. But I believe that this morning God is leading me to do some acts of service and kindness for our neighbors. I also believe He is not displeased with me trying to protect my home from further damage. I remember Jesus teaching the religious leaders in Luke 14 about the importance of doing necessary and helpful things on the Lord's day. He said, 'Which of you shall have an ass or an ox fallen into a pit, and will not straightway pull him out on the Sabbath day?' I'm not going to be sitting on the patio, sipping tea this morning. And I know that God knows my heart. He knows that I would prefer to be at church."

Joe was convinced that he was doing the right thing. The rain had picked up again, and he thought about the damage that it was doing to homes missing part of their roofs. Yet, there was that very tiny doubt, ever so small, that questioned the same as Rob. Again, he wished he had been a Christian longer and that he knew, without a shadow of a doubt, what was the right thing to do in every situation. However, in discussing the topic of knowing God's will with a godly older man in his church one Sunday, the man had stated, "Don't think you'll ever

THE DELIVERY

reach a point where everything is crystal clear. At least that's not true in my life. I think you have to pray, study the scriptures, and allow the Lord to direct you. And remember, God knows your heart. He knows when you're just making excuses for the benefit of others and when you really and truly mean what you're saying." That helped.

So the morning was spent, patching and cleaning things up. Joe was especially pleased that he could do an act of kindness for Peter and Jane Udeen. "Lord, I pray that somehow You might use this to honor Your name. Help them to learn of Your love for them."

At lunch, an exhausted Joe reported on the progress being made in the community.

"So it just missed us?" Meghan asked.

"Apparently so," Joe replied.

"It's a good thing we prayed," Rob said. "Or the tornado might have . . ." he hesitated, looking at Pete. It was obvious he didn't want to frighten the little guy again. He need not have worried much, however, since Pete was busy munching on his sandwich, apparently oblivious to this conversation. ". . . well you know what I mean," Rob finished.

Joe thought about what Rob said. "Yes, we did pray. But is it possible that the tornado might still have come right over us?"

"It didn't," Rob answered.

"Yes, but could it have?"

"I guess so," Rob said. "But we prayed, and . . ."

"That's my point. Children," Joe began, looking around at his family, "prayer is a powerful thing. We're talking to God, the Creator and Sustainer of the universe. However, just because we ask something doesn't mean we'll get it. That's why we always pray that not our will, but God's will be done. It is quite possible that the tornado might have hit us last night, even though we prayed. Don't you imagine that some folks over at Foxboro subdivision were praying just like we were? Just as sincerely? Just as fervently? I think they probably were. God answers our prayers in a way that is consistent with His own will. Remember that sometimes 'bad things' can and do happen to Christians. We're not immune from pain and suffering and tornadoes." It was a topic they had discussed before, but one that needed to be raised from time to time, as his young family matured.

Joe took a bite of his sandwich. Laura, who had been watching her dad closely during his discussion, watched him swallow. She was suddenly intrigued.

"Daddy, what is that lump on your neck?" she questioned, pointing to Joe's neck. She honestly couldn't remember ever having seen it and wondered if maybe the pressure of the tornado had somehow caused it, or maybe that he had worked too hard this morning and that 'muscle' was all stretched out.

"You mean this?" Joe asked, touching his Adam's apple.

"Yes!" exclaimed Laura, surprised that Dad would touch it so nonchalantly. "How did you get it?"

Joe laughed. "That's called my Adam's apple. It moves up and down as I swallow. Here, I'll demonstrate." Joe held a drink of water in his mouth, then while he tilted his head up to the ceiling, he swallowed.

"Wow." Laura was obviously impressed. "Can you make it come all the way out the other way?" she asked, motioning with her hand, indicating that she wanted him to spit out his Adam's apple.

"No," Joe said, laughing again. "It needs to stay right there where it is." He then explained a little about

THE DELIVERY

what its purpose was and why it was important for it to remain in his body.

Laura thought that all made sense. Then, she suddenly lifted her chin toward the ceiling and asked, "Can you see my apple, too?"

Everyone laughed. "Yes, we see your apple, too," Amy answered. "It's a good bit smaller than Dad's, but it's supposed to be."

That afternoon, the family continued to help clean up their house, as well as work at neighbors' houses. As they did so, Joe couldn't get out of his mind that he was forgetting something. *Is it something I'm supposed to do? Or ask someone? Or what?* Try as he might he could not remember what it was. *Oh well, I suppose it will come to me eventually.*

Chapter Fifteen

It took a full twenty-four hours before the Reynolds' power came back on. During the next week, things slowly got back to normal, at least for folks in Joe's subdivision. Joe's insurance adjuster came by and approved an application to get the roof and kitchen window fixed. The sound of saws, hammers, and chain saws was common from morning until night.

It would take months, and in a few cases even years, before the people in the Foxboro neighborhood could piece their lives together again. Even though Joe didn't personally know anyone in that subdivision, he and several of his friends went over after work that week and offered to help in any way they could.

Things at work went as usual. Casey was obnoxious. Perhaps even more troubling was the language that he used. Joe had no desire to use or even think of the words and phrases that Casey often used, yet he found himself thinking those same words and thoughts from time to time. It was irritating that the world was having an impact on his life, and he decided he would like to have a talk with Isaac about the matter. Isaac had been a Christian for many years, and perhaps the wisdom and maturity of his relationship with God would help Joe.

It was Saturday before Joe had an opportunity to visit with Isaac, who was out washing his car.

"Hello, Joe! Sounds like a better weather forecast than we had last weekend," Isaac said in a friendly tone of voice.

THE DELIVERY 155

Joe looked at the clear, blue sky. "Yes," he agreed. "Of course, at about this time of the morning last Saturday, they weren't exactly predicting tornadoes. Still, I doubt if we have anything to worry about."

"Heard anything from the Udeens? Did they make it to New Jersey in time for that birthday party?"

"Haven't heard a word." Joe picked up a sponge and helped Isaac wash the wheels of his car. "How's your week been?"

"Pretty good," Isaac said. "It's hard to believe that we just have about four more weeks of classes at the university. This spring has really flown by for some reason."

"I know what you mean," Joe agreed. "Say, you've talked a few times about what it's like there on campus. I imagine there are some people who don't speak the way we do."

"What do you mean?" Isaac said, standing up to look at Joe. "We do have some international students."

Joe laughed. "No, I was thinking about the vulgar way in which some people talk. You know, taking the Lord's name in vain, and filthy speech."

"Oh sure, we certainly have our share of that," Isaac said sadly. "Often, it comes from faculty, who should know better. Of course, the students aren't little children, they should know better also."

"How do you handle it?" Joe asked suddenly.

"Handle it?"

"Yes. I mean, does it affect you?"

"Sure. I wish they wouldn't do it," Isaac said, not understanding why Joe wouldn't realize that fact without asking.

"No, I mean, does it affect you personally. Do you find yourself, instead of becoming an example of godly speech for them, falling into the same sin they are in? Do you ever start saying or thinking what they say out loud?"

Isaac put down his wash rag. "I see what you mean," he answered slowly. "I'm afraid it does affect me. No, I don't use the words and phrases they do, even when my Christian brothers aren't around to hear me. But there have been times, mostly when I first started teaching and especially when I'd been around certain people a lot, that I found myself thinking those same words. It bothered me."

"Is there no hope?" Joe asked.

Isaac laughed. "Joe, there's always hope! Listen, you and I both know that God is not pleased with those words or thoughts. And it is His desire to conform us to the image of His Son. And He has promised us that the Holy Spirit would help us live a victorious life."

"So, what's the answer?"

"I found several things to help," Isaac said, reflectively. "First, as much as possible, I tried to stay away from people who use bad language. Wait. I know what you're going to say. 'I can't! I work with them!' I understand. So do I. But there are times when I can avoid these people and still do my job. For example, I have to be in meetings with them, but I don't have to go to lunch with them. I have to pass them in the halls but I don't have to stop and listen to their talk and jokes. I guess I'm just saying that I don't have to spend as much time with them as most people might think."

"But how can you be a testimony to them?" Joe asked honestly. "I mean, if you're going to avoid them, how will they ever see your life and want what you have?"

THE DELIVERY

"Excellent questions," Isaac praised. "Excellent. I agree that we need to be salt and light in the world we live in. I agree that we should share the gospel with the people we work with. I believe we should let others see our lives lived for Christ. However, if someone else is dragging down my walk with Christ, if someone else is causing me to sin and want to sin, shouldn't I avoid that evil? Shouldn't I trust that God will use my life and the lives of others to accomplish His will for that work? I think so. Romans 12:9 says to "abhor that which is evil; cleave to that which is good." Keep in mind, I'm not telling you what you have to do. I'm just telling you what I feel the Lord has taught me and what has helped me with the problem you're talking about."

"I hear what you're saying," Joe nodded. "But our pastor is always talking about how important it is to be a missionary right where we work."

"I agree," Isaac said kindly. "And I try to do that too. You do what you feel you need to do. I'm not suggesting you become a hermit, or avoid any contact with those folks. But I don't think God expects you to have to sin in order to accomplish His will in someone else's life. Look at it this way. Would you sit in a room and watch your coworkers take illegal drugs just so you could be a witness while they're doing it? Of course not. All I'm saying is that you need to avoid sin in your own life and avoiding certain people at times is one way to accomplish that."

"I hear you," Joe repeated, thinking about what Isaac had told him. "What other things do you recommend?"

"Well, I would also suggest you pray to God, asking Him to clean your mind and keep it pure and holy. I would suggest you memorize a verse or some verses and then every time you start to think or say something that isn't pleasing to Him you can think or say that verse.

You can meditate on the verse. One that I meditated on was James 4:7-8: 'Submit yourselves therefore to God. Resist the devil, and he will flee from you. Draw nigh to God, and he will draw nigh to you. Cleanse your hands, ye sinners; and purify your hearts, ye double minded.' Of course there are lots of other verses that you might want to memorize and meditate on.

"If you follow that plan, I can't help but believe that God will honor your heart and help you. The Bible says in I Corinthians 10:13, 'There hath no temptation taken you but such as is common to man: but God is faithful, who will not suffer you to be tempted above that ye are able; but will with the temptation also make a way to escape, that ye may be able to bear it.' That promise tells me that God will provide a way out of your temptation."

"So you recommend prayer, scripture memory, and avoiding as much as possible situations where I am exposed to evil speaking," Joe summarized.

"That's pretty much what I would recommend," Isaac agreed. "That, and making yourself accountable to someone. You probably remember what James 5:16 says: "Confess your faults one to another, and pray one for another, that ye may be healed. The effectual fervent prayer of a righteous man availeth much." If you have a problem you're wrestling with, it can be helpful to have someone else praying specifically for that problem."

"I would like to be accountable to you. And I would surely appreciate you praying for me, Isaac."

"I will. Let's do it right now. Lord, thank You for the promises in scripture. Thank You that You want us to be men of God whose whole desire in life is to please You and glorify Your name. Help Joe with this problem he is experiencing. Please bring him to my mind often, so I can lift him up in prayer. And please help me not to

THE DELIVERY

be full of pride, lest I fall myself. In Jesus' Name. Amen."

"Thanks, Isaac. I don't want you to think that I have a major problem with it. It's just that I don't want to have one at all. I'll try to come up with some verses and do as you suggest."

"Well, hello Elaine! I didn't know we were going to have the honor of your presence at our lunch table today!" Joe exclaimed as he came home for lunch. "It's always a treat to have you here."

"Thanks," Elaine said a little shyly. "I hope I'm not a bother."

"Not at all," Joe said sincerely. "We love to have you here. What's for lunch, Amy?"

"Salad, sandwiches, and ice cream," Amy replied, kissing Joe on the cheek.

"Let's eat," Joe called. "Time to eat!"

Children amassed from all directions.

Amy looked a little embarrassed. "It's not quite ready, dear."

"Shoo! Off with you, children!" Joe laughed. "Sorry. We'll try it all again in a few minutes." Laughing and giggling, the children walked back out of the kitchen.

Finally, everything was ready and a blessing was offered. "Did the insurance adjuster come to your place?" Joe asked Elaine.

"No, he is supposed to come next Monday," she replied. "But he said it wouldn't be any problem. He just has to take a picture and write up some report."

"Good," Joe said. "Let us know if you need any help."

Talk turned to other current events. "I got a letter from my nephew in Troy today," Elaine remarked. "He was involved in a water-skiing accident."

"Water-skiing can be so dangerous," Amy agreed. "I never was very good at it anyway. I'm sure I couldn't water- ski today!"

Rob noticed a smile on Joe's face. "Did you water-ski, Dad?"

"Yes, I did," Joe replied. "When I was in my late teens and early twenties, I spent a lot of time on a pair of water-skis."

"Do you think you could still do it today?" Rob asked.

"Yes, I imagine I could."

Laura couldn't believe it. "Dad, how can you ski now, when Mom can't? You're lots older than she is. You're forty-two and she's only thirty-nine!"

Everyone laughed. "I'm not ancient, you know!" Joe retorted.

"In fact, when I was a teenager my father bought a ski boat," Joe began. "It wasn't much of a boat, but it was one we could afford. I remember that the man we bought it from had stored it in his back yard for years, but he promised it was seaworthy. We took the boat home and cleaned it up some. We probably should have spent more time going over the boat, but we were impatient to get it on the water and see how fast it would go."

"Well, what happened?" Rob asked. "Did you take it to a lake? Did you have fun?"

"Yes, we took it to a lake. Before we could, though, we had a few items to buy. Like skis, an extra gas tank, one rowing paddle, a marine battery, a ski tow rope, some outboard marine oil, a trailer hitch and light kit for the car, a license for the trailer, some life vests, a few

THE DELIVERY

cushions, and we had to pay to register the boat with the state. That cheap boat was ending up costing us plenty! All that stuff cost us just about as much as the boat itself! So we have this boat and accessories, but we still haven't ever had the boat in the water yet. And there was no way to tell if the motor was good, because it had to be in water before you could start it."

Joe saw he had the family's undivided attention, and smiling, he continued.

"Finally, the big day arrived. It was a beautiful sunny day. But a little chilly. Probably because of the high wind. *No problem!* we thought. *We're not going skydiving, just water-skiing. What difference could a little wind make?*

"On the way to the lake, that wind whipped the boat and trailer back and forth. There for a while I thought we might lose it. My dad never did slow down for anything, and wasn't about to slow down just because we had a little trailer behind us.

"When we got to the lake, it looked like maybe they were giving away five-hundred dollar bills or something to whoever would bring their boat that day. I mean that parking lot was crammed full of cars, trailers, and what looked like half the population of town milling around. Now to my knowledge, my father had never ever driven with a trailer before and had no idea how to back one up. It's easy enough going forward, but backing one up is a real art.

"He whipped in that parking lot, throwing more dust in the air than a man had a right to do. I noticed several angry looks by people standing by their cars and trailers. 'So where do we put the boat in?' Dad asked, confused by all the parked cars and trailers.

"'I think you're supposed to pull up along that paved place and then back the trailer into the water,' my older brother Jerry replied.

"So that's what my father did. At least that's what he tried to do. Only thing is, that every time he started backing, the trailer started to jackknife on him, like this." Joe illustrated the problem with his hands scissoring together.

"Every time it jackknifed, he had to pull forward and try again. Now a couple of more boats had arrived and were waiting their turn. At first they were patient about Dad's inability to back the trailer. Everyone has a bad day, you know. I would say for about two, maybe three minutes they were patient. Then the horns started to blow.

"That didn't calm my father down a bit. He started accelerating even harder every time he had to move forward or backward. I can still hear the tires squealing right now. Sqquueaalll! The car lunges forward. Sqquueeaaallllll! The car jerks backward until the trailer almost collides with the side of the car and nearly flips over. With car horns blaring. And Dad shouting, 'What's the matter with this trailer? Did we get a lemon, Judy?' Finally he asked Mom to get out and see what was wrong.

"My mom obediently got out, but she sure didn't have any suggestions. Every time she would signal for him to go to the left, my dad would twist the steering wheel hard to the left and the trailer lunged to the right instead. 'Joe, get out there and help your mother. I don't think she knows how to give directions for a trailer. She's all backwards!'

Everyone at the table laughed at the picture Joe was painting, except Laura. "You see, Laura, when you're backing a trailer up, if you want the trailer to go to the

THE DELIVERY 163

left, you have to steer to the right. If you wanted to go to the right, you have to steer it to the left," Skip explained. "That's just the way trailers work."

"Right," Joe agreed. "Anyway, we had been there maybe ten minutes, kicking up dust, making a lot of racket, and blocking traffic. About that time a park ranger came over. I think he thought Dad must be drunk. But he wasn't. The ranger leaned way over near Dad's face and asked, 'You need some help, sir?'

"'Well, I reckon so!' my dad blurted out. 'There's something wrong with this trailer. Would help if you could get everyone to stop blaring their horns so much, too!' The nice ranger got in and backed the car up for us. Right into the water. He did it so smoothly and perfectly and easily.

"Dad didn't like to be shown up. 'I must have finally gotten it straight before you jumped in,' Dad remarked. 'Thanks to you, sir.'

"Now we had to get the boat off the trailer. That wasn't hard. We undid some straps, released the cable sprocket, and zzooooommmmm, the boat went flying down the trailer into the water. With no one in it. Not exactly what you would call a controlled-boat launch! It just bobbed in the waves (it was a very windy day remember) and Dad hollered, "Go get that boat, Jerry!'

"By now, there was a group of about fifteen or twenty people hanging around watching to see what dumb thing we would do next. Probably better than going to the circus. Well, Jerry jumped in, swam to the boat, and toppled in. He looked at Dad as if to say, 'Okay, now what?'

"'Row it over to that dock,' Dad instructed, pointing to a dock made just for that purpose.

"'With what?' asked Jerry. The paddle was in the back of the car, because Dad had been afraid it would blow away on the trip over. And he should have been worried about it, too. We learned later that two boat cushions had blown out on the way! I ran to the car, got out the paddle, and threw it into the water. A set of waves washed it right back to shore where I was standing. The crowd laughed loudly.

"'Give me that paddle,' Dad instructed. He threw it as hard as he could, and it would have probably been a good throw, except for one thing. That wind. It blew it off course and the paddle landed about ten feet to the left of the boat. Now we just had to wait longer for the paddle to drift to shore. The crowd laughed some more, and a few people from the swimming area of the lake started walking our way to watch the fun. It's too bad I didn't think of selling tickets.

"'Dad had had enough fun, and decided to swim out to the boat with the paddle. He was a good swimmer and made it there in no time, especially since the action of the wind and waves had caused the boat to drift closer to shore. Climbing aboard, he proudly put the paddle into the water and commenced to paddle as hard as he could, trying to get the boat to that dock.

"Now I don't know if you've ever tried to paddle a heavy, sixteen-foot ski boat with a single three-foot paddle, but it's not easy. I'm not even sure it's possible! Not on a calm day. But especially with a wind whipping up. The boat just went in a lazy sort of circle around and around, bobbing in the waves.

"By now, the boat had drifted all the way back to the shore and was hitting up against the empty trailer. One of the tail lights got smashed. 'Judy, move that trailer before we destroy it!' Dad shouted. The crowd roared. Mom jumped in the car, but found that Dad had the keys.

"'Here, I'll toss them to you,' he called to Mom."

"Oh no," Rob cried out. "He didn't, did he Dad?"

THE DELIVERY

"Yes, he certainly did, Rob. He threw those keys to Mom. Dad's got pretty good aim and a strong throwing arm. But his hand hit the windshield as he was releasing the keys, and they merely dropped on the front of the boat and slowly started sliding toward the water. I thought the crowd was going to go crazy. We all watched as Dad tried jumping over the windshield to catch the keys. He almost did, too. Almost is a sad word.

"Plunk. The keys disappeared into the murky, muddy lake. Dad was furious, I was trying to keep from laughing, and Mom was trying to keep from crying.

"To me he said, 'Joe, dig around with your toes and see if you can find them.' Then addressing Mom he yelled, 'Just use your keys.'

"Mom mumbled something and Dad shouted for her to repeat it. The crowd leaned in her direction to keep from missing what she said. 'I didn't bring my keys, honey. You said I wouldn't need my purse.'

"I was digging in the soft muddy bottom with my toes, but didn't find any keys. I started being afraid that maybe I was burying them by accident. Jerry didn't help matters any when I heard him tell Dad, 'I told you we should buy one of those little floating key chains.' Again, the crowd roared. The boat bumped into me from time to time as I searched. Dad was reaching out with his paddle, trying to keep the boat from ramming our trailer.

"A few boys jumped in the water and started digging around with their toes, too. I suspect that some parents put them up to it. After all, as long as we were around, they were getting some free entertainment. One of the boys shouted that he had found them. Sure enough, he pulled a muddy, slimy set of keys up from the water and threw them toward Mom. I think a few bystanders were upset that he didn't toss them to Dad instead.

"While she was moving the car and trailer, Dad was trying to get the engine started. The paddle was totally useless. Why, he couldn't get himself to shore with one paddle if the lake was as smooth as glass. So, he tried to get the engine started using the electric starter. He cranked and cranked. Nothing happened.

"Someone on land called out, 'Do you have the gas tank turned on?' Dad looked sheepishly down at the gas line and saw that it was in the off position. 'Thanks,' he called to shore. Another round of howls and laughter.

"By this time, Mom had the car parked and was standing on the dock watching the boat bob in the water. I had crawled in the boat, so she was the only one out. 'Do you want me to swim over?' she called meekly. 'I really don't mind, honey. It might be the easiest thing to do.' That was too much for our gallery of onlookers and the hoots sprang forth.

"But about that time, Dad got the engine going. You've never seen the like of blue smoke that came pouring out of that engine. I wondered if maybe Dad had mixed the gas and oil incorrectly. I doubt if he read the directions on the bottle of oil to learn how much gas it was supposed to treat. Well, that smoke cloud floated over to shore, and helped dissipate the crowd just a little bit. A few hung around, though, figuring we weren't through with our entertainment just yet. I'm afraid they were right.

"Dad apparently had never driven a motorized boat before and we went lurching over the waves toward the dock where Mom was waving at us. As we got closer, I guess Mom got afraid that we were going to run over the dock, and she ran screaming off the dock with her hands in the air. Dad didn't hit it however, not so much because he was a good helmsman, but due more to a

THE DELIVERY

sudden wave that sucked the boat away from the dock right before impact.

"The boat, doing all it knew to do, started floating away from the dock. 'Hurry, Judy, before we lose you!' Dad shouted. Mom came running down the dock, jumped in the boat, and landed hard about halfway into one of the seats. With that Dad gunned the engine and we went tearing away from shore. I guess he had had about all the humiliation he could stand.

"With the boat flying along the water, things started looking up. For a few minutes anyway. Then they started coming out. First one, then a few more, then a whole bunch. Wasps. There was a wasp's nest under the seat that Mom had jumped onto. I guess that impact was enough to jar them into action. Back home, when we had been looking over the boat, we had noticed wasps, but didn't think they had a nest in the boat. They did.

"Mom screamed. Dad tried to slow the boat down to see what was wrong, but moved the throttle in the wrong direction. It lurched forward causing me to just about fall out. Then, almost immediately, Dad, figuring he should pull the throttle in the opposite direction, pulled the throttle all the way back, causing the boat to come to an instant standstill. That, too, almost caused us to fall out of the boat.

"As it turns out, Dad had a can of insect killer ('I'm always prepared, aren't I?' – he praised himself) and started attacking the wasps. While he was doing that, Jerry and I jumped into the water. Mom crawled over the windshield and positioned herself on the front of the boat, as far away as possible from those wasps. I noticed some people on shore pointing at us. But before long, Dad had the whole thing under control."

Joe stopped as if he was not going to go on. "Then what happened, Daddy?" Laura asked excitedly.

"Well, I'm glad I wasn't a bug about that time. The air was so saturated with bug spray that that's about all we could taste in our mouths the rest of the afternoon. But we all got back in our seats and Dad started off again, this time a little slower. He took a few turns around the lake and I noticed that some people on shore were waving at us. I waved back.

"'Who wants to be the first to go skiing?' Dad asked, as though he did this kind of thing every day of the year, and that nothing at all out of the ordinary had happened since we pulled into the park.

"Jerry always did beat me to the draw, and he said 'yes' first. So, in the water he went. Jerry was a pretty good skier and I didn't think he would ever drop and let someone else ski. When he finished, Dad asked Mom if she wanted to ski. She was busy trying to tie something on her head to keep the wind from blowing her hair to Africa. 'No thank you,' she said a little sulkily. I was excited since I knew who would be next. After everything that had happened, things were finally looking up.

"'Well, Joe, I guess it's time for you,' Dad suggested. Eagerly I jumped overboard and got in position. 'We'll take it slowly,' Dad assured, knowing that I was a marginal skier at best.

"I couldn't get up the first few times I tried, but finally I did manage to keep my balance and let the boat pull me out of the water. Dad was cheering and Mom was waving. Jerry had a sort of 'I can't believe it' look on his face.

"I wasn't very good though, I can tell you that. And the waves were pretty high, thanks to all of that wind. I had no confidence and knew if I got nervous that I would lose my concentration and fall down.

"All of a sudden, Jerry says something to Mom who looks at the floor of the boat. Pretty soon, Dad is turning

THE DELIVERY

around looking at something Jerry is pointing at. Then, Dad pulls the throttle forward as far as it will go and off we shoot!

"Now it's about all I can do to hang on. I'm bobbing over those waves with my skis about to fall off. I thought that maybe Dad had lost his mind. I was about to drop the tow rope when Jerry saw what I was going to do and motioned frantically for me not to drop. 'Stay up, Joe! You've got to stay up! Don't drop!' he shouted over and over, with both his thumbs pointing upward. Mom was hanging onto her scarf for dear life.

"Dad had steered the boat directly toward the shore where we left our car. But he wasn't lowering the throttle at all. *Is he going to drive the boat clear up on land?* I wondered. He didn't, but he got so close to doing it that some people shouted at him to slow down before we were all killed. Dad powered down, and bobbed up to the dock. Actually, what he did was sort of run into the dock, but he'll deny that today if you ask him.

"Me, I'm left out there in the lake, at the end of the tow rope. But now that the boat has stopped, I sort of just slide down into the water. Swimming to the boat, I see my dad bailing water out of the boat with a bait bucket just as fast as he can. Mom is running toward where the car is parked and Jerry is laughing. A few people walk down the dock to see. What an adventure!"

"What was wrong?" Skip asked, laughing at the emotion in Joe's voice.

"The boat apparently had a few leaks that the previous owner didn't know about, or at least failed to tell us about. In fact, we later learned that the whole hull had filled with water while we were in the lake. Water was spouting three inches into the air though a few small holes in the flooring. Dad was afraid that if we stopped out in the middle of the lake, the boat would just sink.

That's why Jerry told me I had to stay up until we got to shore."

"Did the boat sink?" Rob asked.

"No, and that's a shame actually," Joe answered laughing. "You see, if it had simply sunk right then, we wouldn't have had to spend so much money on it over the years and have some of the adventures we had."

"Tell us about your other adventures on the boat!" Meghan pleaded.

"I'm afraid I would just bore you all," Joe said, smiling. "Besides, I was thinking of having a picnic at the lake this afternoon. Without a boat, of course, Amy! What do you all think? Elaine, you'd be mighty welcome, too."

"I'm sorry, but I need to get back home," Elaine said. "But you all should have fun. It's a beautiful day."

"What about the rest of you?" To the enthusiastic response, Joe added, "Good, then we need to get a few things done before we go. Skip, please get the grass cut; Meghan, you can help your mom get the food together; Rob, please find our cooler and get it washed out; Laura, please find the fishing poles; and Pete . . . what can Pete do?"

"Let him find some worms!" Rob suggested.

"That's a good idea," Joe agreed. "Pete, you can find some worms for us to fish with. Okay?"

Pete didn't say anything, but he did nod his head.

"I think he might need some help," Amy suggested. "Pete probably doesn't know what a worm is or where he can find them."

Pete wasn't happy about this statement. "I can find worm!" he insisted.

THE DELIVERY

"Okay," Joe agreed. "But Rob, you . . ." Joe didn't finish his sentence with words, but nonverbally he told Rob to also be responsible for finding some worms.

Chapter Sixteen

That afternoon everyone worked hard on the tasks they were assigned. Pete got up from his nap around 2:30 and immediately went out into the yard to look for worms, carrying an empty tomato paste can his mommy had given him.

At 3:00, Joe called his family together. "Are we ready?" he asked.

"Food's ready," Meghan reported.

"Cooler is cleaned out, and ice is in it," Rob added. "And I got some you-know-whats."

"Grass is cut," Skip said happily.

"I forgot what I was supposed to do," Laura admitted, gloomily.

"Did you find the fishing poles?"

"Oh yes, that's what I was supposed to do!" She brightened. "Yes sir, they're in the car. Skip helped me put them in so we wouldn't forget them."

"Then I guess we're ready to go. Everyone go to the bathroom and then load up."

"My stuff," Pete said. "Got my stuff!"

Joe got down and looked at Pete. "What's that, Pete?"

"My stuff!" Pete handed Joe his can of "worms."

Inside was a hodgepodge of things. There was a dead fly, an old spark plug, an empty piece of cardboard that used to hold sewing needles, and something very smelly. "Anybody have any idea what that thing is?" Joe asked, holding it up.

THE DELIVERY

"Could it be a part of that dead bird that's been in the ditch for a few weeks?" Skip asked, laughing.

Joe shuddered, and dropped it back into the can. "I think these can stay home, little helper. We have some worms that we can use. Thanks for your help, though."

"You're welcome," Pete said with a pleased countenance.

"Let's go wash those hands!" exclaimed Amy.

There was the usual chaos surrounding an exit by the Reynolds family, but eventually everyone was buckled in their seats.

At the lake, their favorite picnic table was already taken by another family. Skip was annoyed. "Why did they take that table? They're not even looking at the water!"

"Yeah, they could have just as easily used a table that wasn't even near the water," Rob agreed. Somehow it just didn't seem right for the Reynolds to be denied their table.

"I guess they have just as much right to use that table as we do," Amy interjected. "It's not our table, you know."

"Yes, but they're not even eating now. Looks like they are ready to go home. Why don't they leave it so we can take it?"

"That might be a nice thing to do, but we can't expect others to do what we wish they would do," Joe reminded. "It is a good lesson for you, however. If you're ever in the same situation, I would hope you will remember to do unto others as you would have them do unto you. That's a simple lesson, but if everyone would follow it, we'd have a much happier world."

The late afternoon was spent taking a walk around the lake's edge and fishing. This was Pete's first time fishing, and he was thrilled. Of course, he didn't have a clue what he was doing, but that didn't stop him from laughing and dancing around as Joe put bait on his hook.

"He's going to scare all the fish away," Rob complained. "Look at the way Pete is splashing the water with his pole. The fish are going to leave. I don't blame them."

"Yeah, Dad," Skip agreed. "Can't the rest of us go somewhere else to fish? That way Pete could still have his fun, and we could have ours as well."

"You can move down some, but I want you to be where I can see you," Joe instructed. "We're fishing together as a family for fun, not so we can put food on our plates. Besides, if Pete scares the fish away from his pole, that doesn't mean they won't go near yours."

The new fishing arrangement worked well. Pete, with a lot of assistance from Joe, caught a small bream. He couldn't have been happier. And Rob caught a large mouth bass. Skip kept getting nibbles, but no bites.

While they were fishing, a car could be heard approaching the picnic area. It sounded like an old car, but as it came around the bend, the family could see it was actually not that old. Just needed a muffler. Loud music was blaring from the open windows.

The driver pulled it right next to the Reynolds' car and the occupants got out. Five older teenage boys and one girl. They were laughing and shouting in an uncontrolled kind of way that made Joe suspect either drugs or alcohol. When one of the boys opened his car door, it hit the Reynolds' car. He shouted to a friend what he had done and loud laughter echoed across the park.

"Honey," Amy said to Joe. That's all she said, but she was obviously concerned.

THE DELIVERY

"I see," Joe returned, eyes narrowing slightly. "You children come back down here and fish right next to me," he called to Skip and Rob who had moved down the beach. They were taking their time doing so, so he called out, "now!"

The rowdy group hung around their car for a while, drinking and laughing. Joe wasn't sure what was going to happen next, but he knew he was responsible for his family's safety, whatever did happen.

"What is it?" Skip asked, somewhat irritated at having been called back so soon. "I was starting to get some bites. You said we could..." Then he noticed the boys near their car. He stopped talking.

Pete noticed that the atmosphere had changed at the picnic. He didn't understand why his family wasn't talking much and why they were all standing close together, but he knew something was up.

"Should we leave, or...?" Amy asked.

"Hang on, Amy," Joe answered, cutting her off. "Before I decide what to do, I want to see what they are going to do."

The boys at the car continued to drink. One of them reached over and knocked his buddy's hat off. The boy pushed him away and the first guy just laughed. Joe noticed the gleam of metal sticking out of one of the boy's pockets. If that was a gun, there could be real trouble.

Joe looked at his family. They were all staring at the gang. "You children turn around and fish," Joe commanded with authority. "I'll tell you when I want you to turn around again."

The situation was tense. Joe kept an eye on the rowdy group, but didn't stare at them. It wasn't Joe's intention to raise their attention to him and his family. He also didn't want to appear to be challenging them.

"Let's move down the lake some," Joe suggested, softly. "Come on, let's go!" Following the authority in his voice, the family moved slowly, never questioning Joe's wisdom. Little by little, the family moved further and further away from the potential danger. Now they were a good fifty yards away from the rowdy bunch, and nearer to another group of picnickers. Joe kept good tabs on what was happening up there by the car.

After a while, the group of boys and the girl walked toward the lake. But they didn't walk near the Reynolds. Getting to the lake, they laughed drunkenly and threw their beer bottles in. Joe had been praying for wisdom during the ordeal, and now he asked God to know what to do.

The group apparently decided to move in the opposite direction from the Reynolds and started walking around the lake, laughing and trying to push each other into the water. Joe was relieved, but still acted quickly.

"Children, I'm afraid we're going to have to leave now. I'm sorry, but I think it's best. Maybe we can go by the ice cream parlor for a treat."

"That's fine!" Meghan said. Rob and Laura agreed.

Amy seemed relieved. "Hurry now, and do what Dad said. Let's load up . . . No, don't worry about those leaves you found. We'll get more when we come back the next time." In a few minutes the Reynolds were in their car.

"Do we have everyone?" Joe asked, buckling up.

"Yes, I think we have everything," Amy answered, happily. It looked like they were going to avoid any confrontation with the group of rough kids.

THE DELIVERY

Joe pumped the van once to prime the engine with gasoline, and then turned the key. The car tried to crank, but the engine didn't turn over. "It'll start," he said hopefully to Amy. "I had trouble with it a few weeks ago, but they got it fixed at the shop."

RrrrrRrrrrrRrrrrrr. The starter motor struggled to start the engine. RrrrrRrrrrrRrrrrrrr. Now the smell of gasoline was in the air.

"You didn't flood it, did you, Dad?" asked Skip. "If you did, we may have to sit here for a while." As he finished speaking, the rowdy group emerged from behind some trees, slowly walking back toward their car. One of the boys had a sign that he had stolen from the edge of the lake, stating "No life guard on duty! Swim at your own risk!" For some reason they were laughing loudly.

RrrrrrrRrrrrrrr. The car wouldn't start. *Lord, please help the car to start*, Joe prayed. But it wouldn't.

The group got closer and closer to the car. One of the boys pointed to the Reynolds' car and laughed.

RrrrrRrrrrrRrrrrr. Now the battery was getting weak. *Why didn't the shop get the car fixed?* Joe asked himself softly. *Now this car is putting my family at risk!*

The boys were less than fifteen feet from the car. One of them picked up a large rock, leaned back, and threw it as hard as he could right at the windshield. Joe involuntarily ducked while shouting to his family "Get down!" Pete wailed with fright.

But the rock didn't hit the car. Joe slowly raised himself to a sitting position and looked at the boys. The boy who had "thrown" the rock was laughing so hard he fell to the ground. When he got up, he went through the motions again of what he had done and then acted out what Joe had done and said. Everyone in the gang laughed.

"Hey old man, if I had really thrown that rock, you wouldn't have had time to duck. I don't miss what I want to hit!"

It then dawned on Joe why the rock had missed. The boy hadn't actually thrown it. When he leaned back, he must have dropped it on purpose when his hand was out of sight for a second. He had merely been trying to frighten them. His attempt had been very successful!

RrrrRrrrrrRrrrrrr. Joe tried again. The battery was practically dead.

Their leader motioned for the boys to surround the car. Soon a rowdy gang member was positioned by every door. "Hey, there's a gal back here!" one shouted.

"Now we're going to have some fun!" the leader yelled, starting to reach for Joe's car handle.

Chapter Seventeen

The stench of beer was heavy on the boy's breath as he announced this right next to Joe's face. "Yep, let's have some fun. Who all do we have to play with in this car?" the leader said, looking over the passengers.

"Look..." Joe said manfully, acting decisively. He knew what must be done and he was prepared to do it.

Before he could say or do anything else, however, the leader of the group blurted out, very loudly, "Why, look here, boys. It's Skip!" Moving to the back window and peering in, he continued, "That is you back there. Ain't it, Skip?"

Skip's heart was beating rapidly. His breathing was so excessive that he was on the verge of hyperventilating. He could think of the words to say, but his body prevented them from being said.

The drunken leader thrust his head in the car window and got within a few inches of Skip's face. "Skip?"

"Yeah," Skip squeaked, almost inaudibly.

The leader, JoBo, stepped back from the car and shouted. "Okay, get back, you guys," he commanded his followers.

"But there's still a gal back here!" one said.

"I said get back! And I mean, now!" JoBo said, reaching his hand into his pocket. The other gang members reluctantly obeyed. "Get in the car!" he commanded to his followers.

One of them slammed his foot into the Reynolds' car before obeying. As he did so, he spat on a window.

When this gang member walked in front of JoBo to get in their car, JoBo hit him in the back of his neck.

The young man screamed in pain. "I said to get in our car, Fluffhead. Not hit their car! You do as I say, not what you want to!" Fluffhead, holding his neck, was pushed into their car roughly by JoBo.

In a few minutes all of the gang members were in the car. JoBo, who had walked back over to Skip's door, leaned over and said, "Didn't know you was in there, Skip." Without saying anything else, JoBo walked to his car, started it, and drove away. Two gang members shouted something and gestured meanly as they drove off.

"Thank You, Lord Jesus," Amy gulped, as tears began to stream from her eyes. The stressful ordeal seemed to finally be over.

"I think you know why I need to talk to you," Joe began.

"Yes sir," Skip answered, looking down.

"Well, why don't you fill me in? Start from the beginning."

It had been several hours since the incident had occurred. Getting a jump start from another family, Joe had finally been able to get the car started. But the picnic was ruined. No one felt like getting ice cream, so the family had driven straight home.

Right now, sitting on the edge of his bed, Joe felt a heaviness of heart like he couldn't remember ever having felt.

"Dad, honestly, I've never done anything wrong," Skip began. "I don't know any of those guys from tonight and I've never seen that girl. The only one I know is JoBo."

THE DELIVERY 181

"Seems like a pretty rough character to know, son," Joe said sternly. "From the beginning, please!"

Skip painfully but meticulously gave his dad all the details about the camping trip, JoBo, and delivering packages. "Dad, I never did anything wrong. I promise you that!" he concluded.

Joe sighed long and hard. He rubbed his hands together and then opened them, examining the creases in his hands. Joe didn't say anything for four or five minutes. When he did, it was with emotion. Joe was having trouble talking and there were tears forming in the corners of his eyes.

"Skip, do you know how much I love you? How many hours I've spent praying for you? How much time I've taken to try and make the best life for you that I possibly can? Skip, if you only knew!" With that, Joe began to cry. He was so filled with emotion that it was heart breaking. Skip had never seen his father cry like that.

Tears formed in Skip's eyes, too. Still, his father didn't stop crying. Skip tried not to cry, but couldn't help it.

"Oh, how I wish you could just know," Joe said finally, wiping his face. "I just wish you could know my love for you. And know God's love for you."

Skip didn't know what to say. For the last few hours, he had been rehearsing what he would say to his dad. He had worked out several lies that would cover his tracks, but when the time came to present them, Skip had only been able to tell the truth. Why, he couldn't say.

Then, as he was telling Joe what all had happened, Skip couldn't help thinking about what his dad was going to say in return. *I'll be grounded for a year. I won't be able to leave the house. He'll take away my driver's license. He'll make me confess to the police. He'll lock me up in anger. He'll say he wishes I was never born. He'll say that I don't fit in and would I please just leave his home.*

Yes, Skip had lots of things he was sure his father would say or do. But right now his dad hadn't done any of them. Instead he had said, "I love you."

"How . . . how can you love me? Can you really mean that?" Skip asked. "I've let you down. I've let our whole family down," he finally admitted.

"I love you, just like God loves you, Skip. Unconditionally. Not based on what you've done. Not because you have done good or kind things for me. But just because I love you. God has given me the love I have for you. He is the source of my love for you. And nothing can take it away."

Skip was confused. His father had always said that he loved Skip, but then again, Skip had never done anything that was terribly unlovable. Oh sure, Skip knew he got on his dad's nerves at times and that his dad wasn't pleased that Skip didn't care about God. But now Skip had done something to make himself terribly unlovable, and his dad still claimed to love him!

Although it was one of the lowest moments of his life, and Skip had no idea how it was all going to work out, he suddenly had a peace like he had never experienced before. He felt and knew he had his father's unconditional love. Wow! The enormity of it all caused Skip to start trembling.

"D. . . a. . .d," he stumbled. "I believe that you love me. I really do. It's hard to believe, after the way I've let you down, and all." Skip looked at his hands as though he was struggling with something he needed to say. Finally, he stated, "And I don't always say it. But . . . well, I love you too. I do know how hard you work so

THE DELIVERY

that you can do things for us kids. And I appreciate it. Honestly. I . . . I know I cause you grief sometimes. I'm sorry, Dad. I don't mean to hurt you. I don't sit up at night thinking 'how can I get Dad mad at me.' It just seems that I'm . . . well, that I'm different from the rest of you, somehow. I feel like I don't belong sometimes, although I know you all love me."

"You're right, Skip when you say that we all love you and want what is best for you."

"I know, and that makes this whole thing not seem so bad. Knowing you all love me, and all," Skip concluded.

"It's important to remember, though, that love doesn't make what you did right. You do understand that, don't you?" Joe asked. "And that you will have to be punished. There are consequences of what you've done."

Skip thought about that for a moment. "Yes, I know there are consequences. I feel some of them in the pit of my stomach right now. I know I'll be punished. And I know that we have to do something with this . . . this situation with JoBo. I'm at a loss what to do now. What can we do? I'm afraid!"

"I'm going to have to pray about that," Joe answered. "And get some godly counsel. For now, I need to know from you that you are through with JoBo and his kind forever. Deal?"

"Forever!" Skip exclaimed, holding up his right hand. With that word he felt a finality about the whole ordeal and a peace that had been lacking in his life for the last several months.

"Here's a rule for now. You're not to say anything about this to anyone, not even in our family. Do you understand?"

"Yes sir," Skip replied. Looking into his father's eyes, he pleaded, "Dad, I'll make it up to you. Somehow. I promise. I hope you'll forgive me."

"I'm glad you're willing to try to make up for this, Skip," Joe said, slapping him gently on the back. "Of course some things can never be 'made up' or erased." Joe stopped to let that truth sink in.

"I do forgive you, though, and I'm willing to move on. Right now, I think the most important thing you need to do is to go before the Lord and tell him what you've done and seek His forgiveness."

Skip was uneasy. It was one thing to think that his father could forgive him. However, Skip knew that God kept score of rights and wrongs. You couldn't just erase the scoreboard. He admitted this belief to his dad.

"Skip, it is true that God knows all things we do. Even what we think. And it's true that He will examine each of our lives someday in heaven. However, the Bible also makes it very clear that He can and will forgive us if we but ask Him to. Our responsibility is to ask His forgiveness. He is then responsible for forgiving our sins. Why will He forgive us? Because Jesus Christ died to pay the price for our sins."

Joe looked at his son carefully. It was obvious that this message wasn't sinking in. "Look, you know how I truly do love you now, even though you have sinned against me. Right?"

Skip nodded.

"But I still love you, and forgive you. God, who is the author of love, can still love you even though you have sinned. The Bible says so. If He didn't, then no one could ever be saved and we would all be doomed to hell."

THE DELIVERY

"It would be nice to ask God to forgive me. Really it would. But I'm . . . well, to be honest, I'm not like you, Dad. You've made your peace with God. Mom too. I haven't. I . . . I can't."

Joe stood and paced the floor a bit, silently talking to God. *Oh Holy Sprit, I pray that you would call on Skip. I can't say or do anything else. Skip needs Your presence. Please, God, call Skip to Yourself! Give him the faith to believe that Your Son died for his sins, regardless of what those sins are. Help him to ask Your forgiveness.*

Skip sensed what his father was silently doing. He squirmed uneasily on the edge of the bed. *I can't help who I am,* Skip thought to himself. *It would be nice to be like Dad, but I'm just not! I wish Dad would understand.*

"Skip," Joe began after pacing a few minutes. "I know you feel like you can't make your 'peace with God' as you phrase it. But you can. With the power of the Holy Spirit, accepting the grace that God offers you, by the blood of His Son, you can 'make peace with God.'"

Skip sat staring at his hands. After a time it became obvious that he wasn't going to say anything else.

Joe sighed and walked toward the door. "I'll keep praying for you, Skip. And I'll let you know what I think our next step should be with JoBo." With that Joe walked out of the room.

Chapter Eighteen

On Wednesday of the following week, Joe asked Skip to come out to the backyard with him. "We need to talk about what we're going to do." Joe spoke softly, not wanting to draw Rob's attention. Rob was busy reading a well-worn copy of *Paul Revere: Midnight Rider* and didn't hear a thing.

"I've given the matter some prayer," Joe began. "And I've talked to one godly man whose wisdom I trust."

"But, Dad," Skip protested. "Did you have to tell anyone else? I mean, what if he starts telling everyone about what I've done?" Strangely, Skip was worried about his reputation, something he obviously wasn't as concerned with just a few weeks ago.

"Don't worry," Joe reassured. "I know your concern. I didn't go and talk to lots of men. In fact, one of the criteria I used choosing the man was that I knew he would be discreet. And I'm not even going to tell you his name, so you won't have to worry about seeing him and wondering what he must be thinking of you. I explained it all to him and told him of your true repentance of the whole thing."

Skip seemed relieved. "What did he say?"

Joe somewhat ignored Skip's question. "Based on prayer, and the counsel I received, here's what I think we should do. I believe we should contact the police and tell them what we know. I can do it in a way that is anonymous if you prefer that."

THE DELIVERY

At first Skip seemed to like the idea of anonymity. But then he felt guilty about the whole situation and said, "No, Dad. I think I should talk to them myself. It's the right thing to do." Still, in the back of his mind, Skip couldn't help remembering JoBo's admonition to not talk about their little business arrangement with others.

A few nights later, a police officer in an unmarked car pulled up in the Reynolds' driveway. It had been arranged for Amy to take everyone else shopping for birthday presents for Skip, whose birthday was coming in about three weeks' time.

"Come in," Joe greeted, introducing himself to the officer. "Would you like a cup of coffee?"

"Thanks, that would be nice," Officer Hamilton responded. "Just black will be fine." Then turning to Skip, he held out his hand. "You must be Skip."

"Yes sir," Skip replied, having trouble looking Mr. Hamilton in the eyes.

"You sure have a nice place here," the officer commented loudly, so Joe who was in the kitchen could hear. "Lived here long?"

"About eight years," Joe replied, walking back into the living room. "Here you go, Mr. Hamilton. I just noticed that we also have some chocolate cake. Can I cut you a slice?"

"No thanks. I'm afraid the missus has been on me to cut the size of my stomach. And just call me Phil." Phil took a drink of coffee. "That's good. Thanks. Now, your dad said you had some things you might want to tell me," Phil said, addressing Skip.

"Yes sir," Skip answered. "A few months ago I learned about a way to make some money. It sounded too good to be true. All I had to do was deliver a package and I'd make $40. So I tried it out."

"Did you get paid?" Phil asked, looking up from writing in his notebook.

"Oh sure, that's not the problem. It's just that I'm not exactly sure what was in that package."

"Uh huh," Phil said, seeming to suggest that Skip should continue. Phil was looking at his notebook, not at Skip. That helped.

"I didn't look in the package. But I have a bad feeling about the whole thing. I delivered it to a man's house."

"Did you ask what was in the package?"

"Yes, but the man I worked for refused to tell me."

"That must have raised some suspicions?" Phil speculated.

"It sure did. Oh, I tried to pass it off at the time. But I knew in my heart that it probably wasn't something I should be delivering. Especially the way that JoBo acted."

"JoBo?" Officer Hamilton asked.

Skip looked at his dad. "Go ahead, son. You're going to need to trust Phil."

So Skip told all he knew, beginning with the camping trip. Confessing it to the police lifted a cloud from Skip. But it created new anxieties. *What if JoBo were arrested? Wouldn't he find out that I was responsible for it? And wouldn't he find a way to punish me? Or my family? And is it possible for me to be arrested? Especially if I've done something wrong.* Actually, these questions had been nagging Skip for some time and he struggled with them. Skip was learning the hard way the bad consequences of his actions.

Phil reviewed his notes and asked a few follow-up questions about the deliveries Skip had made. Then he closed his book and sighed a long, heavy sigh.

"What would you do now, if you had it all to do over again?" Phil asked, staring at Skip with even, calculating eyes.

Without hesitation Skip replied, "I wouldn't even consider doing it! There were too many warning signs that I disregarded. I was . . . well, I guess I was just being immature."

"But you're mature now?" Phil asked with a smirk on his face. "When did you say this started?" he asked, turning back in his notes. "Just a few months ago. In just a few months you've gotten mature? You really expect me to believe that?"

Phil looked at Joe. "I'm afraid I've heard that line before, sir. Boys get in all kinds of trouble, then promise never to do it again. A few weeks or months later, they show up at the police station again. Happens over and over."

The officer's evidence seemed too strong for Joe to refute. Phil looked back at Skip. "Well?"

"Mr. Hamilton, I know that basically I'm the same boy I was a few weeks ago. I know I can't change overnight. But I promised my parents and even God that I wouldn't do anything like this ever again."

"Sure. Look, I'm glad you're sorry, and that you've made promises to God," Phil said. "But lots of boys claim just the same thing you do. 'I've got religion! I'll be different!'"

Skip was uncomfortable with Mr. Hamilton's choice of words. He hadn't exactly 'found religion' the way Mr. Hamilton was using the term, but didn't feel comfortable correcting him. To do so certainly wouldn't have helped his case any. "I guess I'll just have to leave that to you, Mr. Hamilton," Skip said. "Over the next weeks or months, we'll all have to see if my life is any different. I can tell you what I intend to do, but I understand why you might not believe me."

Skip shuffled his feet a little. "Look, I'm sorry for what I've done. Really sorry. I agreed with my dad that we should call you to try and make things right. I would think that is some evidence that I want to change. I guess, though, that you'll just have to see what happens with me in the future." Skip was learning that it was his life, not his talk, that convinced people.

Phil took another long drink of coffee before answering. "You're right there. It does provide some evidence that you want to change. Or, that you want to get off scot free and let someone else hang instead."

Phil looked at Skip and Joe. "I've seen it all. This job has made me more skeptical than most people. Well, what do you think we should do now?" he asked Skip.

"I don't know," Skip answered. "I'll do whatever you tell me to do."

That's not the answer Phil was expecting to hear. "I thought you'd tell me that, since you called me and gave me this information on JoBo, I should just forget your involvement in the whole affair."

"I don't know what you should do," Skip answered truthfully. "Should you just forget that I was involved? I don't know. I know I would like it all to be over for me, but that doesn't look possible." It all seemed such a big mess to him that he couldn't see any good way out of it.

Phil closed his notebook and put it in his pocket. "Here's what I'm going to do. I'm not going to act on the information you've given me, Skip. By that I mean that I'm not going to arrest JoBo, or question him right now, or anything like that."

THE DELIVERY

"I see that you don't understand," Phil continued, looking at Skip and Joe. "*Why?* you're probably wondering. Simple. If I arrest JoBo or question him right now, he might put two and two together and figure out you are the one who turned him in. That might not be too safe. For you or your family. No, what I'm going to do is file this information away and keep an eye out for Mr. JoBo and his friends. If he is up to some bad things, and based on what you've told me I believe he is, chances are we'll never need your testimony. We'll let Mr. JoBo make a mistake. And when he does, we'll be there and grab him. Your testimony will give us further assurance that we're moving on the right person."

Skip was relieved. How could it have worked out so well? "But aren't you afraid he might never get caught?"

"Skip, I want to catch folks who are into drugs and other illegal things. But the reality is that we get a ton of tips just about every week from people who suspect or know that something is going on. These characters are pretty slick. They cover their tracks. Just like using you, Skip, a clean-cut looking guy, to cover their tracks. We have to wait until we have a substantial amount of evidence before the prosecutor is willing to take a case to court. Often we know all about what someone is doing, but we don't arrest them until we think we can build a case against them. That takes evidence, something that is hard to come by.

"Thank you for calling, Mr. Reynolds," Officer Hamilton said. "We need more concerned citizens like you and Skip. We'll let you know if there is anything else we need. Goodbye." With that the officer thanked Joe again for the coffee, and walked out the door.

"I can't believe it," sighed Skip, relieved. "That's it! They won't question me any more and my picture won't be in the papers or anything!"

"It doesn't look like it," Joe replied. "You need to thank God for that."

"Yes, I do," Skip agreed. "I just can't believe there won't be any bad consequences."

"That's not true," Joe reminded him. "Chances are there are bad consequences already. Remember, that the drug money or the drugs or pornography or whatever it was you delivered will be used by someone. And the harm it will do them is certainly a bad consequence of your actions."

"You're right, Dad." Skip was sad again. In his elation of being "set scot free," he had forgotten that others in the transaction had been harmed.

"But I am pleased with the way you handled yourself tonight," Joe praised. "My only prayer is that you would come to know the Savior. As far as I'm concerned that would erase the final obstacle to this whole episode."

Skip made no reply.

Chapter Nineteen

On Tuesday following the meeting with Officer Hamilton, Joe arrived at work earlier than usual. "You're here early!" Martha, who was making coffee, exclaimed.

"I had to put my car in the shop again," Joe answered. "The guy who gave me a ride has to be at his job at 7:00. So, here I am." Joe had intended to spend some time reading his Bible, but the TV was blaring in the break room and an older man was watching it while drinking a cup of coffee. Sometimes, Joe sat in his car to have devotions or think, but today that wasn't possible.

So Joe sat in the break room, trying to read the scriptures, but having trouble concentrating with the noise level so high. He got angry that the man didn't have the common courtesy to ask Joe if he wanted the TV cut down. But the man didn't. *I can't believe he is so rude as to not care about whether it is bothering me or not!*

Joe continued to read, or attempt to read, Isaiah 34. He read one passage over and over:
> 'It shall not be quenched night nor day; the smoke thereof shall go up for ever: from generation to generation it shall lie waste; none shall pass through it for ever and ever. But the cormorant and the bittern shall possess it; the owl also and the raven shall dwell in it: and he shall stretch out upon it the line of confusion, and the stones of emptiness.'

Not only was Joe having trouble knowing what a bittern and cormorant were, but the noise level just made comprehension almost nonexistent. *Now I know what persecution is!* he finally thought. *I have a right to read this Bible, and that rude man won't let me.* He felt rather sorry for himself. Privately, he sort of suspected that most Christians would be happy to just close their Bibles and watch TV.

A few hours later, Joe had his mail sorted and was driving toward his first stop. Walking part of his route, he tried to forget about his problems, and focus on his work. He never wanted his own thoughts or desires to interfere with what he considered one of his primary acts of worship to be: delivering the mail, as unto the Lord. That simply meant that delivering the mail was his job, and Joe realized that he was to do all things to the best of his ability, as though he were performing the job directly for the Lord.

He enjoyed delivering at Mrs. Condee's house, because it gave him a chance to see how his bird friends were doing. Joe had enjoyed watching some robins build a nest under the overhang of the porch. Now their hatchlings were growing up and it didn't look like it would be long before they were able to fly. God had used the object lesson of the birds to help Joe remember that his own nest of children would grow up all too soon. Did he supply all of their needs? Had he prepared them for the world? When they "flew away from the nest" would they have the right training and moral fiber to live godly, productive lives? Not that these little birds reflected on such questions, but Joe sure did.

As Joe drove up to make his delivery to a fraternity house, he noticed an unusually large group of students milling around the yard. Several kegs of beer were stationed around the yard, as were a couple of huge

THE DELIVERY

charcoal grills. It looked like yet another party was under way. The music was loud. Too loud. Joe wondered what the neighbors thought.

Actually, he didn't have to wonder. He had heard them complain often about the noise. "But what can we do?" Mrs. Austreg asked one afternoon. "The police seem not to care."

The music blared, "I don't care what nobody say, I gonna do what I wanna do! Yeah, I'm gonna do what *I* wanna do!"

"Hey man, want a burger?" a student asked Joe as he walked toward the house. Saluting Joe, he added, "Our fraternity supports men in uniform!"

"No thanks," Joe answered, continuing to walk. Then he turned and asked, "Looks like a big party. Classes canceled today?"

The young man laughed, spilling his beer a little in the process. "They're **always** canceled when there's a party, man!"

A girl standing next to the young man heard this and laughed too. Then she flushed a little. Joe couldn't help thinking that this was or was at one time a very nice young lady. She answered Joe's question. "No, sir. Classes aren't canceled. But some of us have our classes in the morning, you know. My classes . . ."

Before she could finish her sentence, the boy whispered something to her and the two walked toward one of the kegs. As they did so, Joe noticed the girl had a chain around her neck with these letters: WWJD, which stands for 'What Would Jesus Do?'

Joe turned and walked toward the house, troubled by the encounter. *What's she doing here?* he thought. *That could be my Meghan or even Laura in a few years. I wonder if her parents know what she's doing? I wonder if they know how she's spending her time?*

As the day wore on, Joe reflected on the incident in the break lounge this morning. At first he was sure it was an open and closed case of persecution. However, he finally had to come to grips with the possibility that the man hadn't noticed his Bible. In fact, the man seemed so preoccupied that it was possible that he hadn't paid much, if any, attention to Joe. Joe began to imagine what the man was thinking of. What if the man was having trouble at home? Or had a loved one in the hospital? Or was struggling with sin? Or was considering giving his life to Jesus? The fact is that Joe had no idea. However, that hadn't stopped him from judging the man for not turning off the TV.

Joe began to feel selfish. *I had no right to consider myself persecuted*, he thought. *For one thing, if that is called persecution, then what do I call it when Christians are tortured or killed for their faith?* No, it didn't seem strong enough to call it persecution.

What I should have done instead was to pray for the man. And not just pray that he would turn the TV off, but that God would work in the man's life as He saw fit. If that involved me, then I needed to be ready to help. Joe realized it would be hard to have a servant's heart toward a man with whom you're really angry.

Joe was convicted to ask God's forgiveness for his attitude that morning. He finished his prayer with these words: "Help me to be available for Your use, whenever and wherever You want to use me. Help me not to judge, but to love, just as You loved me. Amen."

"Hey, Dad. Got a minute?" Skip asked when Joe got home a few hours later.

THE DELIVERY

"Sure. You want to take a short walk before supper?" Joe suggested.

As they walked, Skip related a conversation he had that afternoon with JoBo. "Dad, I never intended to talk to him again. But he called me this afternoon asking me if I would make a delivery for him."

"What did you tell him?"

"I said, 'No thanks. And I'm not interested in delivering any more packages, either."

"What did he say to that?" Joe asked.

"He wasn't happy about anything I told him. He said, 'Look, I counted on you for this delivery today. Now you've got to do it. After today, we can split with no hard feelings. But today, you deliver for me! Understand?' I was so scared I didn't know what to say for a minute. Finally, I said, 'No, JoBo. Not today or any other days. Sorry, but I have to go. I've got some work I have to do. Goodbye.' Then I just hung up. I didn't slam down the receiver or anything. I just gently hung up the phone."

"Whew!" Joe whistled softly. "Well, at least I guess he knows exactly where you stand."

"Dad, did I do the right thing? I mean do you think I've made him mad and he's going to try to get even with me or something?"

Joe walked for a while before answering. "Skip, I think you probably did the right thing. It was probably best that you not explain a lot about the reasons you're not going to deliver any more. Is he going to try to get even in some way? I honestly don't know. I suppose time will tell. I think it would be best for you to stay close to home for the next couple of weeks. That way, if he does see you, he will have had a chance to cool off a little. Maybe he'll just forget it."

Skip seemed unsure. "I don't know. He seems like someone who could hold a grudge a long time. Besides, he might figure out that I talked to you, or even the police."

"That's just something we will have to deal with, if it ever becomes an issue. Let me give you some advice. Don't dwell on it. Don't spend your time worrying about what *might* happen. The Bible says in Matthew 6:34: 'Take therefore no thought for the morrow: for the morrow shall take thought for the things of itself. Sufficient unto the day is the evil thereof.' Instead, we are to seek the kingdom of God and His righteousness. Let's just leave this matter in the Lord's hands and trust Him for this." Joe stopped and voiced a short prayer addressing the issue.

Skip felt better after Joe prayed. "Thanks, Dad. I kind of knew it would be better after talking to you."

"Good," Joe nodded. "It usually does feel better when you share something with someone else. And with God."

Chapter Twenty

A few days later, Joe paused while loading his mail truck. Something seemed wrong. *What is it? Ever since I got to work, it seems like something is wrong, somehow. Did I forget to do something for Amy before I left? Did I say something unkind to a coworker?*

But try as he might, Joe couldn't think of what it could be. "Is there anything special I'm supposed to do today?" he asked his supervisor.

"Like what?" Larry asked.

"Beats me!" Joe responded. "It just seems like I'm forgetting something."

"Got all your mail loaded up?"

"Sure."

"Then . . . I'd say you're ready to go!" Larry politely suggested, looking at his watch.

Joe walked to his truck, stepped inside and said a quick prayer asking God to bless his day and keep him safe from all harm. As he started his engine, he suddenly knew what was missing.

Stopping the engine, he jumped out of the truck and walked to the maintenance closet in the back of the post office. The door was slightly ajar and a light was shining inside but no one was in there. Joe sniffed, but didn't detect the familiar odor of aftershave he often smelled there. Leaving that area, he walked quickly throughout the post office. He noticed a person sweeping the front area. It was someone he had never seen before.

Hmm, Joe thought. *I wonder . . .*

Climbing back in his truck, Joe started on his route. "Is it possible? No, probably not. Just out sick with a cold," he said to himself. "It's too much to hope that Casey has quit."

But all day long he couldn't help but think about life without Casey at work. Too good to be true!

Arriving back at the post office, he suspiciously walked through the building, expecting any minute to have Casey dive from behind a mail bin and shout "Surprise! You'll never get rid of me, Reynolds!" But Casey was nowhere to be seen.

"Where's Casey?" Joe finally asked Denise, a customer service counter employee.

"Isn't it nice?" she said, dreamily. "Not once today have I had to worry about one of his practical jokes."

Joe had to ask again, "Okay, but where is he? He hasn't... quit, has he?" Joe couldn't restrain his enthusiasm, and Denise just laughed.

"I see you've had a better day yourself, Joe! But no, he hasn't quit. I heard from Mabel that he was in Coleman County Hospital. Pneumonia, emphysema, or something like that."

"Oh." Now it was hard for Joe to restrain his disappointment. Again Denise laughed. Joe seemed embarrassed.

"You don't have to apologize. I doubt if he has more than two friends in this whole place." Denise lowered her voice. "You ever wonder how Casey keeps his job?" She looked around to make sure no one was listening. "I've heard he is related to the postmaster somehow. Second cousin or something like that. I know there are many times I would like to boot him out the door, or toss him out with my bare hands. In fact, I've thought of a

THE DELIVERY

few different things I would like to do to him before I retire..."

Joe wasn't really interested in hearing Denise's savage plans to get back at Casey for his meanness. He mumbled something about having to go, then headed to his car.

Another day's work was over. It was a bright, beautiful sunny day. Something central Alabama was practically famous for. It was rather humid, however.

As he got in his car, Joe thought about Casey. *I wonder how many days he will be out from work?* He smiled at the thought of not having to hear Casey's foul language or crude jokes. Yes, life was going to be much more pleasant, for a while anyway.

"How was your day, honey?" Amy asked pleasantly as Joe entered the kitchen.

"Great!" Joe exclaimed.

Amy looked at him a little suspiciously but didn't say anything. Joe walked over and opened the oven door. "Hey, what's in here?"

"Cake," Amy replied. "And be careful when you close the oven door. If you let it slam, it'll make the cake fall."

Joe carefully closed the oven door. "Wouldn't want a fallen cake!"

Amy couldn't resist asking the question that was on her mind. "You didn't have a ... confrontation with Mrs. Webber, did you?"

"No, why?" Joe asked. "I didn't see her. Haven't seen her for some time. And when I have, there's been no problem."

Amy went to the cupboard and retrieved some paprika for the Cuban chicken she was making. "I don't know. I guess ..." She was having trouble saying what she was thinking. "I guess I just wondered when you said you had a great day."

Joe walked over and hugged his wife. "I have a great day when I see you! Besides, if I had a 'confrontation' with Mrs. Webber, that wouldn't have made it a good day. It would have made it a very bad and stressful day." Joe knew that Amy struggled a little bit with jealousy over Mrs. Webber. Joe didn't know anything else to do about that, except to pray for Amy and show her how much he loved her.

"Want to know the real reason I had a great day?" he asked, lowering his voice as though he had a very special secret. "Casey wasn't there."

"Did he quit?" Amy asked quickly, hope on her face. She knew what a problem Casey was for Joe.

"No, but he's out sick. Sounds like he will be out sick for a while, too. Imagine, days without Casey!"

Amy smiled. "Should I make a cake to celebrate?"

"I think you already have," Joe replied, sniffing the air.

Joe walked to the living room and picked up the mail. Sitting down in his chair, he looked out the window at his children playing. Laura and her friend Jenny from down the block, were dragging a large stick back and forth across the lawn. Joe tried to figure out what they were doing, but finally gave up. *Children,* he thought. *There's no telling what they are pretending.*

Joe intended to read his mail, but his mind went to Casey again. *He'll be gone for a while. How long? Maybe a week? Who knows? Pneumonia can be a pretty nasty thing sometimes. No Casey at work. Wonderful!*

But then he had a thought that he tried to dismiss. *Am I behaving as Christ would act? Should I be happy that Casey is sick?*

THE DELIVERY

Joe picked up a *Focus on the Family Magazine* and scanned the first story. His mind drifted, however. *But I'm not really happy that Casey is sick! It's just that I won't mind him not being around. After all, Isaac suggested that one of the best things I could do was avoid being around people who sin repeatedly. Couldn't Casey's sickness be a blessing from God? A way that God was removing Casey from being an influence on me?*

Joe had to admit that God might have done just that. But maybe not. Joe thought about the girl at the fraternity house a few weeks ago. Her WWJD necklace summed up his thoughts right now: What Would Jesus Do? If Joe was upset that the girl didn't seem to be following WWJD, was Joe any better right now?

Okay, what would Jesus do? Joe reflected on that. He opened his Bible and read from Matthew 25:31-40:

> When the Son of man shall come in his glory, and all the holy angels with him, then shall he sit upon the throne of his glory: And before him shall be gathered all nations: and he shall separate them one from another, as a shepherd divideth his sheep from the goats: And he shall set the sheep on his right hand, but the goats on the left. Then shall the King say unto them on his right hand, Come, ye blessed of my Father, inherit the kingdom prepared for you from the foundation of the world: For I was an hungred, and ye gave me meat: I was thirsty, and ye gave me drink: I was a stranger, and ye took me in: Naked, and ye clothed me: I was sick, and ye visited me: I was in prison, and ye came unto me. Then shall the

righteous answer him, saying, Lord, when saw we thee an hungred, and fed thee? or thirsty, and gave thee drink? When saw we thee a stranger, and took thee in? or naked, and clothed thee? Or when saw we thee sick, or in prison, and came unto thee? And the King shall answer and say unto them, Verily I say unto you, Inasmuch as ye have done it unto one of the least of these my brethren, ye have done it unto me.

There were other verses that spoke to the situation, but Joe didn't need to look them up. It seemed obvious what he should do. He picked up the phone book, looked up Casey Weaver, and then dialed the phone number.

"Joe, where do you keep . . . Oh, I'm sorry," Amy apologized more quietly, when she realized Joe was on the phone.

"That's okay. No one has picked up yet," Joe replied. "I'm calling Casey's house to talk to his wife."

Amy had a queer look on her face, but walked out of the room. In a few minutes, Joe followed her.

"Amy, I got to thinking. I had the wrong attitude. God showed me I ought to be concerned for Casey, not just glad he was absent from work. I'm going to the hospital to visit him."

"Did his wife say how he was doing?"

"There was no answer," Joe responded. "You know, now that I think about it, I don't even think he's married. I can't remember him ever saying anything about a wife."

After supper, Joe drove to the hospital and was directed to the intensive care wing. "I came to visit Casey Weaver," he stated. "They said downstairs that

THE DELIVERY

only family could visit, but I thought I could leave a note for him."

"You can see him if you want," the nurse said. "He doesn't have any family that I'm aware of and has had no visitors. He's right this way."

Joe was a little shocked that Casey was so all alone. But the more he thought about it, the more sense it made. It was because Casey was so unfriendly. Or maybe Casey was so unfriendly because he had no family or real friends.

Joe was also shocked when he saw the physical deterioration of Casey. Tubes were leading out of his mouth and monitors were attached all over his body. An IV dripped the contents from several bags into his veins. *Can this be the same obnoxious, strong Casey Weaver that I know?* Joe wondered.

"He seems to be asleep."

"Yes, he was in a coma yesterday," the nurse replied. "He's been a very sick man. He has opened his eyes several times this afternoon, but we're not sure if he can recognize anything."

Here I was glad that Casey was not at work, and look how bad he is! Joe felt very embarrassed. He spent the next fifteen minutes or so sitting by the bed. Casey never woke up. Finally, Joe felt it was time to leave, but he wrote a short note and handed it to the nurse.

Casey,
    Sorry I missed seeing you. My family and I will be praying for you. May God have compassion on you and restore you to health soon.
                    Sincerely, Joe

Joe couldn't think of anything else to write.

The next night, Joe stopped by the hospital on the way home from work. Joe thought he saw Casey's eyes get big when he walked into the room. Apparently Casey still couldn't talk with all the tubes.

"Hello, Casey. I imagine you're surprised to see me. I was here last night but you just wanted to sleep. You better get well soon. The post office is starting to look kind of ragged." Joe continued talking to Casey, trying to joke with him and lift his spirits. Whether he was having any success or not, Joe had no idea. Casey just stared at Joe.

After about ten or fifteen minutes, Joe said, "Well, I better go now. I'm sure that Amy is wondering why I'm not home yet. You take care of yourself and get well. Okay?" Then Joe said a prayer for Casey.

As he was about to turn and walk out, Casey lifted his hand and waved weakly, IV tubes dangling from his wrist.

Joe visited Casey over the next few days. On Friday, Joe was surprised to find that all the tubes had been removed from Casey's mouth.

"Well, you're sure looking better," Joe greeted, trying to be cheerful even though hospitals always made Joe feel sick. Casey didn't say much, and when he did it was a hoarse whisper.

"The tubes . . ." Casey struggled to say. "The tubes messed up my vocal cords."

"That's okay, you don't have to talk." Joe brought Casey up to speed on what was happening at the post office. Casey listened with interest but made very few comments. Joe then showed Casey some get-well cards that Joe's children had made.

THE DELIVERY

When it was time to go, Joe again had prayer with Casey. When Joe opened his eyes, he noticed that Casey had had his eyes closed for the prayer.

I wonder if all of this is helping Casey see his need for Jesus Christ? thought Joe. Once again, Joe spoke of the Lord and talked about the need for the redeeming blood of Christ. Casey listened but made no response. As Joe walked out of the room, he noticed there were still no flowers from anyone, other than the ones Amy had ordered. No other cards were anywhere around either. The nurse said that Joe was still the only visitor Casey had.

The next day, Casey was moved to a regular room. And he could talk much better. But this was a very different Casey than the post office janitor that everyone knew. Joe hoped that perhaps Casey's heart was softening. As Joe left, he handed Casey a book as a gift. Joe meant the gift to entertain Casey. It also had the plan of salvation as a part of the story line. Joe prayed with Casey before going. "Would you like to pray, Casey?" Joe asked when he was through.

"No," Casey replied, still hoarse. "You do a good job. I don't know how to pray anyway."

"It's really very simple," Joe replied. "All you do is talk to God. He's in the room right here with you, because God is everywhere. And He is listening to what you are saying. Even what you're thinking. You don't have to have any special words or go through any special motions. Just tell God whatever you want to tell Him."

Casey looked at Joe for a long while before he said anything. Then he bowed his head slightly and said, "Thanks for Joe Reynolds." That's all he said, but it sent a flood of joy over Joe. The Lord had used Casey's sickness to teach Joe a few lessons about humility and servanthood and judging others.

"I'll stop by tomorrow after work again," Joe said, getting ready to go. "Can I get anything for you? Do anything for you?"

"No," Casey said slowly. "They said I might go home tomorrow."

"That would be great!" Joe cheered. "Would you like me to arrange to take you home?" Joe knew that no one would come and get Casey.

"No," Casey replied. "But thanks anyway. I'll be seeing you at work before too long." Joe knew that was true. It was amazing how much better Casey looked today than even yesterday. The nurse had told Joe that Casey was much improved, and hinted that Joe's visits had helped. Casey still had to have breathing treatments several times a day and he continued to cough, but he had a more healthy look in his eyes.

"Well, I'd be happy to drop by your house," Joe volunteered. "You know, to see if you need anything."

"No thanks," Casey repeated. "I'll be okay."

Joe was disappointed, but what else could he do or say?

"Joe," Casey called as Joe was about to cross the doorway. "I do appreciate all you've done for me. I don't think anyone has ever been as nice as you have."

"I thought I'd never say it, but I've enjoyed it, Casey. Really. And everything I've done has been in the name and with the love of Jesus Christ."

"I know," Casey said. "I know that. You've made that perfectly clear. Joe, keep praying for me."

Chapter Twenty-One

The next several weeks seemed to fly by. Thankfully, JoBo never did call Skip again, and there was no evidence that he was going to do anything in the way of revenge toward Skip. Needless to say both Joe and Skip were thrilled by that. However, both kept in the back of their minds that it was always going to be a possibility. Skip learned a lesson the hard way: there can be long-term consequences of one's actions.

Joe was kept busy during these weeks, working on small projects around the house and occasionally visiting Elaine to work on some things she needed doing. He was encouraged with the maturity that Rob was showing. That day Joe and Rob worked together a few months ago at Elaine's had created a strong bond between father and son.

Summer was nearing its end. Some nights were starting to cool down a bit, and a few times Joe was even able to turn off the air conditioner at night. Not that he could ever shut it down completely, not in central Alabama, anyway. Why, he could remember running it in February before!

And now it was early Monday morning. Time to put on the postal uniform and deliver the mail. Joe stretched and looked over at Amy. "Do you have a busy day planned today?" he asked.

"No," she replied. "I'm thinking about taking the children to the mall and look for some fall clothes. And shoes of course, too. I can't believe how fast Rob is outgrowing shoes! Those feet of his seem to grow about a half a size each month!"

"I'll be home a little late," Joe commented. "I promised Dave I would stop by and help him carry an old freezer out of his house. He said he could probably do it, if it weren't for those narrow back porch steps. It shouldn't take long, though."

After breakfast, Joe headed to work. He thought about the upcoming day, trying to anticipate what might come up. Things at work were going pretty well. Since that incident months ago with Mrs. Webber, he had no more encounters of that kind. He was really glad, but wondered what his reaction would be if it occurred again. *I hope and pray I know what my reaction would be, but you never know until it comes up, exactly what will happen. Lord, help me to be strong in You.*

Joe's relationship with Casey seemed to be better in the weeks since he had returned to work. That didn't mean that Casey showed Joe any kind of friendliness. Joe had assumed that Casey was having trouble knowing how to relate to Joe. After all of the years of abuse, it must be hard to change overnight. *Probably he wonders what everyone would say? After all, Casey has something of a reputation to uphold, even though it is a bad one.*

But at least Casey wasn't obnoxious like he used to be. In fact, Joe couldn't remember a single thing Casey had said or done that irritated him since the hospital visit. *I'm encouraged. Maybe he is coming to the Lord!* Joe felt led to say a silent prayer for Casey.

Turning into the parking lot, Joe noticed a commotion at the loading dock. Several men were lounging against the wall, smoking. Casey was in the middle of them. He looked over as Joe got out of his car. Joe could hear laughter erupt from the group.

THE DELIVERY

"Hello, guys," Joe said in a friendly voice. A mingle of "hello's" and "Hi ya, Joe's" were voiced. Casey didn't say anything to greet Joe.

Walking into the building, Joe went to the message board to see if there was anything new there. Then he went to his box. Inside was an envelope with "Joe Reynolds" written on the outside. *I wonder what this is all about?*

Inside was this note:

Joe,

I know you did a lot of stuff for me when I was sick. At first, I couldn't figure it out. Nobody ever did much for me. I sort of look out for myself, if you know what I mean. Well, I finally figured it out! You was doing it just so you could try to get me to come to church. I've read how your kind is always trying to get other folks to come to church. There was a show on TV about it. Well, I'm a little busy on Sundays, thank you very much. So, you just go to church if you want to and I'll do what I want to. Casey

Joe's happiness vanished. *Oh no,* he sighed. *That's not what I was trying to do. Lord Jesus, please help Casey understand that my motives were pure!* Joe resolved to talk to Casey as soon as he could and try to help him see the truth.

But an opportunity didn't present itself before he left on his route. Joe suspected that Casey was avoiding him. *Satan is controlling him. If only he would listen.*

That cloud followed Joe the rest of the day as he made his deliveries. In the afternoon, returning to the post office, Joe sought out Casey specifically to have a talk.

Casey was talking to one of the customer counter representatives when Joe found him. It seemed that

Casey was purposefully extending the conversation just to avoid talking to Joe.

However, Joe wasn't going to be thwarted. He stood there, politely out of ear shot, waiting for Casey to finish. Finally, even Casey apparently ran out of things to say, and he turned and walked quickly toward his janitor's closet.

"Casey, I need to talk to you," Joe said, following closely behind the retreating figure. "It's about this note you put in my box."

Casey realized that Joe wasn't going to stop pursuing him. Finally, he turned and stared at Joe. Instantly Joe recognized what he saw there. The old Casey. Those eyes filled with hate and mistrust. The Casey who hated Joe and all he stood for. "Why don't you leave me alone?" Casey bellowed. "I don't want you nor the religion you're spouting off about! Understand? Want me to file a complaint against you for trying to tell me about God on Post Office time?"

Joe was almost frantic. "Casey, that's not it at all. All I want to say is that you have it all wrong. Sure, I would be happy if you became a Christian. But that is not what caused me to come visit you in the hospital. Truly, I did it because I thought that was what I was supposed to do. Please accept my kindness for what it was intended for."

"I aint' going to accept nothin' from you, Reynolds," Casey blurted out. "Cause you ain't got nothing I want. Now leave me alone."

Joe saw the hopelessness of explaining it to Casey. Head dropping, he slowly moved away. *Lord Jesus, it is in Your hands. Only You can help him see the error. Please let him know the truth. And Lord, please do bring him to Yourself. Amen.*

THE DELIVERY

As Joe was walking to his car a few minutes later, Casey stuck his head out the back door of the post office. "Hey, Joe! Better call home first and see if you're supposed to bring something home for the missus! I would hate to see you tomorrow with a black eye!" Laughing crudely, he closed the door.

When Joe got home after stopping by Dave's house, he saw Isaac trimming his hedges. Joe decided that he could use a nice talk with a friendly Christian man. Walking over, he stated, "How are you doing, Isaac?"

"Fine," Isaac replied. Then he took a few steps into his garage and retrieved something. "Say, Joe. We bought this new telescope for the grandchild. That's Tim, John's oldest boy, you know. We can't figure out how to use it. You ever use one before?"

"No," Joe answered. "I guess I always thought you just looked through one end and everything in the sky would be lots bigger."

"Yeah, that's the way it's supposed to work," Isaac agreed, laughing. "But we went out last night with this telescope and honestly, I could see things better with my naked eye than I could with this telescope. What's up with you?"

"Oh, just another day at work," Joe started, then decided to be candid with Isaac. He told about Casey and what had happened today.

"That's tough," Isaac said. "Really tough. I'm sorry, Joe."

"It's not so much that Casey hasn't come to know the Lord," Joe began, "although that is the most important thing he could do. I'm afraid what is more disturbing to me right now is the misconception he has of my motives for seeing him in the hospital."

"Well, you know what the Bible says," Isaac reminded him. "There is a strong battle going in the spirit world. I'm reminded of Ephesians 6:10-12:
> Finally, my brethren, be strong in the Lord, and in the power of his might. Put on the whole armour of God, that ye may be able to stand against the wiles of the devil. For we wrestle not against flesh and blood, but against principalities, against powers, against the rulers of the darkness of this world, against spiritual wickedness in high places.

"The forces of Satan are strong, Joe, don't forget that. My guess is that Satan is being pretty victorious in Casey's life right now."

"Yes, that's what I thought, too," Joe agreed. "But I feel so helpless."

"You are," Isaac reminded him. "Remember, you can't save anyone. And you can't force someone to understand the truth if that person is fighting the truth. About all you can do is pray. I'll pray for him, too." With that, Isaac said a short prayer for Casey. That was one of the things Joe respected so much about Isaac: the way he went to God in prayer right then, not later. His example had been responsible for a lot of Joe's growth in his prayer life.

Joe felt better after talking to Isaac for a while. *It's great to know another Christian man I can talk to*, he thought. *It helps me not feel so all alone!*

After supper, his family had their time of Bible reading and prayer. They had finished the New Testament, and were now working their way slowly through the Old Testament. "I believe we're ready for Exodus 15 tonight," Joe stated, then read the chapter.

THE DELIVERY

After he was finished, he asked, "Who remembers what we read last night?"

Laura raised her hand. When called on, she answered, "They crossed that ocean and the Egyptians got drownded."

"You're right Laura, although it wasn't really an ocean. It is called the Red Sea, and sometimes we call seas oceans, don't we? Anyway, you're right. The children of Israel went across on dry land when God miraculously parted the waters. They were delivered because when the Egyptians tried it, the waters closed in on them, and the Bible says 'and there remained not so much as one of them.'

"Well, in the scripture we've read tonight, Moses is singing a song of praise and worship unto the Lord. I imagine I would feel like singing, too, after seeing what God had just done. What did those verses say?" Joe looked at his Bible closely.

"Verse 11 says, 'Who is like unto thee, O Lord, among the gods? Who is like thee, glorious in holiness, fearful in praises, doing wonders? . . .' Is there any person or anything that is as powerful and holy as God?" Joe asked his family.

Everyone shook their heads. "That's right," Joe praised. "We all know that is true. We all believe it. And the important thing is to keep believing it no matter what happens. No matter what obstacle gets in your path. No matter what temptations you might have. No matter what others might tell you about their gods or about our God.

"What should our response to other people be?" Joe continued.

Meghan answered quickly, "We should worship and praise God, just like Moses did after the Red Sea."

"That's right," Joe agreed. "We should always praise God for who He is. Let's look a little later in this chapter and see what God also instructed the people to do." Joe began reading in verse 26. "'. . . If thou wilt diligently hearken to the voice of the Lord thy God, and wilt do that which is right in His sight, and wilt give ear to His commandments, and keep all His statutes . . .' then God promised that He would protect them. So, in addition to praising God with songs, prayers, and meditation, we also need to remember that God is pleased to see us obey Him. Remember, He has delivered us from darkness and brought us into light. In fact, to claim that we praise Him and then not obey Him is hypocrisy." Joe continued teaching about the truths that were displayed in Exodus 15.

"Who is our Christmas card from tonight?" Joe asked Amy.

Amy picked up a card and looked at it. "It's from Anita and Donald," she said, passing the card to Rob. "Remember, they are the ones with a little boy with cancer. Let's pray that God would heal little Timothy, within His will."

The family had a time of prayer, then sang a few songs before Joe announced that Bible time was over. "Okay," he said, rising. "I'm going to get a little exercise while helping you out, Amy."

Amy seemed surprised. "How are you going to accomplish both of those goals?"

"I'm going to wash the windows that I promised to wash last spring! Actually, I'm looking forward to it. I love the view out a clean window."

Before long, Joe was busy washing the windows at the back of his house. Washing and thinking. His thoughts kept coming back to Casey. Finally, he admitted to himself, *Casey hasn't changed. He's the same old*

THE DELIVERY 217

Casey and it looks like he's going to keep on being the same old Casey. Life's not perfect, Joe Reynolds. Joe sighed. *No, life's not perfect!* Life here on earth was never going to be perfect. According to Genesis 3, not since God cursed man's time here on earth due to his sins had life been perfect. Nor was it going to be perfect. An important lesson to learn. But a hard one to accept.

For a few moments, Joe was saddened by his thoughts. Then, the Lord brought verses and sermons to his mind which reminded Joe that heaven was his home. 2 Corinthians 5:1-2 said it well: "For we know that if our earthly house of this tabernacle were dissolved, we have a building of God, a house not made with hands, eternal in the heavens. For in this we groan, earnestly desiring to be clothed upon with our house which is from heaven." How often lately he had felt the groaning that the verse referred to. So, while he was still sad about Casey, Joe was encouraged by the hope of an eternity of perfection: heaven.

It was while Joe was struggling with these thoughts that Skip came walking around the corner. "Hi, Skip!" Joe called down from the ladder. "Can you toss me up that roll of paper towels that seems to dislike heights?"

Skip did so. It took two throws before he was successful. The first throw was a little short, and a long trail of paper towels flew like a flag as the roll raced back to the ground. The second throw almost hit Joe in the face, but Joe caught it before it did.

Skip kept hanging around the ladder. "So, what are you up to?" Joe questioned, squirting some cleaner onto the window.

Skip shuffled around a bit, then answered, "Nothing much." It was obvious something was on his mind, but Joe didn't rush him. Over the years, Joe had learned that each child had a different style of bringing up difficult topics. Rob just blurted out his questions or concerns, while Meghan, the quiet one, almost never expressed her innermost thoughts. Skip was somewhere in between the two extremes.

Skip tossed a rock toward the back fence. Finally, he said, "Dad, I've been doing a lot of thinking about some things you've said lately. What you've said makes a lot of sense to me, but I still don't know how to . . . well, I'm feeling a little confused."

Joe got off the ladder and collected some used paper towels from the ground. By acting a little nonchalant, Joe was trying to help Skip express himself, without feeling threatened. The same approach had worked many times in the past for Skip. "Did you say confused? About what, son?" Joe moved the ladder to the next window.

"I can't help but think about that talk we had that night, Dad. You remember, the night of our trip to the lake?"

"Uh huh," Joe replied, looking up at the window and adjusting the ladder a little.

"You said that your love was unconditional. And that God's love was unconditional, too. That sounds good, but I'm confused. How can that be true? After all, you're my father. But we're talking about God here. How can He just be willing to wash away all the bad stuff I've done?"

"You're still searching for peace, aren't you?" Joe said, looking into his son's eyes.

"I guess I am," Skip admitted. "I want to have peace, but I don't know how to get it!"

"I think I know what you mean, Skip. You may not believe this, but I was right where you are now just a few years ago. Let me tell you the truth, the truth that Satan

THE DELIVERY

would not have you believe: you **can** make peace with God! Right now. If you wait until you deserve His love, you will never do it. Know why? Because you'll never deserve His love. Just His wrath. That's why His love is a gift to you. A gift that you don't deserve, but a gift nonetheless."

Joe put down his window cleaner and leaned on the ladder. "Satan wants you to believe that it can't be done. That's just not true. Think about the Bible reading we had last night and tonight. That Red Sea looked hopeless. The Egyptians were about to overtake the Israelites. There was nowhere to turn, no way to safety. An absolutely hopeless situation! Probably kind of like you feel right now." Joe paused to let Skip see the analogy.

"But God opened up the sea. The people didn't do it. God delivered them from the hand of the Egyptians.

"God has opened up a Red Sea for us, Skip. Even though we don't deserve it, just as the Israelites didn't deserve it. He has made a way for us to come to Him, even though we are sinful and He is holy. He has delivered us from our sins through the death of His Son, Jesus Christ, who paid the price for us when He died on the cross."

Skip looked thoughtful and Joe offered a silent prayer before continuing. "Accept His gift, Skip. Ask God to forgive you of your sins. Ask Him to help you turn from sinning and live a life that is pleasing to Him. Tell Him you believe that Jesus died for your sins. Promise to make Jesus the Lord and Master of your life. Tell Him that you're willing to suffer anything for Him, who has already died for you. That's the only way to truth and peace and joy."

Skip stood looking at the ground. Right then he wanted something more than he had ever wanted anything before in his life. He wanted God's forgiveness for his sins. As the Holy Spirit filled his heart, he bowed his head and closed his eyes, in a reverence that Joe had never seen displayed by his oldest son before. Skip prayed and became a brother in Christ Jesus.

Praise the Almighty! Joe prayed silently, watching this with tears in his eyes. *Praise the Almighty!*

The End

What Is a Christian?

Over the years, if you're like most people, you've probably asked yourself questions such as: *What is the meaning of life? Why am I really here? How can I find true joy? Is there any hope for the future in this crazy world we live in?* We would like to briefly share with you how we found meaning and joy and hope. It's really quite simple. The most important thing in anyone's life is their relationship with God.

First, you must understand that there is something called sin. You've sinned just like we've sinned. Everyone has sinned (Romans 3:23). To sin is to do something that displeases God, disobeying Him — not doing what God has commanded us to do (I John 5:17; James 4:17). God is holy and just, and demands payment for sin. The payment He requires is that we die and go to the place He created for sinners, called Hell (Romans 6:23). Hell is a real place and there are people there right now. They are in anguish and pain continually (Luke 16:23-24). People who are punished by being sent to Hell are never allowed to leave it (Matthew 25:46).

Now, for the good news. God decided to let someone die in our place, so that we don't have to go to Hell because of our sins. That someone is Jesus Christ. Jesus is God's Son, whom God the Father allowed to come to earth. While He was on earth as a man, Jesus never sinned (John 8:46). He lived a perfect life. When he died on the cross, God allowed Jesus' death to be the payment for our sins (Hebrews 1:3; John 3:18). Jesus was buried, but the grave couldn't hold him. When God raised Jesus with His power He came back to life (Mat-

What Is a Christian?

thew 28). After some time of teaching His followers, Jesus then returned to Heaven to be with God the Father (Mark 16:19).

So, since Jesus died for our sins, no one has to go to Hell anymore, right? Wrong. People still go to Hell (Romans 2:8-9). How can you avoid Hell? There is only one way. First, you have to admit to God that you are a sinner (people want to pretend that they're not sinners, but all of us are). Then, you have to believe that Jesus is God's Son and that Jesus rose from the dead for your sins (Romans 10:9). You must start obeying God and keeping His commandments (Romans 6:12; I John 1:7-9). God will even help you learn to obey Him. Finally, you need to tell others what you have done (Romans 10:9). When you do these things, you become a Christian. It's important to realize that you don't become a Christian just by believing there is a God or by living a "good life" (Acts 4:12).

Now, what about those questions you were asking? Let's take a look at them from the viewpoint of a Christian.

What is the meaning of life? Why am I really here? The reason you are here is to glorify God and live for Him (Philippians 2:10-11). It is why you were created and why you are alive right now. Doing what God wants you to do won't always be easy. You'll still be tempted to sin (I Corinthians 10:13). Others may not like the fact that you are a Christian (Matthew 5:11). However, it is an important task and one which God will help you to perform (John 14:26).

How can I find true joy? As a Christian, you will find joy that cannot be found anywhere else (John 14:27; Philippians 4:4). You will have joy in knowing that God

What Is a Christian?

cared about you so much that He sent His only Son, Jesus Christ, to die for the sins that you've committed (John 3:16). You will have joy in knowing that those sins are truly and completely forgiven (Romans 8:1). You will have joy in knowing that God promises you that He will never leave you or forsake you in any way (Hebrews 13:5). You will have joy in knowing that nothing, absolutely nothing at all, can separate you from His love (Romans 8:35-39). Please understand that you'll still be sad and lonely and sick and hurting at times. But you will find joy in knowing that God loves you and that there is a reason for everything that happens in your life (Romans 8:28).

Is there any hope for the future in this crazy world we live in? Yes! As a Christian you can know where you will spend your future--in heaven with God Himself (2 Corinthians 5:8; John 14-2-4).

There is no way that this short discussion can tell you everything about being a Christian. We encourage you to do several things. Please get a Bible and read it. In the paragraphs you've just read we included the location of some verses for you to look up for yourself so you can see why we said what we did. God Himself will help you understand what you are reading, through the power of the Holy Spirit, and how it relates to you as an individual.

Please make contact with someone who can answer any questions you might have. You might want to contact a pastor at a local church. There are also some folks you can talk to on the phone who can help you learn more about what it means to become a Christian and live a life that is pleasing to God. We're not officially affiliated with any of them (we're really and truly just a press). Although phone numbers can change, you might try these:

1-888-NEED-HIM
1-800-772-8888 (Canada 1-800-663-7639) Insight for Living
1-719-531-5181 (Canada 1-800-661-9800) Focus on the Family

If none of these work, feel free to write us and we'll try to help. Our address is on the back cover of this book.

After you become a Christian, please link up with other believers so you can continue to grow as a Christian and help others in their attempts to please God. You can do this best by meeting on a regular basis with other believers and studying the Bible. If you can't find other believers in the area where you live, the organizations we just listed may be able to help you find them.

FINAL THOUGHTS

When we placed this material in this book, it was done so with a prayer that you would find the peace and joy that we have found. We continue to pray for you right now. May God richly bless you!

Castleberry Farms Press

Our primary goal in publishing is to provide wholesome books in a manner that brings honor to our Lord. We believe in setting no evil thing before our eyes (Psalm 101:3) and although there are many outstanding books, we have had trouble finding enough good reading material for our children. Therefore, we feel the Lord has led us to start this family business.

We believe the following: The Bible is the infallible true Word of God. That God is the Creator and Controller of the universe. That Jesus Christ is the only begotten Son of God, was born of the virgin Mary, lived a perfect life, was crucified, buried, rose again, sits at the right hand of God, and makes intercession for the saints. That Jesus Christ is the only Savior and way to the Father. That salvation is based on faith alone, but true faith will produce good works. That the Holy Spirit is given to believers as Guide and Comforter. That the Lord Jesus will return. That man was created to glorify God and enjoy Him forever.

We began writing and publishing in mid-1996 and hope to add more books in the future if the Lord is willing. All books are written by Mr. and Mrs. Castleberry.

We would love to hear from you if you have any comments or suggestions. Our address is at the end of this section. Now, we'll tell you a little about our books.

The Courtship Series

These books are written to encourage those who intend to follow a Biblically-based courtship that includes the active involvement of parents. The main characters are committed followers of Jesus Christ, and Christian family values are emphasized throughout. The reader will be encouraged to heed parental advice and to live in obedience to the Lord.

Jeff McLean: His Courtship

Follow the story of Jeff McLean as he seeks God's direction for his life. This book is the newest in our courtship series, and is written from a young man's perspective. A discussion of godly traits to seek in young men and women is included as part of the story. February 1998. ISBN 1-891907-05-0. Paperback. $7.50 (plus shipping and handling).

The Courtship of Sarah McLean

Sarah McLean is a nineteen-year-old girl who longs to become a wife and mother. The book chronicles a period of two years, in which she has to learn to trust her parents and God fully in their decisions for her future. Paperback, 2nd printing, 1997. ISBN 1-891907-00-X. $7.50 (plus shipping and handling).

Waiting for Her Isaac

Sixteen-year-old Beth Grant is quite happy with her life and has no desire for any changes. But God has many lessons in store before she is ready for courtship. The story of Beth's spiritual journey toward godly womanhood is told along with the story of her courtship. Paperback. 1997. ISBN 1-891907-03-4. $7.50 (plus shipping and handling).

The Farm Mystery Series

Join Jason and Andy as they try to solve the mysterious happenings on the Nelson family's farm. These are books that the whole family will enjoy. In fact, many have used them as read-aloud-to-the-family books. Parents can be assured that there are no murders or other objectionable elements in these books. The boys learn lessons in obedience and responsibility while having lots of fun. There are no worldly situations or ﾻuage, and no boy-girl relationships. Just happy and ﾻome Christian family life, with lots of everyday woven in.

Footprints in the Barn

Who is the man in the green car? What is going on in the hayloft? Is there something wrong with the mailbox? And what's for lunch? The answers to these and many other interesting questions are found in the book <u>Footprints in the Barn</u>. Hardcover. 1996. ISBN 1-891907-01-8. $12 (plus shipping and handling).

The Mysterious Message

The Great Detective Agency is at it once again, solving mysteries on the Nelson farmstead. Why is there a pile of rocks in the woods? Is someone stealing gas from the mill? How could a railroad disappear? And will Jason and Andy have to eat biscuits without honey? You will have to read this second book in the Farm Mystery Series to find out. Paperback. 1997. ISBN 1-891907-04-2. $7.50 (plus shipping and handling).

Midnight Sky

What is that sound in the woods? Has someone been stealing Dad's tools? Why is a strange dog barking at midnight? And will the Nelsons be able to adopt Russian children? <u>Midnight Sky</u> provides the answers. Paperback. 1998. ISBN 1-891907-06-9. $7.50 (plus shipping and handling).

Other Books

Our Homestead Story: The First Years

The true and humorous account of one family's journey toward a more self-sufficient lifestyle with the help of God. Read about our experiences with cows, chickens, horses, sheep, gardening and more. Paperback. 1996. ISBN 1-891907-02-6. $7.50 (plus shipping and handling).

Call Her Blessed

This book is designed to encourage mothers to consistently, day by day, follow God's will in their role as mothers. Examples are provided of mothers who know how to nurture and strengthen their children's faith in God. Paperback. 1998. ISBN 1-891907-08-5. $6.00 (plus shipping and handling).

The Orchard Lane Series: In the Spring of the Year

Meet the Hunter family and share in their lives as they move to a new home. The first in our newest series, In the Spring of the Year is written especially for children ages 5-10. Nancy, Caleb, and Emily learn about obedience and self-denial while enjoying the simple pleasures of innocent childhood. Paperback. 1999. ISBN 1-891907-07-7. $8.00 (plus shipping and handling).

The Delivery

Joe Reynolds is a husband and father striving to live a life pleasing to the Lord Jesus Christ. Having been a Christian only seven years, he has many questions and challenges in his life. How does a man working in the world face temptation? How does he raise his family in a Christ-honoring way? This book attempts to Biblically address many of the issues that men face daily, in a manner that will not cause the reader to stumble in his walk with the Lord. The book is written for men (and young men) by a man – we ask men to read it first, before reading it aloud to their families. Paperback. 1999. ISBN 1-891907-09-3. $9.00 (plus shipping and handling).

Shipping and Handling Costs

The shipping and handling charge is $2.00 for the first book and 50¢ for each additional book you buy in the same order.

You can save on shipping by getting an order together with your friends or homeschool group. On orders of 10-24 books, shipping is only 50¢ per book. Orders of 25 or more books are shipped FREE. Just have each person write a check for their own total, send in all the checks, and indicate **one** address for shipping.

To order, please send a check for the total, including shipping (Wisconsin residents, please add 5.5% sales tax on the total, including shipping and handling charges) to:

Castleberry Farms Press
Dept. TD
P.O. Box 337
Poplar, WI 54864

Please note that prices and shipping charges are subject to change.

CASTLEBERRY FARMS PRESS
P.O. BOX 337
POPLAR, WI 54864

Description	Quantity	Unit Price	Total
The Courtship of Sarah McLean		$7.50	
Waiting for Her Isaac		$7.50	
Jeff McLean: His Courtship		$7.50	
Footprints in the Barn (hardback)		$12.00	
The Mysterious Message		$7.50	
Midnight Sky		$7.50	
Our Homestead Story		$7.50	
Call Her Blessed		$6.00	
In the Spring of the Year		$8.00	
The Delivery		$9.00	
Shipping and handling charge ($2.00 for first book, 50¢ for each additional)*			
Wisconsin residents must add 5.5% sales tax (on total, including shipping costs)			
TOTAL DUE			

Your name and address:

Note: If you know others who might like to have a catalog, please send us their names and addresses and we'll send them one. Thank you.

ve on shipping! Get an order together with your friends or homeschool On orders of 10 or more books, shipping is only 50¢ per book. Orders ore books are shipped FREE. Just have each person write a check total, send in all the checks, and indicate **one** address for

CASTLEBERRY FARMS PRESS
P.O. BOX 337
POPLAR, WI 54864

Description	Quantity	Unit Price	Total
The Courtship of Sarah McLean		$7.50	
Waiting for Her Isaac		$7.50	
Jeff McLean: His Courtship		$7.50	
Footprints in the Barn (hardback)		$12.00	
The Mysterious Message		$7.50	
Midnight Sky		$7.50	
Our Homestead Story		$7.50	
Call Her Blessed		$6.00	
In the Spring of the Year		$8.00	
The Delivery		$9.00	
Shipping and handling charge ($2.00 for first book, 50¢ for each additional)*			
Wisconsin residents must add 5.5% sales tax (on total, including shipping costs)			
TOTAL DUE			

Your name and address:

Note: If you know others who might like to have a catalog, please send us their names and addresses and we'll send them one. Thank you.

*Save on shipping! Get an order together with your friends or homeschool group. On orders of 10 or more books, shipping is only 50¢ per book. Orders of 25 or more books are shipped FREE. Just have each person write a check for their own total, send in all the checks, and indicate **one** address for shipping.

Shipping and Handling Costs

The shipping and handling charge is $2.00 for the first book and 50¢ for each additional book you buy in the same order.

You can save on shipping by getting an order together with your friends or homeschool group. On orders of 10-24 books, shipping is only 50¢ per book. Orders of 25 or more books are shipped FREE. Just have each person write a check for their own total, send in all the checks, and indicate **one** address for shipping.

To order, please send a check for the total, including shipping (Wisconsin residents, please add 5.5% sales tax on the total, including shipping and handling charges) to:

Castleberry Farms Press
Dept. TD
P.O. Box 337
Poplar, WI 54864

Please note that prices and shipping charges are subject to change.

Call Her Blessed

This book is designed to encourage mothers to consistently, day by day, follow God's will in their role as mothers. Examples are provided of mothers who know how to nurture and strengthen their children's faith in God. Paperback. 1998. ISBN 1-891907-08-5. $6.00 (plus shipping and handling).

The Orchard Lane Series: In the Spring of the Year

Meet the Hunter family and share in their lives as they move to a new home. The first in our newest series, In the Spring of the Year is written especially for children ages 5-10. Nancy, Caleb, and Emily learn about obedience and self-denial while enjoying the simple pleasures of innocent childhood. Paperback. 1999. ISBN 1-891907-07-7. $8.00 (plus shipping and handling).

The Delivery

Joe Reynolds is a husband and father striving to live a life pleasing to the Lord Jesus Christ. Having been a Christian only seven years, he has many questions and challenges in his life. How does a man working in the world face temptation? How does he raise his family in a Christ-honoring way? This book attempts to Biblically address many of the issues that men face daily, in a manner that will not cause the reader to stumble in his walk with the Lord. The book is written for men (and young men) by a man – we ask men to read it first, before reading it aloud to their families. Paperback. 1999. ISBN 1-891907-09-3. $9.00 (plus shipping and handling).

Footprints in the Barn

Who is the man in the green car? What is going on in the hayloft? Is there something wrong with the mailbox? And what's for lunch? The answers to these and many other interesting questions are found in the book Footprints in the Barn. Hardcover. 1996. ISBN 1-891907-01-8. $12 (plus shipping and handling).

The Mysterious Message

The Great Detective Agency is at it once again, solving mysteries on the Nelson farmstead. Why is there a pile of rocks in the woods? Is someone stealing gas from the mill? How could a railroad disappear? And will Jason and Andy have to eat biscuits without honey? You will have to read this second book in the Farm Mystery Series to find out. Paperback. 1997. ISBN 1-891907-04-2. $7.50 (plus shipping and handling).

Midnight Sky

What is that sound in the woods? Has someone been stealing Dad's tools? Why is a strange dog barking at midnight? And will the Nelsons be able to adopt Russian children? Midnight Sky provides the answers. Paperback. 1998. ISBN 1-891907-06-9. $7.50 (plus shipping and handling).

Other Books

Our Homestead Story: The First Years

The true and humorous account of one family's journey toward a more self-sufficient lifestyle with the help of God. Read about our experiences with cows, chickens, horses, sheep, gardening and more. Paperback. 1996. ISBN 1-891907-02-6. $7.50 (plus shipping and handling).

Jeff McLean: His Courtship

Follow the story of Jeff McLean as he seeks God's direction for his life. This book is the newest in our courtship series, and is written from a young man's perspective. A discussion of godly traits to seek in young men and women is included as part of the story. February 1998. ISBN 1-891907-05-0. Paperback. $7.50 (plus shipping and handling).

The Courtship of Sarah McLean

Sarah McLean is a nineteen-year-old girl who longs to become a wife and mother. The book chronicles a period of two years, in which she has to learn to trust her parents and God fully in their decisions for her future. Paperback, 2nd printing, 1997. ISBN 1-891907-00-X. $7.50 (plus shipping and handling).

Waiting for Her Isaac

Sixteen-year-old Beth Grant is quite happy with her life and has no desire for any changes. But God has many lessons in store before she is ready for courtship. The story of Beth's spiritual journey toward godly womanhood is told along with the story of her courtship. Paperback. 1997. ISBN 1-891907-03-4. $7.50 (plus shipping and handling).

The Farm Mystery Series

Join Jason and Andy as they try to solve the mysterious happenings on the Nelson family's farm. These are books that the whole family will enjoy. In fact, many have used them as read-aloud-to-the-family books. Parents can be assured that there are no murders or other objectionable elements in these books. The boys learn lessons in obedience and responsibility while having lots of fun. There are no worldly situations or ˈguage, and no boy-girl relationships. Just happy and ˋsome Christian family life, with lots of everyday ˋ woven in.

Castleberry Farms Press

Our primary goal in publishing is to provide wholesome books in a manner that brings honor to our Lord. We believe in setting no evil thing before our eyes (Psalm 101:3) and although there are many outstanding books, we have had trouble finding enough good reading material for our children. Therefore, we feel the Lord has led us to start this family business.

We believe the following: The Bible is the infallible true Word of God. That God is the Creator and Controller of the universe. That Jesus Christ is the only begotten Son of God, was born of the virgin Mary, lived a perfect life, was crucified, buried, rose again, sits at the right hand of God, and makes intercession for the saints. That Jesus Christ is the only Savior and way to the Father. That salvation is based on faith alone, but true faith will produce good works. That the Holy Spirit is given to believers as Guide and Comforter. That the Lord Jesus will return. That man was created to glorify God and enjoy Him forever.

We began writing and publishing in mid-1996 and hope to add more books in the future if the Lord is willing. All books are written by Mr. and Mrs. Castleberry.

We would love to hear from you if you have any comments or suggestions. Our address is at the end of this section. Now, we'll tell you a little about our books.

The Courtship Series

These books are written to encourage those who intend to follow a Biblically-based courtship that includes the active involvement of parents. The main characters are committed followers of Jesus Christ, and Christian family values are emphasized throughout. The reader will be encouraged to heed parental advice and to live in obedience to the Lord.

truly just a press). Although phone numbers can change, you might try these:

1-888-NEED-HIM
1-800-772-8888 (Canada 1-800-663-7639) Insight for Living
1-719-531-5181 (Canada 1-800-661-9800) Focus on the Family

If none of these work, feel free to write us and we'll try to help. Our address is on the back cover of this book.

After you become a Christian, please link up with other believers so you can continue to grow as a Christian and help others in their attempts to please God. You can do this best by meeting on a regular basis with other believers and studying the Bible. If you can't find other believers in the area where you live, the organizations we just listed may be able to help you find them.

FINAL THOUGHTS

When we placed this material in this book, it was done so with a prayer that you would find the peace and joy that we have found. We continue to pray for you right now. May God richly bless you!

What Is a Christian?

cared about you so much that He sent His only Son, Jesus Christ, to die for the sins that you've committed (John 3:16). You will have joy in knowing that those sins are truly and completely forgiven (Romans 8:1). You will have joy in knowing that God promises you that He will never leave you or forsake you in any way (Hebrews 13:5). You will have joy in knowing that nothing, absolutely nothing at all, can separate you from His love (Romans 8:35-39). Please understand that you'll still be sad and lonely and sick and hurting at times. But you will find joy in knowing that God loves you and that there is a reason for everything that happens in your life (Romans 8:28).

Is there any hope for the future in this crazy world we live in? Yes! As a Christian you can know where you will spend your future--in heaven with God Himself (2 Corinthians 5:8; John 14-2-4).

There is no way that this short discussion can tell you everything about being a Christian. We encourage you to do several things. Please get a Bible and read it. In the paragraphs you've just read we included the location of some verses for you to look up for yourself so you can see why we said what we did. God Himself will help you understand what you are reading, through the power of the Holy Spirit, and how it relates to you as an individual.

Please make contact with someone who can answer any questions you might have. You might want to contact a pastor at a local church. There are also some folks you can talk to on the phone who can help you learn more about what it means to become a Christian and live a life that is pleasing to God. We're not officially affiliated with any of them (we're really and

CASTLEBERRY FARMS PRESS
P.O. BOX 337
POPLAR, WI 54864

Description	Quantity	Unit Price	Total
The Courtship of Sarah McLean		$7.50	
Waiting for Her Isaac		$7.50	
Jeff McLean: His Courtship		$7.50	
Footprints in the Barn (hardback)		$12.00	
The Mysterious Message		$7.50	
Midnight Sky		$7.50	
Our Homestead Story		$7.50	
Call Her Blessed		$6.00	
In the Spring of the Year		$8.00	
The Delivery		$9.00	
Shipping and handling charge ($2.00 for first book, 50¢ for each additional)*			
Wisconsin residents must add 5.5% sales tax (on total, including shipping costs)			
TOTAL DUE			

Your name and address:

Note: If you know others who might like to have a catalog, please send us their names and addresses and we'll send them one. Thank you.

*Save on shipping! Get an order together with your friends or homeschool group. On orders of 10 or more books, shipping is only 50¢ per book. Orders of 25 or more books are shipped FREE. Just have each person write a check for their own total, send in all the checks, and indicate **one** address for shipping.